BOOTED

BOOTED

A novel

by

RICHARD BADER

BOOKS

Adelaide Books
New York / Lisbon
2020

BOOTED
A novel
By Richard Bader

Published by Adelaide Books, New York / Lisbon
adelaidebooks.org

Editor-in-Chief
Stevan V. Nikolic

For any information, please address Adelaide Books
at info@adelaidebooks.org

or write to:

Adelaide Books
244 Fifth Ave. Suite D27
New York, NY, 10001

ISBN: 978-1-954351-11-0
Printed in the United States of America

For Catherine

[chapter 1]

Flying at night only made things worse. It was bad enough that the tin can of an airplane carrying Victor Barstow careened through the sky like a four-year-old in a bounce castle. But when the sun went down and that bounce castle turned black, the absence of visual cues started Victor's stomach churning, a process aided by the presence there of a largely undigested slice of pepperoni-and-sausage pizza he had purchased and eaten in a rush before takeoff. Victor fumbled in the seat pocket for a barf bag, but found only a yellowed copy of evacuation instructions and a half-eaten bag of pretzels, and he didn't want to ask the pilot for one, lest he appear weak to that woman sitting up there next to him in the cockpit. When the plane swooned into a left-leaning tilt, Victor decided he should prepare to die, possibly in a pool of his own vomit. But then two rows of lights appeared on the ground marking the outline of a landing strip on the otherwise black landscape. Then Victor felt relief. Along with trepidation.

There were only four passengers on the plane, which had a maximum capacity of seven, for a total of five people if you counted the pilot, so there was really no need for the woman to sit up front next to him in the copilot's seat. Yet that's where he had instructed her to sit, mumbling something about "balance." Weren't there F.A.A. regulations against that? Victor doubted that the pilot, who looked to be of an age where he should be bagging groceries after school, could spell F.A.A. Of course the woman's seating placement had nothing to do with balance, and everything to do with the fact that she was gorgeous. The pilot spent an inordinate amount of time fiddling with his right-hand-side controls, the ones in plausibly accidental touching distance of the place where her coat had fallen open to reveal a generous expanse of black-panty-hosed leg. And was that black leather way up there where the leg disappeared into skirt fabric? Victor suspected that the plane wasn't the only thing that had lifted off and climbed to flying altitude. *Cockpit.* What a word.

The pilot's name was Buck. He had announced this back in Albany when everyone was on board and he'd gone through the safety procedures. He'd pointed to his nameplate as he said it, as if to prove his point. *No, seriously—my name really is Buck.*

Victor told himself to keep a close eye on the woman, and not because of the endless miles her leg traveled before it reached the hem of her skirt. Victor wasn't like the Bucks of the world. He was a mature and happily married man away on an important business trip, and he needed to keep a close eye on her because he she was his competition. He knew this because of the logo on the luggage Buck had stowed away for her, the same logo that was on the shoulder bag she carried on board, with the distinctive *nD* drawn to evoke a mountain range. Nanda Devi—possibly the most powerful outdoor gear company on the planet. Which meant Victor was in trouble. Only the monogrammed purse that she took from her carry-on shoulder bag to address a lipstick issue lacked the company brand. Like the woman herself, the purse looked expensive, made of what Victor assumed was un-faux snakeskin, though he was no expert on these matters. It bore the initials EP. Evil Princess, maybe? Why is it, he wondered, not for the first time, that women think it's perfectly okay to touch up their lipstick when they're out among strangers? Like he would ever think to stop and reapply deodorant in the middle of a shopping mall.

Well, Victor was a *married* man, anyway. The *happily* part he was becoming less and less sure of.

"Like Buck Rogers," EP had said back before takeoff when Buck introduced himself, and she had reached out to place a slender hand on his uniformed forearm, leaving it there just long enough for touch to register. He grinned broadly and flushed red and lost his train of thought on the finer points of seatbelt operation, and Victor was pretty sure he had no idea who the hell Buck Rogers was. And EP, Victor suspected, was just warming up. He felt the odds drop on his chances of winning the contract he had come to win.

The other two passengers were college students who spent the whole ride sucking each other's faces in the seats behind Victor. Or *seat*, more accurately, as the girl was all curled up in his lap. What did that do to the *balance*, Victor considered asking Buck, though chose not to.

The plane bounced a few times before making reliable contact with Earth, then rolled to a stop near a Quonset hut doing a feeble impression of an airport terminal. The four of them deplaned and then stood around while Buck retrieved bags, helped by an overweight kid with bad skin and an enormous down jacket patched with duct tape. Snow was everywhere and it was beyond cold, the cold having broken through to some new and intensely frigid realm where a simple word like *cold* seemed like an insult. Victor heard a crackling sound, and worried briefly that they might all be standing on breaking ice, until he realized that the sound came from his nose hairs freezing and thawing as he inhaled and exhaled.

In a parking area exhaust billowed from the tailpipe of a shiny black Lexus SUV, and after EP got her suitcases—their Nanda Devi logo announcing to the world that they were made sturdily and cost more than any reasonable person would ever pay for luggage—she made her way to it. The driver, a large Black man in a black overcoat and a black chauffer's cap, got out to put her bags in the back.

Victor looked around the tarmac for the car he had reserved, knowing he'd requested a compact but wishing he had gotten a free upgrade that would deliver him something that wouldn't feel cheap next to the Lexus. "I'm supposed to have a rental car," he said to the terminal kid. Now they both looked around the tarmac. There were two other cars parked near the Quonset hut, a beat-up Honda Civic with a New York Rangers bumper sticker—that would be terminal boy's—and an equally beat up Ford something-or-other, into the trunk of which the college kids were loading their duffels.

Terminal boy shrugged. "Don't see one," he said, stating the obvious. There weren't many places for a rental car to hide.

"They said it would be here when I landed."

The kid looked around again. No car had materialized. He shrugged again.

The Lexus rolled across the tarmac to where Victor and terminal boy stood and eased to a stop. Its tinted passenger-side window slid down. EP looked toasty-warm in her white down overcoat and furry Cossack hat, long black hair shimmering on her shoulders in the beam of a single halogen lamp atop a tall pole.

"Are you heading in to Granite?" she asked, her lips red and full, her mouth just possibly betraying a hint of a smirk.

There was nothing to identify Victor as her opponent—he had no company logo (consistent with the fact that had no company)—but he felt sure she knew his purpose in flying to this ice-cube hell was to compete for the same turf she sought to claim.

"Yes," Victor said. He wondered if she could hear the sound his nose hairs were making.

"Would you like a ride?" she offered, in a way that conveyed just how insignificant an obstacle he posed. EP was not, he suspected, a woman who experienced rejection often. But Victor was nothing if not a proud man, and accepting her offer could only make him more insignificant than he already was. "Thanks," he said, "but I'll call a taxi."

"As you wish," she actually said, like she was going to click her heels and cast a spell. Who says that except in fairy tales? She disappeared as the tinted window rose and the Lexus drove off. Victor felt a twinge of regret as the car's last remnants of exhaust dissipated in the cold night air.

"Dude, you so should have gone with her," terminal boy said. "One, she's super hot. And B, there's no taxis around here."

"No taxis," Victor repeated.

"There's a guy that does shuttles, but not this late. It's like midnight." Victor looked around. It was indeed like midnight. It was like the midnight where other midnights went to die. There were supposed to be mountains out there somewhere, but it was too dark to see anything outside of the halogen-powered circle of light they were standing in, no reassuring glow of civilization on the horizon, nothing.

"I'll call an Uber, then," Victor said. He took out his phone and saw he had no signal.

"What's an *oober*?" the kid said. Victor put the phone back in his coat pocket.

Victor did not want to spend the night sleeping on a bench in the Quonset hut alone with terminal kid. He needed a good night's sleep if he was to appear remotely competent in his presentation in the morning. Plus, he had lost all feeling in his toes.

The beat-up Ford rolled over to where Victor and the kid stood and the driver's-side window went down, creaking like a rusty door hinge. "Hey mister," the college boy said. "You wanna come with us?"

★

"Nate," the boy said, reaching around to extend a hand after Victor pushed aside some old Burger King wrappers and climbed into the back seat. He shook it. "Fiona," said the girl, who glanced back at him and smiled but did not offer a hand.

"Victor," Victor said. "Victor Barstow." He hoped the car's heater worked.

"What brings you to Granite, Victor Barstow?" Nate asked. He was a skinny kid with a dirty blond ponytail trailing out from under his ski cap—dirty blond less because that was its color and more because it looked blond and dirty. The question—*What brings you to Granite?*—struck Victor as almost metaphorical in nature, as in that moment he felt heavier than a lunk of dense, cold stone. But by Granite the kid meant the town by that name, which Victor figured had to be somewhere nearby, seeing as how they were in the parking lot of the ambitiously named Granite International Airport, *international* by virtue of the fact that anyone with a middling arm could throw a stone across the river that ran beside the runway and hit Canada on the other side.

"Have you heard of Winklers?" Victor said. They hadn't.

[chapter 2]

The Winkler legend began with Maximilian Winkler, a once-struggling Salzburg cobbler whose fortunes turned when he was recruited to manufacture boots for the Central Powers at the start of what would later—and in retrospect, ironically—be called the War to End All Wars. The opportunity unleashed something in Max, and the boots he crafted were exquisite, heralded for both their warmth and remarkable comfort even when their grateful wearers were soaking wet and covered in mud in the trenches of the Western Front.

The boots' reputation spread rapidly. Along with gold fillings and wedding rings, they became a highly prized battlefield commodity, and were commonly removed from owners who were dead, or dying, or wounded, or sometimes just soundly sleeping, a process that in a hurry—in the midst of battle, say—might be performed swiftly with the aid of a bayonet or some other sharp instrument that would remove both boot and foot, the foot to be discarded later. Indeed, after a time any poor soul whose corpse was found footless on the battlefield was said to have been "Winklered."

All of this brought a measure of notoriety to Max Winkler and his boots from participants on both sides of the conflict. Sadly, as the war wound toward its bloody conclusion, poor

Max began heading toward his own bloody conclusion. He contracted tuberculosis, and lived his remaining time on Earth coughing, then coughing blood, then doing those things while bedridden. Before his illness confined him to a bed, Max Winkler managed to teach his craft to his young son Nicolas, and although demand for Winkler-made boots declined some in the post-war years, even as a teenager Nicolas managed to keep the business afloat. Nicolas had been taught well and developed into a gifted craftsman, more gifted, some said, than even his father, and his skill elevated Winkler boots up close to the realm of art. He was also a young man of varied appetites, one of which was for an Italian prostitute of gypsy ancestry named Isabella. When Isabella, tiring of her profession, became pregnant with a child she insisted could only be his, he married her.

They named the baby boy Marco. Not long after Marco's birth, showing keen intuition as to the side on which his bread was likely to be buttered, and understanding that the Nazis in neighboring Germany were growing in power and treating the gypsies as least as horribly as they were the Jews, Nicolas took Isabella and baby Marco and fled Europe as Hitlerian rumblings rumbled across the continent. They worked their way westward and escaped via a cargo ship that left Le Havre bound for New York City six days before German tanks rolled into Austria at the beginning of the Anschluss.

The young family settled in the remote, tiny, and incongruously named hamlet of Paradiso in upstate New York, which Isabella chose because it had the same name as a favorite mountain in northwestern Italy and because it gave them clear views of the mountains to the south, whose rounded peaks were an inferior but close-enough-under-the-circumstances approximation to their beloved Alps. With a few glasses of wine in him, Nicolas saw in those beloved mountains a resemblance to the even more beloved Isabella's perfect breasts, especially in winter when the snow turned them white. He could gaze at them for hours.

The War to End All Wars hadn't ended anything at all, and the Second World War proved to be even more lucrative for Winkler boots than the First. The family business thrived, and this time with the added advantage of manufacturing for the winning side. And the boots themselves, with Nicolas's craftsmanship, and seasoned with Isabella's Italian influence, became even better—warmer, dryer, more buttery, more stylish. Nicolas's strength was boot-making, not marketing, and only a few people outside of the military had heard of his boots until the *New York Times* ran a front-page story about workers at a distribution center who stole several crates from a shipment bound for France and sold them on the black market on the streets of New York City. Not long afterward "Winklers," as they would thenceforth be called, started appearing on the feet of well-heeled Manhattanites aiming for an outdoorsy, military-chic look.

This new niche in the world of urban fashion proved to be neither sustainable nor entirely welcome—Winklers, so the Winklers maintained, were meant for more important purposes than wardrobe accessorizing. Alas, urban fashion alone lacked the power to keep business thriving, and after the war ended demand plummeted, forcing Nicolas to lay off dozens of workers and drastically scale back production. After a few years he began talking with Isabella about simply shutting down the business and retiring on their war earnings, but she rejected the idea, and a smaller-scale version of Winklers, Inc. kept making boots.

In February of 1954 Nicolas, Isabella, and a teenage Marco were on a ski vacation in Kitzbühel when Nicolas, a good skier, though not quite the expert he believed himself to be, lost control on a patch of ice and crashed into a tree. He crushed his head and snapped his spine and died on the spot, making it a toss-up as to which was the fatal blow. Isabella flew back to New York with his body and buried him in a small plot on their property in Paradiso, on a hillside with a view of the mountains to the south. It was supposed to be a small family-only funeral, but dozens of Winkler acolytes managed to learn about it, and they hiked in and stood around on the periphery looking forlorn and outdoorsy in their plaid shirts and Winkler boots. It's worth noting that all were men. Winklers at this time were only made for men, and the few women who had a pair possessed them only because a boyfriend or husband had given them to her.

The arrival of the acolytes touched Isabella, and it triggered an idea. Her former profession had given her keen insight into the nature of desirable objects and the massive sums of money people were willing to part with in order to enjoy them. And though she had no formal training in economics, Isabella demonstrated an intuitive grasp of the workings of a supply-demand curve. As she stood graveside on a miserable March day watching her husband's casket get lowered into the ground—with a mix of snow and sleet starting to pelt her black veil and with all those Winkler-wearers standing around looking somber but well shod—the grieving widow saw the future. When she put a hand on the shoulder of sixteen-year-old Marco standing next to her, he looked at her, held her dark, intelligent eyes with his own, saw the glimmer of an idea there, and understood—he had been anointed.

Isabella Winkler's new business model ran so counter to the prevailing post-war religion of growth and bigness as to be a stroke of genius. They would slash production to a couple of hundred pairs a year, shrink the workforce to a tiny handful of the world's very finest bootmakers, and create the Stradivarius of hiking boots, for each pair of which customers would not only willingly, but gratefully, fork over a small fortune. They would also have to make a pilgrimage to Paradiso to have their feet custom-measured. Boot construction would take several days, during which time customers would pay another small fortune to stay at the Winkler estate, sleeping on thousand-count bed linen and eating gourmet meals. If owning Winklers had become a mark of status, then acquiring them would become an experience of the senses, something akin to a vacation at an expensive and exclusive spa. Customers weren't just buying boots, Isabella understood—years before an upstart sneaker company in Oregon reached the same conclusion—they were buying a lifestyle. And if the expense of buying Winklers meant that their owners would afterwards struggle to pay rents and mortgages, well at least their feet would be well equipped for a life lived outdoors.

Acquiring a pair of Winklers became less like buying an item of clothing and more like joining a fraternity, and membership was restricted. Before any prospective boot owner was invited to make the pilgrimage to Paradiso, he had to be deemed worthy. Would-be candidates would send in requests in writing, submitting a 500-word Statement of Desire (Isabella's name of choice for the particular document, erotic undertones being essential to her marketing plan), a photo of themselves, and a résumé. Outdoor credibility was one criterion—after the dockworkers' theft and the boots' redistribution to city dwellers, Isabella was determined not to have the boots wind up on the feet of rich New Yorkers whose most ambitious expedition had been to trek from their Upper West Side apartment to the taxi stand at 95th and Park, or whose highest climb was to their 6th floor Chelsea walkup. A poetic nature was another. Ever the romantic, Isabella had as much interest in the souls of Winkler wearers as she did their soles. With Marco's blessing, she instituted a new policy of giving away one pair of boots for free each year to a candidate in financial hardship whose life story struck her as especially poignant. The Winkler mystique grew.

Marco, a genius craftsman, possibly the finest his family had produced, oversaw quality control and personally stitched at least part of every boot the company manufactured. To verify authenticity (and boost value), each boot had the letter "W" branded on the inside of the ankle in a confident if somewhat blocky font specially designed for them by a legendary typographer who was an old family friend. Beneath the "W" was the production number; the lower the number, the higher the value. By 1961 the price of a pair of early edition Winklers in good condition had climbed close to that of a new Volkswagen Beetle.

Requests for the boots streamed in by the thousands. When the waiting list grew to two years, Isabella raised boot prices and instituted a $50 application fee that would be counted toward the purchase price if the application was accepted, and pocketed by the Winklers if it wasn't. This failed to dim interest, and soon the company employed almost as many people to open envelopes and screen candidates as they did to make boots. In a nod to the rising feminist tide, in the mid 1960s the company even introduced the first-ever Winkler's for Women, which bore a more feminine variation of the sturdy W logo. WfW had been Isabella's idea, motivated by two factors. One was that as a woman entrepreneur now running her second successful business, she felt an affinity with the young feminists and their demands for equal rights and privileges.

The second reason was that with a predominantly male work-force and an all-male clientele, it was growing unlikely that the workaholic Marco was going to find anyone with whom he could produce an heir to pass the business on to. Isabella decided he needed to meet some girls. She herself screened all female applicants.

Her plan worked, but only to an extent. Marco thrust himself not only into this intriguing new world of women's boot design, but also into no small number of the female customers themselves when they arrived in Paradiso for "measurements." Marco's discovery and enthusiastic partaking of the pleasures of the flesh heightened his design sensibilities, and elevated to even higher levels, some Winkler wearers insisted, the renowned eroticism that came from the act of slipping on a Winkler boot. Among cognoscenti, The Winkler *Oh!* became a phenomenon.

But Marco valued variety over anything that might have evolved into a stable relationship, and through some combination of his own precautions, his female clients' precautions (the increasing popularity of the pill played a key role here), and sheer dumb luck, no heir had resulted from what he regarded as nothing more than recreational diversions. Or at least no heir that he was aware of.

Then in July of 1980, a young woman in cutoff denim shorts and a dark blue tank top appeared at the entrance to the Winkler compound and positioned herself in front of Isabella's pickup truck as she and Marco were leaving to run an errand. She had sun-streaked hair tied into a long braid and carried a well-worn frame-pack on her back, onto which she had fastened a drinking cup and a pair of drying panties. A sheen of sweat clung to her skin. Trail dust accented her high cheekbones. Her belt held a buck knife in a leather sheath.

On her feet—and a Winkler always noticed a person's feet—she wore a pair of crude hemp sandals held together by duct tape.

Winkler protocol in a situation such as this would have been to deliver a short lecture about how this was private property and visitors were not welcome, and then simply to drive on by. The family summarily rejected walk-ins; the company's delayed-gratification purchase model fed its mystique, and its mystique went to the heart of its brand. After Marco and Isabella left, the mechanized iron gate to the property would have slid shut and locked behind them, keeping the intruder out. But something about this girl struck a chord with both Marco and his mother. For Isabella, it was wanderlust: a girl, alone, hiking in the wilderness, full of all the strength and vulnerability such effort required. The girl evoked memories of Isabella's Romani ancestors wandering through Europe, wary of others, bolstered by their distinctive culture and music, and persecuted everywhere they went. For Marco it was just plain lust, triggered by the girl's eyes, round and earnest, their pale blue the color of morning sky on a clear day, but also liquid, as if that sky were being reflected in a still lake. Then there were her feet, calloused and dirty, with the skin cracked in places, but perfectly shaped, slender and strong with straight toes, suffering none of the havoc that years of wearing ill-fitting shoes wreaks on most feet. And then there was the body that flowed between eyes and feet, strong and lithe and nubile. It was as if Artemis, the goddess-huntress, had materialized there in the family driveway. All that was missing was the quiver of arrows and the bow.

Isabella turned off the truck, got out, and walked to the girl. "May we help you?" she asked.

"I hear you make hiking boots," the girl said.

They gave her the guest room with the claw-foot tub and the view of the mountains. She came down to dinner in a simple black dress that stopped above her knees and was full of wrinkles from whatever nook or cranny of her backpack it had been crammed into, her long, reddish-blond hair freed from its braid and still damp from her bath. Marco's eyes again lowered toward her feet—an occupational hazard in the Winkler household—but they took their sweet time getting there, pausing along the way to take in the full length and contours of her body, and especially her legs, now stubble-free thanks to the razor Isabella had placed on top of the pile of plush towels she had put out for the girl, though crisscrossed with scratches that reminded Marco of comets streaking through the night sky. The girl watched Marco run his eyes over her, but only when his gaze reached her feet did she blush. She was barefoot.

"I don't have any shoes," she said. "That's why I'm here."

She told them her name was Annie, and she had lived in the nearby town of Canton, an only child of a single mother who had died of cancer. Hiking had become Annie's way to cope. She had meandered through the wilderness in sneakers until the soles of her shoes started to detach from their uppers. The sandals were Plan B, and it had become clear that a Plan C would be needed, and that it would have to involve more substantial footwear if she was going to be able to continue. She had met a hiker wearing a pair of Winklers and admired them. He told her where they had come from, so she walked off to get herself a pair. "It's not that simple," the hiker had called after her, but Annie just kept walking, and now here she was.

The next morning, Marco took measurements. Then he retreated to his workshop to transfer the measurements to the materials. That afternoon he began making Annie's boots.

In eight days they were finished. Marco took a little longer than usual because for her, he wanted Winklers' exacting standards to be a little more exacting. Plus, he suspected she would leave when the boots were finished, and he wanted to keep her around as long as possible. She sat in a plush armchair in the Winkler parlor to try them on for the first time, Marco on a low stool in front of her, holding the right boot. At the try-on, all Winkler buyers were barefoot; socks, the family had long insisted, while fine for warmth if the owner so desired, were superfluous in an artfully made boot, and detrimental to proper fit. If the boot had been made to meet Winkler standards of perfection, the sock was unnecessary; if worn, they were to be as thin as possible. "Foot condoms," the workers dismissively called them.

From his seat on a stool in front of her, Marco put his left hand under her calf and guided her bare right foot into the soft leather of the boot. A sound, a rush of air, escaped Annie's lips as her foot eased in. Puzzled, and afraid he'd hurt her (and fearing he'd made some grievous error in boot construction— was a nail poking through?), Marco backed the boot off, and this elicited a similar sound, though one emitted with a bit more conviction behind it than the first. He looked up into pale blue eyes that were intent and focused, a mouth with lips slightly parted. What she felt, he now understood, was not pain. Marco continued, moving slowly. On a little, off a little. On a little further, off a little less, and with each in and out of Annie's foot the noises became louder and more insistent until somewhere around round seven Marco finally slid his perfect boot all the way on to her perfect foot, and Annie's head went back and her back arched and her fingernails dug into the leather on arms of the chair with enough force to leave holes, and she came, loudly and totally, with a force that caused Marco to fall off his stool.

When they'd both recovered, they sat there for a few minutes staring at each other and panting. Then he repeated the procedure with the left boot, and she did it all over again.

Marco and Annie married in a grove of sugar maples near the base of Santanoni Peak, eight weeks after her arrival at the Winkler compound. A boy, Lukas, was born seven months later, in April of 1981, and family legend maintained that his conception resulted from that first union of foot and boot, and not from more conventional methods of procreation, which Marco and Annie indulged in so enthusiastically in the days and weeks after the boot-fitting that boot production slowed and Isabella had to intervene and tell her son to stop fucking around and get to work. A girl, Sasha, came along fourteen months after Lukas.

Annie was a devoted mother. Like her own mother had done with her, she started taking the children into the mountains before they could walk—day trips where she would strap Sasha into a Snugli on her chest and perch Lukas in a frame carrier on her back. Their vocabulary as toddlers was a kind of wilderness poetry, filled with words like chokeberry and wood sorrel and buttonbush. Marco immersed himself in work and seldom joined them on these outings. Seldom turned to never as the children grew older and more mobile, and Annie would take them out for several days or a week at a time. Marco couldn't spare that kind of time.

As the years went on, Lukas became fascinated with the family business. He loved its smells and textures and sounds, and by the age of twelve he had become a capable bootmaker in his own right, good enough for Marco to include him in the production process. But it was clear to father and son that

Lukas would never be the craftsman his father was, and with time his interests gravitated to other aspects of operation that intrigued him more than the bootmaking itself—production efficiency, quality control, marketing, and especially brand management. He majored in economics at Cornell—making him the first Winkler to get a college education—and then went on to get an MBA from Dartmouth's Tuck School of Business. All of this made Marco and Isabella very proud. Annie was proud as well, though a little perplexed and sometimes disturbed by his choices, which struck her as being overly capitalistic and sometimes downright cruel.

It was at Lukas's urging that Marco fired Leon, a Lithuanian man with twinkly eyes who had been one of the first bootmakers Marco had hired after setting up shop in Paradiso. Leon had been Annie's favorite among the Winkler employees. On his days off he would sometimes accompany mother and children on their wilderness jaunts. Leon read the landscape the way some people read novels, and he introduced her to things—the medicinal properties of plant species, animal habits, geographic formations—that enriched her understanding of the forests immensely. He became the father figure she had never had, and a doting grandfather of sorts to her children, who grew to adore him. But arthritis had twisted Leon's once-nimble fingers, and when the productivity chart that Lukas kept on each of the workers confirmed a decline in output, he persuaded Marco to let him go. On his last day Annie helped him pack his tools with tears in her eyes, kissed him on the cheek, and felt her heart break as he walked away.

Sasha was a blend of her mother and grandmother. The aesthetics of the family craft interested her more than maximizing production efficiency or leveraging purchasing power to get lower prices on boot materials. She, too, learned the family trade, and from Marco's perspective this produced good news and bad news. The good news was that by the time she was a teenager she was making boots that were works of art—she became the first and only woman on the Winkler bootmaking team. The bad news was that it took her forever to make them—it could take six months for her to complete a single pair, too slow for her to be fully integrated into the production cycle. But because she was his daughter—and because he didn't have to pay her in the same way he would a normal employee—Marco let her plod along. But then a problem arose. The tiny subset of boot buyers lucky enough to end up with boots that Sasha had made began talking about this newer Winkler, a Winkler that out-Winklered even the normally fantastic Winklers. As the rumors spread the business experienced a minor crisis of quality control—no pair of Winklers was supposed to be better than any other pair; they all were supposed to be perfect. There was talk of having Sasha teach the others to make boots the way she did, but Lukas worried about the production slowdown that would result, and Isabella maintained that the magic Sasha worked with boot leather was her gift, and not something that could be taught. Normalcy returned when at eighteen Sasha, who never had any real interest in a making a career out of making boots, went away to RISD to study sculpture.

After college, Sasha followed a boyfriend to Vermont, where she joined an artists' co-op in Brattleboro and began to establish herself as an artist. Lukas moved to New York City and took a job with a venture-capital firm that funded technology start-ups. He would sometimes use his connections to get his sister shows in small galleries there. She sold well. Meanwhile, the family boot business hummed along.

When the children were in college, Annie continued the wilderness treks on her own, sometimes leaving Marco for a week or more at a time, two or three times a year. She would pack food and clothes in a backpack, tell him she was going, and just walk away. The Winkler property was miles from the mountains, and Marco didn't know if she walked the whole way, or hitchhiked, or what. In his more paranoid moments he worried that she wasn't out hiking at all, but was picked up a mile or so down the road by some burly mountain man driving a pickup truck and spirited away to a clandestine love nest for days of trysting before returning, exhausted but sated, home. These fears emanated from his own guilt. Marco had insisted on maintaining personal control of the WfW line, and he hadn't done so just out of concern for the foot comfort of female hikers. He loved Annie, no one doubted that, but he also loved novelty. His infidelities were a poorly kept company secret. Annie had confronted him about this on more than one occasion, and each time exacted a contrite but unconvincing promise from him that he'd stop.

"You'll lose her," Isabella told her son, speaking as a woman with knowledge of the predicament, as once her entire business model had relied heavily on persuading husbands to partake of the pleasures of someone other than their wives. "You're being a fool." The ever-perceptive Isabella proved to be right on both counts. In July of 2000, twenty years to the day since a teenage Annie had walked into the Winkler compound, Annie left on one of her treks and simply failed to return. Once the children left home she never told anyone the planned end dates for her trips. She would just leave, and then some number of days later she would return. Until this time she didn't.

"Annie's been gone a long time," Isabella said to Marco one day in the workshop as Annie's absence stretched into its third week. "Longer than usual." He didn't look up from the boot he was inspecting.

"Marco," Isabella tried again a couple of days later. "Annie should be back. Something's wrong."

Authorities were alerted. A search was dispatched, first with park officials—foot patrols and helicopters and rescue dogs—but after the local media picked up the story, the acolytes returned, some of whom traveled enormous distances to come help. These were seasoned hikers with thousands of hours of wilderness experience, plus excellent boots. If anyone could find her, they could.

But they couldn't. Not even a trace. After months, on a cold October day when the season's first snow dusted the mountaintops, the family called off the search. They thanked the acolytes and told them to go home. At age sixty-three, Marco had lost the love of his life.

Annie's presumed death may have devastated the family, but word of her disappearance—and the mystery surrounding the body that was never found—only served to strengthen the brand. A legend grew. That she'd fought a bear and lost, and what the creature didn't eat coyotes and vultures had taken care of. That was why no one found a body. Or that she hadn't died after all, but lived out there as a sort of she-wolf, or werewolf, or vampire. Or that in late summer, when the wind blew a certain way through the trees, it made the sound of Annie singing. Winkler acolytes started referring to those warm breezes as "Annies."

Marco became despondent, and dropped into a depressive and wholly unproductive funk that lasted for the better part of a decade, a plummet that deepened when four years after Annie's disappearance Isabella died of heart failure. People who held out hope that Annie might still be alive felt certain she would return for her mother-in-law's funeral. When she failed to show, it ended speculation: Annie must be dead, too.

The family's losses were the company's as well. Isabella had been the spiritual anchor and motivating force. Annie had injected a wild spirit. These were gone. Boots produced during those next years were said to be lackluster. More pairs than ever before got returned for repairs. "This quirky little company that we've grown to love," said an article in the *Wall Street Journal*, "has lost its mojo." The Winklers were reeling.

Lukas, who had worked his way up to vice president at a successful Manhattan venture capital firm, took a leave of absence to try to right the listing Winkler ship. He generated graphs, charts, tables, spreadsheets, PowerPoint decks. He ran numbers on production, labor, machinery, overhead, deferred maintenance, the costs of the leather that Marco insisted on buying from a single provider in Tuscany, despite the fact that there were more cows than people in the part of the world Winklers occupied. He itemized and analyzed. When he presented all of this data to his father it made the old man's head spin, so he cut to the chase with its troubling but inescapable conclusion: "Dad," he said, "the company is in a death spiral. If we don't do something, we'll be gone in five years."

Fears of running into the ground a business that had been in his family for more than a century led to a succession of sleepless nights for Marco. The days found him not in his workshop, but wandering the wooded trails that surrounded the Winkler property, or in the small family graveyard, staring at the stone markers of his mother and wife (Annie's headstone planted there despite the absence of a body), beseeching their spirits to help him.

"What we need is a good war," he announced to Lukas one day at breakfast. The company owed its very existence to war, had risen to prominence on the feet of the young Winkler-shod men who had trudged across battlefields in the name of causes of varying degrees of dubiousness. The fame of Winkler boots was joined at the metatarsal to those who had died more or less nobly wearing them. Lukas, who at that moment was spackling a cinnamon-raisin bagel with cream cheese, paused mid-spackle to point out that although there was no shortage of wars to choose from at present, war was now "off brand" and "not our demographic." Joining the supply line of the military-industrial complex ran the very real risk of alienating Winklers' granola-eating, pot-smoking, tree-hugging core. Besides, troop withdrawals were the order of the day.

Marco went back into the woods.

Then Marco, being Marco, came up with another idea. He would create a pair of boots built to the exact specifications he had used for Annie's. Women from anywhere on the planet could trace the outline of their feet on paper and send it to him (along with a photo of themselves). Those whose foot dimensions looked like the closest fit, he would invite to come to the Winkler estate to try on the boots.

"And then what?" asked Sasha, who lost count of the number of ways this was a bad idea. "The one who the boots fit becomes your princess?"

"Sort of," Marco replied.

"Dad," she said, "that's disgusting."

"I marry her?"

"No, you don't." Since Isabella died, Sasha worried that her father might be losing his mind. This ruse only helped confirm her suspicions.

"It's brilliant! It's Sword in the Stone! It's Cinderella!"

"It's insane. It's beyond wrong." She pleaded to her brother for support.

Lukas agreed with Sasha—Marco's plan was nuts. But the strategic leaking of a *rumor* of the plan—well, that might be something different altogether. What if, he said to Sasha, word trickled out that Winkler's was holding a contest of this sort? The idea was just outrageous enough to attract attention. The free publicity it would generate just might give the company a boost. "It'll mean buzz," he said.

"And what do we say when people ask us if it's true?" Sasha wanted to know.

"We say it's not company policy to discuss company policy."

Lukas used the strategic deployment of an immodest sum of cash to leak the story to a semi-well-connected blogger he knew from the city. It was agreed that Lukas would be identified only as an "unnamed source close to the family."

Sasha was dubious. Who in the world, she wondered, would want to have their foot matched to the foot of the dead wife of a lecherous old man? Well, a lot of people, as it turned out. One afternoon as she was leaving her Brattleboro studio, a TV news reporter intercepted her and thrust a microphone in her face. Is it true? the reporter wanted to know.

"It's not company policy to discuss company policy," Sasha said. Then she went home and took a long shower.

The spark Lukas lit leaped, as he'd hoped, onto social media, where it crackled to life like dry kindling. #WinklerWife became a thing. Instagram was flooded with photos of feet, and more than a few of them also showed other body parts. Feminist backlash was fierce, but it boosted visibility, reinforcing the idea that there really is no such thing as bad publicity. Online discussion threads speculated on Annie's fate, on her relationship with Marco, and, mostly, on her boot size. Foot tracings poured in, each receiving an ambiguously worded response that served to neither confirm nor deny the existence of any actual contest.

Marco was thrilled. The excitement accomplished what Zoloft and Celexa, to say nothing of Viagra, could not. He set to work on the coveted pair of boots.

Meanwhile Lukas tweaked the company algorithm so that a disproportionate number of women entered the Winkler boot queue. When they came to be fitted for boots, the fantasy that they might be under consideration for *the* boots wasn't exactly indulged, but it wasn't rejected either. Sales began to surge. *WSJ* ran a new headline: "The Winkler Mojo is Back!"

But those who live by the Twitter feed also die by the Twitter feed. The revived interest in Winkler boots revived a corollary interest in the fate of Annie, gone more than a decade now, whose body was never discovered. Rumors got layered on rumors. Was she actually alive and in on this fraudulent scheme? Had Marco killed her to reenergize a moribund company and snag himself a trophy wife in the process?

Protests were held outside the Winkler gates, on the very path where Annie had showed up that spring morning all those years ago. Irate Winkler owners felt betrayed by a company whose ethics they had trusted every bit as much as its boots. #Hoodwinklered competed with #WinklerWife. Even the police, who long ago abandoned the search for Annie, came by to ask a few questions.

Lukas drafted a press release debunking all rumors of a boot-fitting contest whose end-game was securing a new wife for the company patriarch. He reaffirmed the company's commitment to women's equality. The furor died down, but business died down with it. Winkler boot sales tapered to a new but unsustainable normal. Lukas, finding himself tethered to a company with a troubled brand in a rural backwater with a population about one-eighth the size of the turnout for a Mets game in a shitty season, decided he wanted out.

"I want to sell the company," he told Sasha on the phone one afternoon.

"Very funny," she replied.

"I'm serious. I'm tired of running it. We're heading into a nosedive, and I'm not the guy to pull us out. But the brand still has potential. Now's the time."

"You can't sell."

"Actually, I can," he said, and he could. Years earlier he had persuaded Marco to sign documents that gave him sole fiscal authority as part of his agreement to try to rescue the company. He explained this to his sister as diplomatically as possible.

"I'll run it," she said.

Lukas laughed. "Yeah, right. And turn it into what? A commune? That'll work."

Sasha sparred a few rounds with her brother over this point, but half-heartedly. He had a point. Lukas had made no effort over the years to conceal his view that Sasha's own business model was insane. The artist co-op she co-managed gave studio and gallery space to any number of artists, most of whom might generously be labeled "aspiring." There were maybe three who were anything close to financially viable, and their earnings shouldered the financial burden in keeping the co-op afloat. Sasha was one of these. In certain circles her name was well known, her abstract sculptures sold well on several arts websites, and she was more or less financially secure. But a larger reason why running Winklers made no sense was that Sasha was perfectly happy with the life she was living in Vermont. Grace, the eleven-year-old daughter she had had with a potter (who, before Grace had turned two, left to study massage therapy in Santa Fe) was thriving and seemed about as well adjusted to life as a middle-school girl could hope to be. And after the potter left, Sasha struck up a relationship with Becca, a jeweler, opening doors of intimacy that she, Sasha, would not have believed were possible just a few years before. It felt new and important and wasn't something she wanted to give up. So no, it made no sense for Sasha to move back to Paradiso and rescue a company that made hiking boots. Still, she felt sad. "A hundred years as a family business, and you want to just throw it all away?"

"Sash," he said, "I've got to get out."

They reached a compromise position. They wouldn't sell the company outright, but they would cede operational control—they would find someone outside the family to run it. If that outside entity ran it successfully, it could use a portion of profits to buy into Winklers, so that over time this outsider would gradually come to own more and more of the company, with maximum ownership capped out at fifty-one percent. The better the business performed, the faster the selected operating team would become majority owner. Sasha, Lukas, and their father would retain minority ownership at a level that would not drop below forty-nine percent of company value. In this way actual, living Winklers would stay associated with Winklers, and if things worked out, the company would generate income for them throughout their lifetimes. And Lukas couldn't determine by himself who would take over control. The Winkler family members would vote.

[chapter 3]

"Winklers are to hiking boots what a Ferrari is to a tricycle," Victor explained, wrapping up, and putting things in terms his SAT-tested audience could easily grasp. "They're works of art. The company is looking for someone to turn operations over to, and I've been invited up to give a pitch."

"So you make hiking boots," Fiona said. She was craned around in her seat to look at him. Fiona was a pretty girl, with an oval face and doe eyes and dark hair that came out from under her ski cap, which she wisely kept on, as the car's underachieving heater kept things not so much warm as less cold.

"Not exactly," Victor said, and struggled with what to say next. Even *not exactly* was a stretch. A simple *no* would have been more accurate, and *I don't know a fucking thing about making hiking boots* would have been more accurate still. This was good practice, to be on the spot like this. The Winklers were certain to have questions like this tomorrow.

"So then why'd they invite you?" Nate said.

This was another excellent question, and another one that Victor didn't have a solid answer to. For twenty years he had been the human resources director for a major Baltimore clothing retailer, but after people stopped buying its clothes, management let go a sizeable percentage of its workforce and outsourced HR to a firm in Richmond. Victor found himself with two months' severance, no job prospects, a schoolteacher wife, and a teenage daughter closing in on college, if he could afford to send her. He took a job selling shoes in a mall, at a place called The Bootery. He went from ninety-five thousand a year with three weeks of vacation and great health insurance to twelve dollars an hour plus a commission based on sales volume. He didn't love it, but it was a job, and he hated it less than he'd expected to. And it turned out he was pretty good at it.

"I'm more on the sales and marketing end of the footwear business," he said to Nate.

"Cool," Fiona said.

When the Winklers' invitation to pitch arrived in his mailbox in Baltimore, he'd thought it must have been a mistake, and his first reaction was to toss it. But he showed it to Carla, his wife, and she convinced him that he must have developed a reputation as a sort of shoe-selling superstar, and this was why the Winklers had invited him. She said maybe someone who had connections to the Winklers had bought a pair of shoes from him at the Bootery and been so impressed that he, or she—and it was far more likely that it was a she, as Victor sold about nine pairs of women's shoes for every one of men's—had recommended him. "You have to go," Carla said. "You have to give it a shot. This could be our big break."

Or it could all be a waste of time, but in the short term at least it was an ego-boosting waste of time, and boosting Victor's ego was not an activity Carla engaged in all that frequently. He began to worry that Carla's enthusiasm for his trip had less to do with her hopes that he'd land the Winkler deal and more with getting him out of town for a few days so she could spend time with Karl, the new science teacher at her school, about whom Carla could not stop talking. But what the hell? Victor thought. He decided to give it a try.

After he'd booked his plane tickets and hotel room, Victor did some research—into Winklers, bootmaking, hiking—and uncovered information that revealed a more plausible explanation for the Winkler invitation, and one that didn't bode well for his chances. But he didn't need to get into it right now with Nate and Fiona. He hadn't even mentioned it to Carla.

"So," Nate said. "The supermodel on the plane. Is she involved in this?"

"Isabel," Fiona said.

"Isabel?" Victor said. "Seriously? That's her name?"

"That's what she said."

How convenient that the Evil Princess just happened have almost the same name as the Winkler matriarch. No way that was her real name, Victor thought.

"Have you heard of Nanda Devi?" he said. Of course they had. They were exactly the kind of kids who would own Nanda Devi things—rich kids whose parents could afford to send them off to an expensive little boutique college out in the godforsaken wilderness, where they could study philosophy and literature and art history and graduate into a life living off their trust funds and selling trinkets on Etsy. They would know Nanda Devi, the maker of widely coveted and ridiculously overpriced outdoor clothing and gear, the company that branded itself as the defender of all things environmental, named for some mountain in Tibet somewhere, the perfect company to fold Winklers into. And who better than this supposed *Isabel* with her phony name to preside over the folding?

"Well, this 'Isabel' is with Nanda Devi. Apparently they're my competition."

No one spoke for several seconds. Victor blew on his hands in an attempt to warm them.

"Dang," Nate said.

"What do you mean, 'dang'?"

"I mean, hot chick, big company like that. I mean you're smoked, Victor."

It was not an unreasonable conclusion to reach. But something in the letter he'd received, the one on Winkler letterhead and signed jointly by Lukas and Sasha Winkler, had hinted at ambivalence within the family. The letter had said, on the one hand, that the Winklers were searching for someone who could "expand the company and improve profit margins while sustaining the reputation for quality on which it had been built." But on the other hand, they sought to retain the "intimate, human scale of operations" and "an unyielding commitment to craft." Those were very different things—one was a growth model; the other aimed to keep things small, and while Nanda Devi did a lot of things well, "small" wasn't one of them. Victor sensed ambiguity, and hoped he could exploit it. It was like the women who would come to him insisting their shoe size was a seven and a half when it was perfectly obvious that their feet demanded nines. You could have your seven and a half, or you could have a shoe that fit, but you couldn't have both. He hoped he might turn out to be the shoe that fit.

"We'll see," he said to the back of Nate's head. He looked out the window at a frozen landscape beneath a moonless sky lit by a gazillion stars. The sky didn't do this in Baltimore. He could make out the dark shapes of the mountains silhouetted in the distance, the White Mountains, or the Green Mountains. He couldn't remember which. Black mountains now, in any event. "What mountains are those?" he asked.

"The Adirondacks," Fiona said.

[chapter 4]

There wasn't much to downtown Granite, just a main street with a few shops arrayed along it—a hairdresser, a hardware store, a few offices, a place that sold antiques, a storefront with plywood in the windows, a small restaurant advertising breakfast all day, with a neon sign over the door that would have said Mercer's Cafe if the second "e" hadn't gone dark. There was snow everywhere, even on the road, and streetlamps managed to give everything fuzzy edges and an orangey glow, like looking at the world through night-vision goggles.

Victor told Nate and Fiona he was staying at the Placid Inn, and they said they knew where it was. As they rolled through town Victor glanced up and down side streets for a sign of it while fighting the creeping feeling that he was being set up for something. Information was being passed wordlessly back and forth between Nate and Fiona in the front seat, communicated with shrugged shoulders and sideways glances and raised eyebrows, ending with Nate's nod of the head. Victor wondered if this was when they robbed him and left him unconscious in an alley, where he would freeze to death in less than a minute, his last few fading nose hair crackles not being loud enough to attract a passerby, not that there would be any out at this hour and in this cold.

"Listen, Victor," Nate said. "Before we drop you off, we were wondering if you could do us a favor," Nate said. Here it comes, Victor thought. Fiona completed the request: "We were wondering if you could buy us some beer."

Beer? That's it? Of course he could buy them beer. Sweet relief swept over him. It made perfect sense. What else could you do up here in North Nowhere on a Friday night, where the single street with a glimmer of a pulse had hours before rolled up and crawled under its down comforter? You got drunk or smoked weed, or both, or, if you had the right resources and connections, climbed even higher on the ladder of mind-altering substances. He was a little surprised that at this point in their college careers they hadn't yet secured fake IDs, but buying them beer was the least he could do to repay them for the ride. "Sure," he said. "My pleasure."

They drove on through town and out the other side about a mile and a half and pulled into the parking lot of a 7-Eleven, a beacon of fluorescence radiating into the darkness.

"We'll wait here," Nate said.

"Bud Light," Fiona added. Victor suppressed a snort, not wanting to make it sound like he was judging her.

"A case, if you don't mind," Nate clarified.

"Cans," Fiona said.

Outside the car the cold hit Victor like an icepick, so he hurried across the parking lot and into the warmth of the store, whose sole other inhabitant was a teenage kid who stood behind the counter and watched as Victor made his way to the refrigerator case where they kept the beer. He found Bud Light in twelve-packs, grabbed two, and took them to the counter. He handed the kid two twenties. "Will that be all?" the kid said. Why do they ask that? Victor wondered.

While he waited for his change, the bright store got brighter as the headlights of another car pulling up blared into it. Victor turned to look, but couldn't see anything past the glare of the lights. Then the headlights on Nate's car went on. And then off. And then on again. And then off. They went on a third time they stayed on, and only then did it dawn on Victor that they were signaling him. And that realization got followed by another: they were moving farther away. Nate's car was backing up, turning, and leaving. "Hey!" he said to no one in particular. He grabbed his change and the beer and ran toward the door, which jingled as he pushed through it, and he all but ran headlong into a large man wearing the unmistakable uniform of a police officer.

"Thirsty?" the officer said, nodding at the two twelve-packs of beer in Victor's hands.

"Stocking up," he said helplessly, flashing a sheepish grin. The taillights of Nate's car were red dots receding into the distance.

"You from out of town?"

"Yes." In a dinky town like Granite, the officer would have known everybody who lived here.

"What brings you to Granite?"

"I'm here for a meeting."

"Ah," the officer said. "Who with?"

Victor didn't want to go all Miranda-rights with this guy, but it was none of his business who he was here to meet. And the last thing he wanted was for word to get back to the Winklers that one of their invitees had been out buying a case of Bud Light the night before his presentation. He didn't know which part of that story would do more damage in Winklerville—his apparent goal of getting wasted or his lousy choice of beer.

"Just a meeting," he said. "For work." He tried to sound nonchalant, but worried that it came out defiant. The cop's fleshy face held the bemused and skeptical expression of someone who's used to getting lied to. He had on one of those trapper's hats with the fur earflaps. A round patch on the front of the hat announced it to be the property of Granite College Security. A campus cop, Victor thought, not a real cop. The hat looked warm. Victor was freezing. "Can we step inside and have this conversation?" he said.

The campus cop didn't move. "Where're you staying?" he asked.

"The hotel," Victor said, nodding in the direction he had last seen Nate's taillights. "The Placid."

"You'll like it," he said. "It's a nice place. Quaint. Homey. Quite a ways from here, though. How were you planning to get there?"

"Oh, walking," Victor said. He worried that his teeth were chattering. "I like to walk. It's a nice night. Clear, brisk. Lots of stars to look at." He looked at the sky—with the store's glare, the stars had all disappeared.

"Six below out here," the cop said, blowing a cloud of breath exhaust to underscore his point.

Victor did a little back and forth thing with his head as if to say, *Well, yeah, but what can you do?*

"So I've got to ask. You weren't by any chance buying beer for those kids, were you?"

"Kids?" Victor said, aware that his voice came out higher than normal, squeaking, fake. Hearing his own voice falseness reminded him that he was not good at pretending things were other than they were, which did not bode well for his meeting in the morning with the Winklers. Also, his mouth was going numb. If any of the cop's questions called for more than a one-syllable answer, he'd be slurring his words.

"Those kids that just pulled out of here in a hurry. Because if you were with them, that would mean you're buying beer for underage kids, and as we both know, that's against the law."

"Right," Victor said.

"Can I see your ID?"

"Offser," he slurred, "ev I done 'thing wrong?" He hadn't. He was going to, but he hadn't, not yet anyway. Victor didn't want to surrender his name, again fearing that all of this would somehow get back to the Winklers. He was disliking this town more and more by the second.

"You're buying beer," he said. "I'm just carding you."

"I'm fifty-three."

"A young-looking fifty-three. Robust. Lots of color in your cheeks. Must be all those cold walks. ID please?"

Victor put the beer down, and with some difficulty took out his wallet and handed over his driver's license. The officer looked at it and squinted. "You sure it's not fake?"

"Oh, come on."

The cop's face broke into a grin. He handed Victor's license back to him. "I'm just yanking your chain. You enjoy your walk back to the hotel, Mr. Barstow." And with that he turned and left to keep Granite College safe from whatever and whomever it needed to be kept safe from. Victor watched the man walk back to his patrol car, where he jotted a few notes on a pad. Then the car backed up, turned around, and disappeared into the night.

Victor went back into the 7-Eleven, rubbing his hands together to try to get some feeling back into them. He went to the counter, where the kid at the counter eyed him uncertainly, wary now after Victor's brush with the law. "How the fuck do I get to the Placid Hotel?" he said.

[chapter 5]

Son of a bitch it was cold out. Bone chilling didn't even begin to capture it. The cold cut like razor blades, a shrewd cold, one that sought out your weaknesses and exploited them. And Victor's weaknesses were many, starting with his clothes, or relative lack thereof. He had on the gray suit he planned to wear to the meeting with the Winklers tomorrow, which he wore because he worried that it might get too wrinkled if he packed it away in his suitcase. Dress shirt, an overcoat that functioned well enough in Baltimore but was overmatched here—and that was about it, and none of it put up much of a defense. On his feet were a pair of expensive Italian loafers that he had bought at the Bootery with his forty-percent employee discount, the idea being that showing excellent taste in footwear would score points with the Winklers. The idea had been Carla's, and Victor understood the logic. But they were cocktail-party loafers, not Iditarod loafers. They pinched his toes and had the insulating value of cellophane. The thin socks he wore with them just laughed at the cold and waved it on through to his feet.

The top of Victor's head, hairless since his late thirties except for some closely trimmed side foliage, went numb before he left the parking lot, and his face was frozen. He held one twelve-pack in his hand and tucked the other under his arm, leaving his free hand to put in his overcoat pocket until the exposed hand got too cold and he had to switch sides, which was about every twenty seconds. The ski cap and gloves he brought from home would have been a big help had they not been in his suitcase, which sat in the trunk of Nate's car. Victor wondered if he would ever see it again.

With the snow and ice creating uncertain footing, and with some minor but not insignificant shortcomings in the directions he'd gotten from the kid at the 7-Eleven, it took Victor the better part of an hour to cover the distance back to the center of town and find the Placid Hotel, a three-story Victorian structure on Lake Street. By this time his hands had frozen into shapes ideal for grasping Bud Light twelve-packs, but of little use for much else, and they resisted his commands that they grab the handle of the Granite Hotel's front door. So he set the beer down and used his left forearm to maneuver his right hand into a position where he could deploy it like a claw to open the door. Weren't hotels supposed to have doormen?

With the rapid transition from subarctic cold to over-heated lobby, Victor worried that his body might crack. At the desk he struggled with a frozen mouth to give the clerk his name—it came out something like *Rictor Rashto*—though eventually his identity and reservation were confirmed and the clerk, an older man with a thin face and wispy mustache and a nametag identifying him as "Oliver," gave him his room key, which he promptly dropped and couldn't with his cramped hands manage to pick up off the lobby's hardwood floor. Oliver came around and got if for him, in the sympathetic but condescending way people have when dealing with the handicapped. Here, let me help you, you poor, sad man.

Oliver helped Victor with his twelve-packs and stood with him as he waited for the elevator. "No luggage?" he said, not even attempting to conceal the judgmental tone behind the question he was really asking, which was, *Just beer?*

"Lost," Victor managed. His mouth was beginning to work again. The icicles that moments earlier hung from his eyebrows dripped water onto his cheeks, making it look as though he was crying. The elevator was in the middle of a hallway that connected the lobby to the hotel's restaurant and lounge. When he looked toward the restaurant his stomach rumbled to remind him he'd eaten only one sketchy slice of pizza since lunch, then the rumbling stopped abruptly when he saw "Isabel" sitting at the bar, looking in his direction. She acknowledged Victor with a tip of the glass of whatever it was she was drinking. Finally, mercifully, the elevator doors opened.

When they reached Victor's room Oliver set the beer on a table and lingered in the professional way of people waiting for a tip. Some life had returned to Victor's hands, and he managed to fish a couple of dollar bills from his wallet. When Oliver left, Victor went to fill the tub for a hot bath.

[chapter 6]

The hot bath took some effort. The tub's drain-stopper mechanism wouldn't close all the way, but with the strategic deployment of a washcloth stuffed around the edges and some repeated refilling, Victor got the tub to hold enough water for long enough to soak even the most stubborn outposts of cold from his body. With his suitcase still in the back of Nate's car, he had no clothes other than those he'd been wearing, and those now hung over him, suspended on coat hangers from the shower-curtain rod, placed there in the hopes that the steam from his bath might work some magic on the wrinkles and creases he'd accumulated during the polar expedition he'd just endured. While the bath had been filling he aimed the hotel-issue hairdryer at his fancy Italian shoes and watched as a radius of gray salt-stain appeared on each. The first-impression gap between him and the Evil Princess was widening.

All Victor could do was hope his clothes would be presentable by morning, and as he was at the moment more in need of sleep than clothes, and tired of refilling the tub, he eventually withdrew himself from its fading warmth and stepped naked into the bedroom. He was surprised to find he had company.

"Victor!" Nate called cheerily from where he sat in the room's only chair. "Want a beer?" He was holding one, as was

Fiona, who smiled from a multi-pillowed perch on the bed, then did a polite averting of the eyes. Victor's suitcase sat in the middle of the room.

A range of emotions fought a quick little skirmish inside Victor's brain. There was anger at them for having abandoned him. Relief that he had his suitcase back. Embarrassment at being a somewhat pudgy middle-aged man standing naked in front of them. Embarrassment won. He ducked back into the bathroom and re-emerged with a bath towel around his waist.

Anger came in a close second: "Where. The fuck. Did you. Go?" he said, breaking up the question into discrete segments so he could communicate his anger without shouting and bringing the wrath of *hotel* security down on his head. A certain flare of the nostrils and a widening of the eyes helped communicate fury.

"Yeah, well, sorry about how that thing at the store went down," Nate said. "We... um... well, you know, the cop and all... We tried to signal you."

"*Sorry?*"

"That cop knows us," Fiona said. "We have a... shall we say... history with him. We're kind of on probation. He catches us again, we get thrown out of school."

"Yeah," Nate said, "and that would really suck because, like, who would ever want to leave a place like Granite?" Fiona giggled.

Here were two ungrateful punks who would let their parents fork over how many tens of thousands of dollars to send them to a fancy college like Granite, where they would piss it all away by getting caught buying beer. Is this what Allie would be doing in the fall? Well, no—not unless he could afford to send her to college.

"You didn't think, maybe, about coming back to pick me up?" he asked.

"Nah, Foxy's onto that one," Nate said.

"Foxy?"

"Officer Fox," Fiona clarified.

"He would have just followed us," Nate said. "He was probably tailing you."

"So you just figured you'd meet me here and drink my beer."

"Where else would you go?" Nate said. "And technically it's our beer. Per our agreement."

"How did you get in here, anyway?"

"Guy at the desk gave us a key."

Victor again weighed options. He could cross the room and punch Nate, or he could retreat to the bathroom and put some clothes on. The fact that he had never punched anyone in his whole life steered him toward the latter option. "Excuse me," he said, and grabbed his suitcase and pulled it into the bathroom, slamming the door behind him.

He emerged a few minutes later in a blue button-down and a pair of brown corduroys. Nate was waiting for him by the bathroom door with an open can of Bud Light, foam bubbling out the top. He held it out toward Victor, a peace offering of sorts. "Take this. You'll feel better." Victor took the beer. "Here, sit," Nate said. He let Victor have the room's only chair, and moved onto the bed next to Fiona.

"We figured if we used someone new to buy for us, someone Foxy didn't know, maybe…" Fiona let her voice trail off.

"*Used*," Victor said. "I think that's the key word here. You used me. And then left me to freeze to death."

"Jeez, Victor," Nate said. "I mean, we gave you a ride and everything. It's a lot shorter walk here from the 7-Eleven than it is from the fucking airport. So, you know, quid quo pro and all that." He got up and helped himself to another beer. Victor counted empties and concluded that Nate was on his third.

"And what if I'd gotten arrested?" Victor said. "Can't you just see me using my one phone call to call the Winklers and say well, gee, I'm sorry I couldn't make it, but I'm in jail for buying booze for minors on my first night in town?"

They both nodded sympathetically. "I think you may have got a little thing on your nose," Nate said.

"A *thing*. What do you mean, a *thing*? What kind of *thing*?"

"Take a look," he said.

There was a mirror over a chest of drawers. On Victor's nose, which was not a small nose to begin with, a red circle about the size of a dime stood out prominently, right in the middle of the tip.

"That might be frostbite."

"Great! That's perfect. I'll go see the Winklers tomorrow looking like Bozo the fucking clown."

"You know, Victor," Fiona said. "Maybe we can help."

"Thank you, but you've done enough already." Now that he was aware of the red spot on his nose, it started to itch. He moved to scratch it and then wondered if that might be a bad idea. What did he know about frostbite? Not much. There was that guy in that book who got left on Mt. Everest and later his nose fell off. Had his itched? Had he scratched it? Victor looked back in the mirror. He found a similar red blotch on his right cheek.

"No, seriously," Fiona said.

Victor walked away from the mirror and sat down, not wanting to stare any longer at a face that had started to look like pink camouflage. "How can you help?"

"Well," she said, "for starters, I can cover that thing up so you don't go into the meeting with a big red spot on your nose."

"Right," he said. "Instead I'll go into a meeting with the family whose entire livelihood is making boots for mountaineers with makeup on my face."

Fiona looked hurt. "I can make it so it won't show," she said.

"Beats Bozo the fucking clown," Nate said. "Plus, how're you going to get there?"

He had a point, one that in the confusion of the night Victor had overlooked. He had planned to drive to the Winklers in the rental car that never materialized. "You're going to let me borrow your car?"

"I was thinking more along the lines of driving you out there," Nate said.

"What's your pitch, anyway?" Fiona wanted to know.

"My pitch?"

"Yeah," she said. "Your pitch. What are you going to say to convince them you should run their company, and not that Isabel person?"

"You want to know my *pitch*?"

"If you have one."

"Personalized service," Victor said. The room went silent while they waited for him to say something more.

"That's it?" Fiona said after several seconds.

"With a story."

"What story?"

Victor told them about Marjorie McGinniss, a woman in her late seventies who had become one of his steady customers after two botched bunion surgeries left her feet deformed in ways that made no shoe fit and any shoe painful. She came to Victor and over the course of three weeks and lots of trial and error and battles with shoe manufacturers and searches for other shoe manufacturers that his store didn't carry, they finally found a distributor that made shoes she could wear in reasonable comfort and were attractive enough that she wasn't too embarrassed to wear them.

"Now she moves like a ballerina," he said. It was a line he'd practiced.

Marjorie McGinnis had sung Victor's praises at the assisted living complex where she lived, which brought maybe a dozen new customers to the Bootery, all of them asking for Victor. It had won him the employee-of-the-year award, which was a pair of bronzed baby shoes the store's owner had inherited from his grandmother.

"That should definitely knock it out of the park," Nate said.

"Don't you see, it's about sharing the Winklers' unyielding devotion to finding the perfect fit," Victor said. It was another line he'd practiced, and that was exactly how it sounded coming out of his mouth.

"It's about an old crippled lady with bad feet," Nate said. "You know any other good stories?"

On the bed, Fiona rested her chin in her hand, and looked at Victor with big round eyes that blinked slowly and more than was normal. "I think we should blue-sky this a bit," she said. Victor had no idea what that meant.

The Winklers' strength, as Fiona explained it, was their dominance of the supply-and-demand curve—at any given moment, people coveted many more pairs of Winklers than the family was prepared to produce. People waited in line, sometimes for years, to get their pair. Customers were buying a concept. They were buying an idea of their better selves that the boots managed to conjure, even, to a degree, while they were waiting in line for them.

"But they're only dominant within the tiny sliver of the market that's willing to put up with that kind of bullshit," she said. "My guess is that the company understands that going forward that's just not sustainable. We're about to see drones deliver things within hours of when you order them by speaking to your cloud-based digital assistant. Unless you haven't already printed them out on your 3D printer. You know, I get the whole *yearning for a time gone by* thing, but the number of people who are prepared to tolerate the kind of delayed gratification that Winklers demands will be too small and too old.

"In class we read about this study where they had people listen to old record albums, on vinyl. When the needle hit that space between songs, people under thirty-five thought something had gone wrong with the record player. They were too impatient to wait for the time it took the needle to move from one song to the next.

"Unless something changes, the Winkler model will be obsolete. They're going to have to have to increase production, speed up delivery, and maybe reduce the price a little to bring the boots within shouting distance of a new generation of hikers and climbers. Thanks to that girl that wrote that book, we're in this age where there's a whole new sub-demographic of young people who look at hiking in the wilderness as a sort of life-fulfilling vision quest. Sure, most of those people will quit after four miles when their legs are tired and their shoulders hurt and they're covered in mosquito bites. But they don't know that when they start out, and that's when we want them to covet these boots. Nobody covets like a millennial. But what you covet needs to be within some sort of realistic reach, or you lose interest."

"What are you majoring in?" Victor asked.

"Studio art," she said.

"With a business minor," Nate said. "And on track to graduate in three years."

"A big part of their spiel has been that you have to come here to be personally fitted to get a pair of boots," Victor said. "I'm not sure they're going to want to move away from that."

"What the Winklers need to move away from is the twentieth century. I mean, write a letter stating why you deserve a pair of Winklers? Really? On what? Papyrus? Parchment? Send it by carrier pigeon? We broaden that, and not just with email, which nobody even uses anymore, but with Facebook, Twitter, Instagram. People can post videos on YouTube of themselves out doing outdoorsy things in their Winkler boots. Give it all a chance to go viral, and then watch how it bends the supply-demand curve. If people want a personal fitting, then great. But let's expand that, too. No more of this tiny bed-and-breakfast approach for two or three people. Open an inn. Make this a vacation destination."

Victor was impressed. The girl could sell ivory to an elephant.

Nate raised his beer can in salute. "To the Barstow Limited Partnership." He and Fiona clinked cans and drank. Victor looked pensive. "What?" Nate said.

"Look," Victor said. "About that Barstow part. There's something I should tell you. There's a chance that I'm not who the Winklers think I am."

In researching the Winklers, and boots, and bootmaking, Victor had come across another bootmaker, in Colorado, a man who, like the Winklers, was carrying on a family legacy that had attracted a modest but cult-like and at one time lucrative following. It wasn't war that had made this family's boots famous—it was mining. The promise of gold and other riches had drawn hundreds of fortune-seekers to the town of Telluride a hundred years before it had transformed into a ski mecca. The mountains yielded gold and silver, zinc, copper, and other minerals. Mining built the town. Miners, like soldiers, needed good footwear, and no one better met their needs than a transplanted Ohio bootmaker named Clement Barstow. He was no relation to Victor, or at least none that Victor was aware of.

The mining died off as the mineral wealth got depleted, and the town nearly died along with it. Then in the 1970s it began capitalizing on a different, more reliable, and renewable resource: snow. Telluride evolved into a ski town, and then into a ski and music and counterculture town, and the Barstow boot-making business evolved to suit evolving tastes. They started making cowboy boots—boots whose popularity skyrocketed when Mary Travers wore a pair at a Peter, Paul, and Mary concert at Red Rocks. Leading the family's resurgence was Clement Barstow's great-grandson, a reclusive eccentric who ran a store on Colorado Ave. called Barstow Bootery. His name was Victor Barstow.

"So I'm thinking that maybe when the Winklers searched for 'Barstow' and 'Bootery,' they somehow got me," Victor said. "They think I'm him."

Nate and Fiona exchanged glances. Nate got up to get another beer. It opened with a *pffssst*, which pretty much summed up the mood of the room.

"Well that complicates things," Fiona said.

This was the first time Victor had spoken to anyone of the Colorado Barstows. Maybe he should have said something to his wife. But why burst her bubble along with his own, he rationalized, though he was increasingly concerned that the sustaining force of Carla's bubble had more to do with quality time with Karl than the relative brightness of Victor's career prospects. What bothered him more than imagining Carla with Karl was how little that thought actually bothered him. Victor's marriage was like one of those mineral veins deep inside the mountains of Telluride, a once-sustaining force that had become tired and too fully tapped out. Now it felt like the only thing golden to come out of their marriage had been their daughter Allie. At best the rest had been zinc. And with Karl in the picture it all felt as flimsy as dented tin.

Another reason for saying nothing of the Colorado Barstows was that once he'd booked his plane and hotel reservations and kicked everything into motion, Victor, with an uncharacteristic burst of optimism, allowed himself to believe that he actually had a chance. It was an invigorating feeling. He stood straighter, walked taller than his five-foot nine-inch frame normally allowed, nodded at the newly confident face he saw in the mirror. Victor believed himself to be a good father, but being a good father overlapped with being a good provider, and with Allie now almost eighteen, being a good provider had crystallized into a single thing: coming up with the money so she could go to a good college. It both touched and pained him to see Allie quit yearbook committee her senior year so she could get a job to help with tuition, but she and Victor both knew that what she made making lattes at Starbucks wasn't going to do much more than pay for a semester's worth of books. Carla's teacher's salary wasn't going to get them very far, either. It would be up to Victor, along with whatever help a college's financial aid office might be able to provide.

So, Victor reasoned, what was there to lose, except for two hundred and seventy dollars on round-trip plane fare, a few hundred more for hotel and meals, and three days of his time, which was the minimum time needed given that only there was only one flight a day out of Granite International that would take him back in the general direction of home. Plus, now, the purchase price of two twelve-packs of bad beer. Worst-case scenario, he loses the bid and goes home to a failing marriage and a job selling shoes. He tried not to think about the worst-case scenario.

The hotel room began to feel uncomfortably warm in the way of hotel rooms everywhere. Fiona removed layers—the down jacket, a sweater, a flannel shirt—until she was down to a black tank top and a scarf, with her ski cap still on her head. A tattoo covered her left shoulder and wound around her arm almost to her elbow—teals and blues and purples, with accents of crimson, vaguely floral, but also wave-like. Victor, normally tattoo-averse, couldn't help staring at this one. He thought of Allie, seventeen, bright but directionless, and wondered what might give her the kind of focus Fiona seemed to have. Would college? Would Allie want a tattoo, and, if she did, would Victor try to stop it? And *how* would he stop it, even if he wanted to, with her off by herself in some Granite-like corner of the planet, though hopefully warmer? Maybe she would be better off living at home and going to the community college after all, so he could keep an eye on her. But that thought felt defeatist. His own financial shortcomings would be the only reason for her to make that choice, so the whole concept undermined his manhood thoughts. If Allie wanted a tattoo—while she was *away* at college someplace—let her get one. Besides, Fiona's was mesmerizing. He caught her eye. She looked at him with a brow furrowed, as if she was wondering why he was staring at her, or working out a problem, which, in fact, she was. His mind had wandered. He was glad someone was staying focused.

"So," she said, "what were you planning to tell the Winklers about this other Victor Barstow?"

"The truth, I suppose."

"That you're not him. That you sell shoes."

Victor shrugged affirmatively.

"What do you think the chances are that they already know who you are and what you do, and don't have you confused with this other guy?"

Victor shrugged, less affirmatively this time. If they knew, why invite him? He thought about snowballs and their survival odds in hell.

"This store where you work, is it your store? Do you own it?" Fiona asked. Victor shook his head. "Are you in charge? Are you the manager, maybe?"

"Not exactly." Not remotely, in fact.

"What does it mean when you say you're on the sales and marketing end of things?"

"It means I work in a shoe store in a mall, and people come in and I help them find shoes they want to buy," he said. He pictured the image going through their minds, of open shoe boxes and clumps of that tissue-paper they stuff inside the toe, of him running back and forth into the storeroom to pull out new styles and sizes for the customer to try, of middle-aged and post-middle-aged women who could sink hours into this exercise. That image was not without accuracy.

"Hmph," Nate said. Victor had lost count of what beer he was on.

Fiona grew quiet, either because she was strategizing or coming to grips with the depth of Victor's hopelessness.

"Maybe we can turn all of this to our advantage," she said eventually. "I don't know about the whole Marjorie What's-Her-Name thing and her bunions, but I think maybe your basic business proposition—all that stuff about unyielding commitment to fit—is pretty close to being on the mark. We build the case that a shoe salesman is exactly what the Winklers need—that you are ground zero for the most important thing they have ever stood for: the place where foot meets boot. We pitch this in a way that says Nanda Devi is just too big and too corporate and too impersonal to be in touch with this fundamental value that's been at the heart of Winklers for nearly a century. You guarantee fit. Nanda Devi guarantees lots of people complaining about fit. With them, Winklers flies headlong into the future in a way that totally wrecks their brand. We move them forward, but in a way that saves their soul."

"There's your tagline," Nate said, grinning, and slurring the words together. "Winklers: Save your sole."

"And you, Victor," Fiona said. "Let's assume inviting you was no mistake. You, Victor, are the savior."

"You're David against Goliath," Nate said. "You're Rocky against… Bullwinkle." He giggled, then excused himself to go to the bathroom, where they heard him throwing up. When he returned he said, "So what time do you want us here in the morning?"

Victor didn't sleep much that night. He mostly lay in bed staring out the window into the cold, black void, wondering about the odds that he would ever see Fiona and Nate again.

[chapter 7]

Saturday morning at nine-thirty sharp Victor heard the knock on his hotel-room door and went to open it. "Let's work on your nose," Fiona said. She and Nate pushed past him into the room.

If it surprised Victor that they'd showed up, it surprised him more how they'd transformed. Nate's youthful resilience had triumphed over what should have been a wicked hangover. He had the androgynous good looks of a Calvin Klein model, in black skinny jeans and a gray Henley sweater, his ponytail now clean and brushed and flowing. Victor figured the Winklers would judge them at least subconsciously on footwear, and hoped Nate's black Converse sneakers were just possibly retro enough to not be a liability. Fiona wore a crimson sweater-dress with forearm-length sleeves that covered her tattoo. The dress clung to her like woolen shrink-wrap before giving way around mid thigh to sheer black tights and black boots that came almost to her knees. A green scarf. Just enough makeup so you'd notice. Even her fingerless black gloves looked stylish. The Winkler men would approve. A black portfolio bag hung off Fiona's shoulder.

"What's in there?" he asked.

"Just some sketches, mostly."

A night hanging in the bathroom had removed most of the wrinkles from Victor's gray suit. Still, he felt stodgy next to Fiona and Nate, like here were these two vibrant young people who'd been forced to bring along their dad.

Fiona took a makeup kit out of her portfolio bag and sat Victor down to address his frostbite blotch. It had changed overnight—it was now less solidly circular and more a mottled blend of pink and white, like well-marbled meat. It took her about five minutes to have it looking more or less like a normal nose. She repeated the process with the spot on his cheek. They discussed strategy. Victor would talk first. Fiona would do a brief bit. Nate would sit and observe, doing his best impression of the creative, silent type. They were as ready as they were going to be.

"Rock and roll, Victor," Nate said as they stood to leave. "Time to go kick some Nanda Devi ass."

The cold was still brutal, but a new variety of brutal, less like a razor cut and more like being hit with a blunt instrument. The skies hung leaden and gray. "It's a little warmer today," Nate said, looking up at the sky, and Victor glanced at him to see if he was joking. "We could see some snow later."

The route to Paradiso and the Winklers went north of Granite on a narrow road that did not rank high on the region's snow-plowing priority list. Their presentation was scheduled for eleven-thirty, and the drive was supposed to take a half-hour, and they had left around quarter past ten to allow some extra time in case they got lost or something. *Or something* turned out to be a slippery road full of frozen-over tire ruts with sections of snow that ranged from a dusting to four inches deep.

They made steady progress, right up until the point where they didn't. Nate's Ford Escort— with front-wheel drive and worn, student-budget tires, and not a sensible Subaru like people in this part of the world were supposed to drive—fought gamely for miles, until they rounded a curve and hit an icy patch that sent them sliding sideways off the roadway toward a row of leafless and unyielding trees. Fortunately the car stopped before the trees stopped them, but less fortunately it stopped in a shallow ditch that Nate's rear wheels slipped into like a foot into a Winkler boot.

"This has happened before," Fiona said, in a tone meant to be reassuring. Victor looked at his watch. Ten thirty-five.

Nate gunned the accelerator and the car strained forward an inch or two before relaxing back into the inevitability of the ditch. He set the emergency brake and got out to survey the situation. "We're going to have to get out and push," he said.

Pushing cars from snowdrifts remains a masculine pursuit, so Nate and Victor got out while Fiona slid over behind the wheel. Giving possibly unnecessary driving instructions is another masculine pursuit. "Give it a little gas when we rock it," Nate said. "Not too much or you'll just dig us in." He and Victor went behind the car. Victor did an assessment. They weren't as stuck as he'd feared. The ditch wasn't deep and the car wasn't heavy, so extracting it didn't seem like an insurmountable challenge.

Nate and Victor rocked, Fiona revved in sync with the rocking, and the front wheels alternately spun and grabbed, spun and grabbed. They made grudging progress, going a little farther with each push, but the car also started to slide from side to side, widening the ditch as much as escaping it. Then suddenly, as if it had become fed up with all of this nonsense, the car lurched forward, skidded sideways a couple of feet, grabbed something solid, and shot back onto the roadway with burst of power that would have impressed NASA. This would have been all good news, except that the sideways skid followed by the lurch forward caught Victor by surprise and he face-planted into the mixture of gray snow and dirt while the spinning car tires threw slush and pebbles at him.

Victor inventoried the damage—mud, stains, and a small horizontal tear in the left knee of his suit pants. He used clean snow to wash as much dirt as he could off his clothes and hands, and hoped the water splotches would dry before they reached the Winklers, which was unlikely given the suboptimal performance of the car's heater. More likely the splotches would freeze, then thaw when they got to the Winklers, so it would look like he had peed himself.

"Shit does seem to happen to you, Victor," Nate said.

Victor checked his watch again: eight minutes to eleven. Barring further tragedy, they still had time, though the margin of error had narrowed. Fiona slid over, Nate got back behind the wheel, and they were off.

They almost missed the turnoff to the Winklers, which was marked only by a mailbox with the company's signature "W" in a big block letter, a larger version of what the company embossed on the inside ankle of every Winkler boot. The turnoff put them on a road worse than the one they'd been on; it hadn't seen a plow in days. But they followed fresh tire tracks made by a bigger and more capable vehicle. They bounced and jostled along until they came to a tall wrought iron fence with a gate, which was closed. They waited to see if someone would come to open it, or if it would open automatically, but nothing happened.

"Now what?" Nate said. Victor didn't know. His watch said eleven twenty-two. He suspected they were being watched, and the discovery of a security camera perched atop one of the fence posts confirmed his suspicion. Maybe this was part of the test. Maybe the game was already over, and they'd barely started to play. Maybe they were being laughed at, with EP and the Winklers sitting in front of a fireplace watching a video screen and drinking hot toddies to toast their new partnership. Fiona got out of the car and walked to the gate. She pulled it and it slid open. Nate drove through and waited. Fiona pulled the gate shut behind them and got back in the car.

"You're welcome," she said.

They proceeded up a narrow and mostly plowed gravel road that stopped at a circular drive in front of the house. The black SUV from the airport was there. Fiona said that was a good sign—it meant Victor would be presenting second, which played into their strategy of positioning themselves in contrast to Nanda Devi, and also gave them a better chance of leaving a lasting impression. Victor, in his torn and splotched suit, felt more anxious about first impressions than lasting ones.

The house was a massive wooden structure built in the shape of a V, with the main door at the elbow. Victor rang the bell and waited. He looked at his watch: eleven twenty-nine— they were on time, but barely. A young woman opened the door. "Mr. Barstow?" she said, and threw a puzzled look at Nate and Fiona. "And...?"

"Associates," Nate said.

"Kirsten?" Fiona said.

The young woman looked at Fiona and tilted her head sideways. "Fiona?"

"What are you doing here?" Fiona said.

"I work here. What are *you* doing here?"

"Business opportunity." She patted her portfolio.

"Look, we're kind of late," Victor said. "Maybe we should...?"

"Please, follow me," Kirsten said. She and Fiona talked as they walked, and Victor and Nate walked behind them. Kirsten, Victor grasped from listening in on their conversation, had graduated from Granite the previous spring and had begun an unpaid internship as executive assistant to the Winkler family.

"What are they like, the family?" Fiona asked her.

"Marco's… interesting," she said. "He's the father, and his two kids, who aren't really kids, they come and go. I don't know them very well. Though I like his daughter a lot. Sasha. She seems nice. She's an artist. She talks to me, at least. Lukas, the son, he's kind of corporate, and sort of off in his own world. I mostly work for Marco."

"Doing what?" Fiona asked.

"Oh, basically I do anything he asks me to do," Kirsten said. "Well, almost anything. Here we are."

She had led them up a grand staircase to the second floor, then down a hall to the closed door they now stood in front of. Kirsten knocked on the door and after a few seconds a man opened it halfway. "Yes?" he said.

"Mr. Barstow is here, sir," Kirsten said. She glanced back at Fiona and smiled. "And associates."

"Excellent," the man said, pulling the door wide. He was about Victor's height, maybe an inch taller, with a business-man's paunch and a green cardigan sweater over a white Oxford button-down open at the collar. "Come in, come in." He extended his hand to Victor, who took hold and shook it. "Mr. Barstow, Lukas Winkler. Delighted you could be here with us today." He looked uncertainly at Fiona and Nate, as if wondering who they were and whether he should let them in. After completing an up-and-down on Fiona, he extended his arm to usher them in. Fiona looked back at Kirsten, who rolled her eyes when Lukas looked away.

They entered a cavernous wood-paneled room. Photographs covered three of the walls—pictures of family, Italy, bootmaking. The fourth wall was mostly windows, overlooking a yard, with forest behind. A crackling fire in the fireplace to their left gave the space a homey glow and may have been its only source of warmth. A pair of bronzed Winkler boots sat on a table. Outside a light snow had started to fall, dusting the pine forest like powdered sugar.

Four people sat at a large oval table in the middle of the room, two of whom were EP and her middle linebacker of a driver. She smiled at Victor, her smile morphing into a smirk as she took in the hole in his pants leg and the water splotch at his crotch. What was she still doing here? Victor fought the urge to panic.

Lukas Winkler handled introductions. "You may know Isabel Forenza and her assistant…"

"Charles," the linebacker said, his voice a deep baritone. It struck Victor as incongruous to see a Black man here, like running into one at the North Pole, or yachting, not that he had been to the North Pole, or on a yacht, for that matter, except for that one company retreat back in the boom years. His daughter would have attributed these instinctual judgments to an imbedded racism. Isabel Forenza sat next to an older man, with her laptop open on the table and a projection screen set up behind her.

"Charles," Lukas repeated. "Charles and Isabel are from Nanda Devi. And this is my father, Marco Winkler, and my sister, Sasha." Sasha nodded at them. She had a kind face framed by dark shoulder-length hair she tucked behind her ears, her shoulders draped in a purple shawl that screamed "craft fair." Marco just sat and stared, his eyes enormous and unblinking behind wire-rimmed glasses with thick lenses.

Lukas continued. "This is Victor Barstow, and…?"

"Fiona O'Brian and Nate Block," Fiona said. "We're Mr. Barstow's associates."

"Fiona O'Brian and Nate Block," Lukas Winkler repeated. "I can imagine you may be thinking it's odd for each of you to be present in the room while the other is presenting. I'll acknowledge that it's somewhat unorthodox, but it is my father's request that we handle things this way." Lukas sounded rehearsed, like a boxing referee reminding fighters not to hit below the belt. "This is a competition of sorts," he continued, "and it is my father's belief that competition is managed with the most respect when the adversaries are face to face with one another. Not to imply that you're adversaries, necessarily. But you are competing, so it's in that spirit… Well, we should get started. Dad, would you like to say anything?"

Marco's huge eyes blinked slowly, the way a ventriloquist's dummy's eyes blink. "War!" he said suddenly. "That's why we're here. That and boots, and it was war that made the boots, or made them famous. Because the Kaiser and the archduke and then the whole thing blew up and it was cold out in those trenches, except then the Ruskies, and you needed good boots if you were going to get anywhere, what with the Japs and Yanks coming into it, and even in Africa, though sand can do a real number on boot leather, and so we moved here, and then there was another one, and another one, but those mountains out there were why, and my own father was a good man—and my God, he made boots!—and the war wasn't here but we helped win it, and the mountains, well, you know he once told me he moved here because they reminded him of—"

Lukas interrupted before mention of his grandmother's breasts could be made. "I think we should get started."

"Isabella, that was my mother's name," Marco said, his watery eyes focused on EP sitting next to him. "That's your name, too, isn't it dear?" She patted his hand and looked at him with an expression meant to convey mournful sympathy.

"Isa*bel*, Dad," Sasha Winkler clarified. "Her name is Isa*bel*, not Isabella."

No it isn't, Victor thought. Not really. He did a quick assessment of the situation. Marco was possibly insane, and EP had positioned herself as the second coming of his mother. Though there was something about Marco's monologue that struck Victor as being less something a crazy person might say and more something someone might say if they wanted you to think they were crazy. He had experience with fake crazy. In his HR days, after his company added a generous insurance rider for mental-health coverage, employee after employee came to him claiming they were crazy in the hopes of qualifying for free meds or an insanity-induced paid leave of absence.

"Ms. Forenza," Lukas said. "Maybe you'd like to get us started?"

Even Victor couldn't deny that Isabel Forenza looked stunning in a dark green velour dress, cut low enough to yield the subtlest hint of cleavage, which the expensive-looking red pendant of her necklace directed your eye to. Marco's eye followed the instructions and stayed there. He was besotted. Victor was in deep trouble.

She stood. "Could we dim the lights, please?" she called across the room. Kirsten, standing ready, dutifully complied, and on the screen a video materialized full of scenes of healthy, outdoorsy people doing healthy, outdoorsy things across all manner of spectacular landscapes—skiers skiing impossible lines down remote and majestic mountains, kayakers plummeting over waterfalls or cavorting with killer whales, surfers riding massive waves, rock-climbers dangling from walls the color of rust, and ending on a trio of breathless hikers panting their way up a ridge to a stunning vista overlooking a wooded valley hung with fog, sweat glistening on their perfect bodies, a perfect sunrise cracking the horizon, all played to a soaring operatic aria. In every scene, on jackets, packs, hats, helmets, kayak paddles, and even on the Lycra-covered and chalk-smeared right butt cheek of the athletic young woman splayed spider-like on a vertical stone wall, you saw the Nanda Devi mountain-ridge logo. At the end of the video came a scrolling list of all the environmental organizations the company supported: the Sierra Club, the Nature Conservancy, Friends of the Earth, something to do with Indians, another involving fish. It went too fast for Victor to keep up. Plus, he'd lost the will to look.

"Lights please?" she said when the screen mercifully went dark.

"Unparalleled reach, uncompromising quality, and an unquestioned reputation for excellence in what every day becomes a more competitive field," Isabel said, her voice deep and rich, like a fine cognac. A smoker's voice. Victor doubted that she'd ever come close to any of the places in her video. "And we combine that with an unmatched commitment to the places where people use our gear. The other companies—Patagonia, Black Diamond, The North Face—we may recognize the names, and they're all fine companies, but they're all vying for second place. Staying at the top means being vigilant in seeking out the best, always looking for ways to improve. We're in a category of one. And that explains our interest in Winklers."

She clicked something in her hand and a still image came onto the screen, of the hikers again, on their mountain vista, smiling with their perfect white teeth. "You'll notice that we don't see their feet," she said. Everyone looked; the image stopped at the trio's shins. "We carry a few brands of hiking boots because people want them. But we have held back from endorsing any particular brand of hiking boots because none have a level of quality to match our exacting standards for craftsmanship and performance. Until now. Winklers meets those standards. Winklers is a brand we feel completely comfortable endorsing. Once Winklers comes in, these others disappear. With Nanda Devi's reach and reputation, we give Winklers an opportunity to broaden your brand in ways you never dreamed of."

She paused here for dramatic effect, looking straight at Lukas and Sasha, and presenting her curvy, silhouetted profile to Marco. Victor decided this pose was intentional. Calculation flowed from this woman like one of those mountain streams in the video she had shown.

"Your boots?" she continued, and clicked again. Now the trio had feet. Another click and the image zoomed in on a close-up of a woman's leg. On her foot she wore a Winkler, with its distinctive "WfW" logo on the ankle. "Your boots are perfection."

The wave of despondency building over Victor started to crash and pound him into the sand. He had no video, no PowerPoint presentation, no multimedia bells and whistles, no close-ups of boot logos. What did he have? He had a talk. And what was his talk about? Maintaining the status quo. Keeping Winklers Winklers. Bunions. Advancing the company exactly nowhere. He was a mediocre shoe salesman here under false pretenses who was going to try to talk his way into having the world's finest maker of boutique hiking boots hand him the reins of their company. He considered getting up and leaving right then and there. Fiona's hand landed gently on his arm. With her index finger she drew his attention to something she'd written in the sketchbook she'd pulled from her portfolio. BIG = impersonal = Nanda Devi. Small = human scale = craft / art = *US!*

Isabel continued her presentation, which spanned her company's legendary origin story—with its eccentric, mountaineer-slash-polymer chemist founder who had lost his climbing partner on the Himalayan mountain that would give the company its name when an equipment malfunction sent him tumbling into a crevasse, and who went on to reinvent the climbing rope, and from there to dominate the outdoor-apparel industry. Victor had heard the story before—everyone familiar with the company knew it—though as he listened to Isabel tell it he wondered if it was all a fable cooked up by some New York ad agency.

Victor looked around the room, trying to gauge reactions. Lukas wore a practiced expression that hovered somewhere between interest and blankness, and fiddled with a pen. Sasha paid attention, but it was an agnostic sort of attention. Marco just stared at Isabel, his mouth hanging open. Outside, the snow had begun to pick up.

There were graphs and Venn diagrams and flow charts. Isabel talked about growth projections and geodemographic segmentation and market penetration. Lukas perked up—she was speaking his language. She went on into hundred-day plans, one-year plans, five-year plans, ten-year plans. Victor had no-year plans. Victor was a fifty-three-year-old bald man in a torn suit whose professional trending lines pointed downward. Half of his support team was a hung-over slacker dude in sneakers whose eyelids had fallen below half-mast and whose head had started to bob. Victor nudged him awake. The other half, however, was the girl, who had opened her sketchbook and started to draw something. To the extent that there was any cause for hope, she was it.

Isabel Forenza finished with a slide showing an awkward mash-up of the Nanda Devi logo with the Winkler W.

"The merger of these two companies," she said in conclusion, "combines stellar reputations for quality with an unparalleled level of business acumen and a keen understanding of the needs of the discerning outdoorsman or woman. It will elevate the reputations of both of us, and carry us forward into the future."

No one applauded, to Victor's great relief.

"Any questions?" she asked.

"My mother's name was Isabel," Marco said.

Sasha shook her head slightly, eyes closed, her fingertips massaging her temples.

"Thank you Ms. Forenza for your excellent presentation," Lukas said. Isabel gathered things from the table, leaning deeply toward Marco, then sat, tossing another smirk toward Victor as she did so. The woman could smirk, he had to give her that. Fiona turned to a clean page in her sketchbook and drew furiously.

"Mr. Barstow?"

Sasha muttered something into her brother's ear. Lukas shrugged, palms up, a *who knows?* gesture. Sasha gave Victor a perplexed look, a look he was sure meant she knew he was an imposter. A fraud. Victor felt as naked as he'd been when he walked out of his hotel bathroom to find Nate and Fiona. And he had the same question Sasha no doubt had—what *was* he doing here? What had made him think that a knack for flattering septuagenarian women who craved flattery more than they craved new footwear could translate into competent leadership of one of the world's renowned bootmaking dynasties? He should just leave now, if that were even possible. Outside the snow came down with greater purpose, not so much falling from the sky as being thrown downward by a god registering his anger at being duped. The trees had disappeared. The world had gone white.

Victor stood. "I'd like to begin with a confession," he said. May as well come right out with it. "I don't make boots. I sell shoes. That's what I do for a living. It's not what I've always done, but it's what I do now, and I'm good at it. Good enough, I have let myself believe, that a company with a reputation as distinguished as Winklers might consider me worthy of the mantle of leadership. In preparing to come here and meet you, I did a lot of research on bootmaking, and in the course of that research one thing I discovered was that I wasn't the only Victor Barstow making his living in the world of footwear, nor was I by any stretch of the imagination the Victor Barstow who possessed the skill set and background that made him most qualified to create boots that come close to meeting your standards. That other Victor Barstow is an actual bootmaker. I work at a shoe store in a shopping mall. But bootmaking isn't the only skill at play here—the ability to *sell* boots is also of paramount importance, and that's an area where I excel. So maybe it's just some quirk of fate that I'm here today, and he is not, but here I am. All this is to say, I may not be who you think I am."

Victor surveyed the Winklers for their reaction. Sasha looked befuddled. And angry. Marco continued to stare blankly. Lukas grinned the grin of a poker player about to lay down four aces.

"Mr. Barstow..." Sasha started, but Lukas raised a hand to stop her.

"On the contrary, Mr. Barstow," he said. "You're exactly who we think you are."

Now Victor was the one to be confused. He looked back and forth between Lukas and Sasha, trying to figure out what was going on. Sasha glared at Lukas, who was determined not to look in her direction. Nate leaned in close and said in Victor's ear, "I think you've been played, man."

"Could we take a five-minute break?" Sasha said.

★

"What have you done?" Sasha demanded of her brother, her face red with anger. They had relocated to an adjacent room, and she spoke in a low hiss so her voice wouldn't carry through the wall to where the others waited.

"I did what you said," Lukas said. It took some effort to keep from looking smug. "I invited Victor Barstow."

"He works in a shopping mall."

"He sells shoes."

"You know what I mean," she said. "We need to stop this process right now and bring in the Victor Barstow who actually knows something about making boots."

"We can't."

"What do you mean we can't?"

"I tried to find him. Letters, phone calls, emails, Google searches, Facebook. I got no response. He's gone. Vanished. Disappeared. Off the grid. He was old, Sasha. He could be dead."

"So what, then? You're prepared to just hand this company over to Nanda Devi? Sell out to…" She waved her hands, searching for the right word. "…to Big Granola?"

"Big Granola," Lukas said. "I like that. You get a vote. I get a vote. Dad gets a vote. Whatever we do, we do it democratically."

"Dad," she said, exasperated. "What do you think he's going to do, with that floozy waving her tits at him."

Lukas shrugged. "You wanted Victor Barstow, I got you Victor Barstow."

"I wanted *the* Victor Barstow."

"You should at least give the guy a chance. He says he can sell shoes."

"You think this is funny."

"They're waiting," Lukas said. "We should go back."

★

"BIG!" Victor said when they resumed, sweeping his arms wide and causing Marco, who may have been falling asleep, to startle in his seat. Victor went on, trying his best to modulate. "If I could sum up Ms. Forenza's presentation in one word, that would be it: big. Her firm will take a company that's built its reputation on skill, and craft, and detail, and *scale*, and fold it into a global conglomerate where it will lose everything that's made it special. By contrast, if you choose me, my goal will be to preserve the traits and values and the human scale—the *intimacy*—that for more than a century have been the Winklers' hallmark."

He continued in this vein, leaving out Marjorie McGinnis and her bunions. Outside, a blizzard raged.

"With Nanda Devi," he said by way of wrapping up, "Winklers will become lost like a size-7 foot in a size 12-boot. By contrast, with Barstow Limited Partnership, you preserve quality and you preserve your identity. We are not about Hollywood-caliber video presentations. We are not about burying Winkler boots on a shelf somewhere in the back of the store. What Barstow Limited Partnership is about is boots—not secondarily, not even first and foremost, but boots, boots, and only boots. *Solely*, you might say, if you'll pardon the pun." He paused for a chuckle that never came. "We are about an unyielding devotion to finding the perfect fit. And for Winklers, we are confident that we are that perfect fit."

Victor sat down, and it was a great relief to do so. He felt okay. He'd made the case he'd intended to make—for human scale over big and corporate, craftsmanship over mass production, art over commerce. Lukas did his best to look unimpressed, but Sasha, while not exactly nodding her head in endorsement, wasn't rolling her eyes, either.

"Does anyone have any questions?" Victor asked.

Sasha, the artist, looked at Fiona. "What are you drawing?" she asked.

As if on cue, Fiona stood. "I've been thinking about ways to bring the Winkler brand into the twenty-first century," she said. "Starting with your logo." She opened her sketchbook to a page on which she'd drawn an accurate rendering of the trademark Winkler W, with its crisscrossing lines in the middle peak. "What you're using now is a typeface whose origins can be traced back to fifteenth century Italy and, if you bring it forward a few hundred years, is related to what became the official typeface of Nazi Germany. This, in and of itself, is probably a good reason for you to consider an alternative.

"Plus, it's just plain *old*. It screams old. It signals that you are a company that's stuck in the past. So…" She turned to a new page in her sketchbook, on which she had drawn a progression of Ws, starting with the current Winkler logo and modifying it step by step. "The thing with Winklers," she went on, "is that on the one hand—or, foot—you're wearing a highly functional item of footwear, a boot that does what it does better than any other boot anywhere. That could suggest that we lean toward something more Modernist, more 'form fits function.' Bauhaus, possibly. Something in a style that emphasizes utilitarianism over artifice or adornment."

Victor worried that Fiona's discourse on typefaces was numbing the audience. She was talking about frigging *letters*, for God's sake. He looked around the table. Sasha hung on Fiona's every word. Even Marco had perked up. He was leaning forward, chin in hand, attentive. Lukas did his best to look bored, yawning and fiddling with his pen. Isabel and Charles looked at each other with a strained expressionlessness that Victor hoped meant they were wondering if they should be worried.

Fiona pointed to several of the designs on her page. "But on the other hand," she said, "when you wear a Winklers boot you're also wearing something that's a work of art, though not the kind to be put on a pedestal and gawked at, and that's exactly what you've tried to do over there." She pointed to the bronzed boots on an adjacent table. "Those are hideous, by the way."

This got a laugh from Sasha, who nodded in agreement.

Fiona continued. "We want something that anchors Winklers in today's world, acknowledges its heritage, but leans in the direction of the future. And we want something original. Something more like this." She turned the page again, and there she'd sketched a pair of Winkler boots—one standing up, one fallen over on its side, laces untied, a few lines in the background to suggest a mountain landscape—with a new Winkler W in place on the ankle of each. Lukas pursed his lips. Sasha nodded. With Marco it was as if a switch had been thrown that transformed him from a drooling geezer into an intelligent craftsman, which made Victor wonder again if the whole village-idiot routine had been an act.

Fiona continued, talking about broadening the market, speeding up delivery, finding a happy medium somewhere between luxury item and affordability, using social media to increase awareness and get Winklers onto younger feet. "It will never make sense," she said, "to take Winklers out of the mountains, but you will not survive unless you come out of the twentieth century and start acting like you belong in the twenty-first."

Sasha interrupted her. "Ramp up production, broaden the market, reach a younger audience—that sounds a lot like what we heard from Ms. Forenza. How is what you're proposing any different?"

"I have the utmost respect for Nanda Devi," Fiona said. "I own a Nanda Devi fleece, a Nanda Devi down vest, and a cute little Nanda Devi ski cap with a big poofy pom-pom on top. And that's just the point. Turn the company over to Nanda Devi, and you have to walk past the fleece jackets, past the puffy things in neon colors, past the hats with their pom-poms, to a wall in the back of the store where you'll find Winkler boots. And not just boots, but also casual shoes, running shoes, Nike, Under Armour, maybe even Birkenstocks." The word elicited a shudder from Marco. "Nanda Devi has grown into a mega-enterprise dominating the outdoor marketplace. There's no way they're going to put your boots front and center. And if your boots are lost in the back of a store, your brand will be, too.

"Another thing Barstow Limited Partnership is proposing is a new but small and elite line of Winkler stores in strategic locations where Winkler boots take center stage—where people can see them and feel them." This was news to Victor, but he didn't object. The girl was on a roll. "One store should be here, of course, and we'll have to think about the others. Maybe you'll sell pom-pom hats in these stores too, but that won't be what people come for. We're talking about finding the sweet spot between commitment to craft and market penetration— you expand not so much that you turn into Timberland, but not so little that you can't survive. And we're not talking about mass production. We're talking about making Winklers the way you've always made Winklers. It's just that more people will be making them. To sustain craftsmanship, we re-institute the apprentice system, bringing in young aspiring bootmakers—men *and* women—piggybacking on the sweeping resurgence in interest we're seeing now in this country in craft. In our mass produced, technologically advanced, Twitter-fed society, people crave things made by hand."

Victor kept looking at Sasha Winkler. She may not have been fully on board, but she was at least walking up the gangplank. He sat there astounded, in part by Fiona's ability to captivate this audience, but more by the realization that there was a decent chance that they had won Sasha's vote. And if they had Sasha's vote, then all they needed was to sway Lukas or Marco, which basically meant swaying Marco, as it wasn't likely that Lukas would come around to their side. Swaying Marco wouldn't be easy. By resorting to sex appeal, EP was exploiting a weakness of Marco's that Victor couldn't exploit. It was not a fair fight.

"You have to change, but we want to find the sweet spot," Fiona continued. "Taking the best of your family's old ways of doing business and bringing them forward in a sustainable way so you don't just survive, but thrive in tomorrow's world. That's the picture we'd like to paint. That's the vision we'd like you to embrace."

What they embraced instead in the next moment was darkness, because no sooner had Fiona finished speaking than the power went out. It had a certain theatrical flourish, like when the lights go down at the end of a play, then come back up so the actors can do their curtain call. Except in this case they didn't come back up.

"Here we go again," Lukas sighed.

Their eyes adjusted as the gray light sifting through the bank of windows slowly filled the room. Outside the snowstorm had achieved new levels of ferocity. There was no foreground, no background, no yard, no trees, no sky, no sense of depth or dimension, no nuance—just white. Victor was fine with that. It held metaphorical meaning. It was a wintry blank slate, a playing-field leveler. The board had been wiped clean, and now anything was possible. For one heady moment, as he looked out at the swirling snow, he felt like he had a chance. Like *they* had a chance. If he was going to win, Fiona was going to be on his team. Nate too, he supposed. In that moment, in the dark room, looking out at the snow, what passed for calm with Victor flowed through him.

The first reaction of three of the people in the room—Nate, Lukas, and Isabel—was to check their cell phones, which lit their faces with a ghoulish glow. Cell phones being as contagious as yawns, Victor looked at his as well. The little row of bars that signaled "signal" was nowhere to be found. Lukas got up and walked to a landline phone on a table. He put it to his ear and put it down—no signal there, either. He walked to the window and tried his cell phone again, with no luck.

The door to the room opened. Kirsten stood in the doorway holding a flashlight that she pointed at the floor. "The power is out, sir," she said to Lukas.

"Thank-you, Kirsten, for that helpful insight," Lukas said.

"Another tree?" Sasha said to her brother.

"What else? The wind. Even the cell tower's out."

"This happens often?" Isabel asked, with something judgmental in her tone, an implicit criticism of these backwoods hicks for having set up business in a place where trees could fall and take out power lines. Good, Victor thought. Let her piss them off.

"Often enough to make it a royal pain in the ass, Ms. Forenza," Lukas said, and Victor thrilled at the edge in his voice, the little crackle of tension thrown back at EP.

"Look," Lukas said, "here's what's going on. The power's out, obviously. The power comes in on one main line that runs along the road all of you drove in on. So if the power's out, that usually means that line is out, and most likely a tree is what took it out. That tree may be lying across the road, or the line could be in the road, or both. Plus, in case you hadn't noticed, it's snowing really hard. What I'm saying is that it's not safe for anyone to leave until we figure out what's going on and clear the road." He looked out the window. "I'm not sure you could get out of here anyway. That snow's pretty deep."

Marco stared out the window as if he saw something there that the rest of them didn't.

"But of course you have a backup generator," Isabel said, in that same judgmental voice, a voice that said, *In the unlikely event that Nanda Devi ever found itself in a remote backwater like this, we would have a generator, or a small platoon of generators, to restore full power. And Nanda Devi would have someone—or a team of someones—out immediately to plow the snow, remove the tree, repair the lines, get the engines of commerce humming again. And those someones would be immune to the elements because they would be dressed in Nanda Devi gear.*

Good, Victor thought. Keep it up. Dig yourself in deeper. In the room's weak light he saw worry in her face. She was a busy woman. She probably had some other big account to fly off to. He, on the other hand, had no such pressing engagements. Time was on his side. Victor breathed slowly. The more he could contrast his own unflappableness with Isabel's irritation, the better his chances.

Lukas walked to a roll-top desk near the fireplace, opened a drawer, and came back with a handful of candles that he rolled across the tabletop. "There's our backup generator, Ms. Forenza. That plus firewood." As if to underscore his point, the fire gave off a loud crack and sent a spark flying out. "And firewood is something we have in abundance. We're all stuck here for the time being, I'm afraid. Overnight, at least. I apologize for the inconvenience, but we have plenty of bedrooms and a good cook. So just settle in until we can get the road plowed and figure out what's going on with the electricity. And, of course, getting back to what brought you all here in the first place, my sister, my father, and I need to talk and come to a decision about what we want to do with the company. Fortunately you've completed your presentations, so I expect we can have that decision for you by tomorrow. Thanks to the snow, we'll be able to give you our decision in person. So," he said, holding up a candle, "does anyone have a match?"

[chapter 8]

Away from the windows, the house was dark. Kirsten, after up-grading to a battery-powered Coleman lantern, led everyone up a flight of stairs and down a windowless hallway of guest-rooms. Outside five of the doors sat lanterns like the one Kirsten carried, each with a supply of backup batteries, plus a small basket of candles. Kirsten talked as she walked. She apol-ogized for the inconvenience. Being prepared for circumstances like this one, she explained, was simply a fact of life here in the North Country. And hosting guests here at the Winklers was nothing new—some of those who came for boot fitting stayed in town, but most chose to stay here at the Winkler mansion. The boot-fitting process could take days, and Marco insisted on keeping some of his clients close through the process. In any event, they were prepared, and she and the Winklers would do everything possible to make this unforeseen stay as com-fortable as they could. They would find down comforters on the beds, and there were extra blankets in their closets, should they need them. There were toiletries and towels and bathrobes. Use candles judiciously, she cautioned, and be sure to please blow them out any time they left the room or when they were about to go to sleep. Most of the house's main rooms, and all of the guest rooms, had fireplaces or woodstoves, and staff had already made fires in each of their rooms and furnished a supply of firewood. Downstairs, down the hall from the room where they had done their presentations, they would find a dining room, and food would be put out for them at seven. "I hope you'll make yourselves at home," she said. "If there's anything you need, please don't hesitate to ask."

Kirsten stopped outside the first of the rooms, its door open. "Fiona, you'll be in here, if that's okay."

"It's perfect," Fiona said. "And Nate and I can share."

"Okay then. Mr. Barstow, you'll be next door to them. Miss Forenza and… I'm sorry, I don't know your—."

"Charles," Charles said helpfully.

"Charles. We have two rooms for you down the hall. I hope these arrangements will be satisfactory."

Nate picked up the lantern and started into the room. Fiona followed, but Isabel stopped her by putting a hand on her arm. "That was impressive work, young lady."

The compliment flustered Fiona. "Thank you," she managed. It came out like a question. She turned back toward her room.

Once again Isabel stopped her. "It's clear who puts the *limited* in Barstow Limited Partnership, and who has the balls," she said.

On the one hand, Victor, watching this exchange, felt encouraged. This little exchange wouldn't be happening if Isabel wasn't worried. On the other, he couldn't just let the insult pass—he had to do something. Though he reasoned that whatever he did should not provoke a counter-something from Charles. He moved close to Isabel, stood inches from her face, struggled to find words. "Your name isn't really Isabel, is it?" was what finally came out.

Isabel laughed and stepped back. She reached into the pocket of her coat, and took out a business card, which she held out for Fiona between two long, slender fingers. "I see a lot of potential in you," Isabel said to Fiona. "Perhaps we should talk later." Then: "Please, Kristen. Won't you show us to our rooms?"

"It's *Kir*sten," Kirsten said politely, and she led them off down the hall.

"Perhaps *we* should talk later," Victor said to Fiona when the others were out of earshot.

"Oh, Victor, don't let her get to you," she said.

"Seriously? Right there in front of your friend Kristen, who works for Marco, she makes you a job offer?"

"*Kir*sten,"

"She's trying to divide us."

"Exactly. Don't let her."

"Can we do this later?" Nate said. "Maybe at dinner? We need a little time to, you know, freshen up."

"Are you sure you don't want me to go into town and buy you some beer?" Victor said. He was worried that his hastily as-sembled but surprisingly successful team was unraveling. "Let me see that card," he said to Fiona. She handed it to him.

He hoped it would say something other than what it ac-tually said, which was Isabel Forenza, Senior Vice President. They could have printed them with a fake name, he concluded.

"Can I have that back?" Fiona said.

"Why?" Victor said, but Fiona just stood there looking at him. A little battle of wills played out there in the doorway. The card stood for trust, for loyalty, for other noble things Victor could probably think of if he had more time to think about it. He handed it back to her. She took it without a word and fol-lowed Nate into their room, pulling the door closed behind her.

"Perhaps *we* should talk," Victor heard Nate say on the other side of the door, mocking him. Fiona responded with a giggle. Victor went into his own room to try to calm down.

His room was spacious but drafty, and smelled like a hamster cage. As Kirsten had promised, a fire had been lit in the woodstove, but away from the woodstove the room was still cool. On his bed lay a puffy comforter, which, if it were real down, might keep him warm but might also trigger a sneezing fit—he was allergic to down. It figured to be a long night.

The room's only chair was next to the woodstove, and Victor sat in it. His first thoughts were gloomy thoughts about trust and betrayal and whether Fiona would turn on him. More optimistic thoughts followed, as he realized that he wouldn't be thinking his first thoughts if things hadn't gone so well with his presentation. Of course, he was still a long shot, but without Fiona he wouldn't have any kind of shot at all. If she crossed over... The needle on his thought meter swung back toward gloomy. Through the thin wall separating his room from Nate and Fiona's came the sounds of them "freshening up" next door. And it wasn't just the sounds. He could swear the wall was moving. He felt vibrations in the floorboards. He moved the chair, though this did little to muffle the multimedia experience.

Now in addition to thinking about trust and betrayal Victor thought about sex, and this got him thinking about Carla, and more specifically about sex with Carla, and this forced him to think pretty far back in time. How long had it been? Weeks? Months? The existence of a daughter stood as proof that at one point in their lives they had been sexual beings. In fact, he could remember a time when they approached sex with all the enthusiasm of Nate and Fiona in the next room. But lately he and Carla had sex with about as much frequency and anticipatory excitement as dentist appointments.

The wall relaxed into post-coital stillness, and in the lull Victor shifted from thinking about sex with Carla to thinking about just plain Carla. "This is your way out," she had said, waving the Winkler letter at him. But way out from what? If he got the contract, it wasn't as if Carla was going to want to pack up and move here. She hated cold. Hated winter. Was his way out an exit door from their marriage? Had that been her plan all along?

The struggles his modest nuclear family was going through weren't all that different from what any number of families went through. He got downsized. It happened. Some men in his situation drank heavily, or contemplated suicide. Victor got a job. Was it a great job? No. Did he come close to making what he'd been making? No. But he made money. They were getting by. They paid their bills, mostly on time. They didn't lose their house, like some people he knew. But now, with Allie in her senior year...

"How is Allie going to go to a good college on what you're making?" Carla asked one Saturday morning in October after he'd dropped their daughter at the high school to take her SATs. By "good college" she meant the kind you're not embarrassed to have decaled onto your car's rear window, the kind that filled the rear windows of the Audis and Lexuses of the Pilates-bound mothers who dropped off their precious progeny at the fancy private school where Carla taught. But she had a point. "I don't know why she even bothers with the SATs," she said. Allie scored a 1490.

Shortcomings. Downsized. Fall short. Can't rise to the challenge. Dud. Given the vocabulary of failure, it was no wonder that their sex life had imploded. "It's good to see someone on your team has balls," Isabel had said. Had she and Carla discussed this beforehand? Had they compared notes? Were they sisters-in-arms of a little anti-Victor coalition?

Next door the call and response between bedspring and floorboard resumed, and now Victor thought about Fiona. Not

Fiona *in flagrante*, but Fiona as business partner. Why should she stay with him? Nanda Devi could make her an offer she couldn't refuse. At age nineteen or twenty or whatever Fiona might command a salary that would dwarf Victor's and Carla's combined income.

Victor got up from the chair. He paced. He put another log in the woodstove. What was that saying about accepting things you can't control? His stomach growled. He hadn't eaten all day. He wondered when dinner would be ready.

★

The dining room was off a long hallway a couple of doors down from the study where the presentation meeting had been held earlier, and as he passed one of those doors Victor could hear a heated argument from within the room. He couldn't make out actual words, but the muffled voices belonged unmistakably to Lukas and Sasha, and Victor figured that unless the argument was about whose turn it was to shovel the driveway, the fact that they were shouting at each other could only be good news for him. True, Lukas had invited Nanda Devi to anoint them, and had invited Victor as cannon fodder. But Lukas needed one other vote to have his way, and the sounds of shouting behind the closed door could only mean he didn't yet have his sister's. A thin, satisfied smile pulled at Victor's lips. He had gone toe to toe with the industry giant and held his own. Or rather, Fiona had held his own. His own had been held, in any event.

He didn't stay satisfied long. In the dining room, at a candlelit table near the fireplace, Nate and Fiona sat with Isabel, with glasses of red wine in their hands, laughing like old friends. Victor had his Coleman lantern with him, and they looked in his direction as this new light source entered the room. The room was substantial, less like a family dining room than a prep school dining hall, and Victor made his way to a dark table away from the fireplace, where he turned off his lantern and sat in the dark and cold. There were candles on the table, plus matches, but Victor chose not to light them; darkness would suit him just fine right now, and it gave him better cover to watch the dynamics across the room.

What could they possibly be talking about that was so funny, Victor wondered, and then answered his own question: they were talking about him. They were laughing at him, maybe retelling the story of yesterday's beer bust with that cop from the college. Had that really only been yesterday? He had he read somewhere that time moved more slowly the closer you got to the poles. Or did it move faster?

A buffet had been laid out on a table between them. Blue Sterno flames cast an eerie light where they reflected off the bottom of metal chafing dishes. Eventually Victor's teammates—or possibly his soon-to-be-former teammates—got up from where they sat with Isabel, shook her hand, and came over toward him. Barstow Limited Partnership, growing more limited by the minute.

"Sleeping with the enemy?" Victor said when they reached his table.

"I wish," Nate said.

"What did she offer you? Something good, I hope."

"CEO," Nate said. "And board chair for Fiona."

"Ha ha."

"Account rep," Nate said.

"Design director," Fiona added. "Decent money, too. Low seventies to start."

"Jesus Christ," Victor said, shaking his head.

"Victor, chill," Nate said. "We didn't defect."

"You turned her down?"

"Yes. Well, no," Nate said. "Sort of. I mean we put them on hold. 'Til after this thing is over."

"This *thing* being...?" Victor said.

"You know." Nate waved his arm. "This. The whole shoe thing."

"Boot," Fiona corrected.

"And what if I win?" Victor said.

Nate snickered.

"Fuck you," Victor said. "You're being bought, and cheap, considering what she stands to gain. She throws a little cash at you, lands the Winkler contract, makes her company millions, then tosses you out like worn-out socks. What just happened wasn't a job offer—it was child seduction."

"Ouch!" Nate said.

"Victor," Fiona said. "She promised that none of this would affect the Winkler deal. And how could it? The Winklers are in a room right now deciding what they want to do with the contract. So this has no bearing on that. Besides, whatever happens with the Winklers, it's not like Nanda Devi is going to go away."

"What if I get the Winklers job? What if I want to hire you? Don't you want jobs with me? What happened to the whole Barstow fucking Limited Partnership?"

"Victor..." Fiona said, but then stopped. He recognized the expression on her face. It was that of a parent looking for a gentle way to tell a child he did not make the travel soccer team.

"You don't think I stand a chance, do you?" Neither of them said a word. "Well let me tell you something. Lukas and Sasha are in a room right now arguing about the contract.

Arguing! This isn't the slam-dunk you seem to think it is. It could go either way, and the two of you are saying that after it's settled, you want out. Is that what I'm hearing?"

Nobody said anything. Victor wondered if he was being delusional.

"Anybody hungry?" Nate said.

[chapter 9]

Victor couldn't sleep. Partly because of the noises coming through his shared wall—even louder now, now that his neighbors had job offers to celebrate—but mostly for other reasons. Because of the look he would get from Carla when he told her he didn't get the contract. Because of how he was letting down Allie. Because he was cold. Because the comforter on the bed was indeed stuffed with down, leaving him with a scratchy throat that was evolving into a sneezing fit. Because this whole fucking trip had become an exercise in subarctic futility. Because nothing he did was good enough, or right, or mattered, not to others, not to Victor himself.

The room. The blanket. The noise. The cold. The smell of stale rodents. Victor got out of bed, put his clothes back on, wrapped up in his overcoat, and went downstairs.

He made his way to the room where the presentation meeting had been held. The fire in the fireplace was all embers and ashes, but after a couple of jabs with the poker and the addition of a fresh log or two it flamed back to life. The room was surprisingly bright for the middle of the night. The snow had stopped, finally. Victor figured the moon was causing the brightness, but when he looked out the window he could find no moon, just a galaxy full of stars in a Milky Way that stood out like it had been drawn with a highlighter, shining down on a yard deep with virgin snow. It seemed impossible that this was the same sky they had in Baltimore—it was so much vaster and more infinite. He thought about stars, and tried to wrap his head around the idea that they had already flamed out of existence, but their light still traveled through millions of miles of outer space to where he stood looking at them through the Winklers' window. There was a metaphor in that someplace, but he chose not to search too hard for it, because he knew a dead-star metaphor would not do him any good. The view was so breathtakingly beautiful that as long as he didn't overthink it, it lifted his spirits. Slightly.

He wondered how much snow had fallen. Without any reference points, it was hard to tell. It lay there like a blanket of fluff, the wind kicking it up in wisps here and there, unbroken except for a single set of tracks leading from underneath the house to somewhere off in the woods. Tracks? Tracks made by what? They looked to be too substantial and indelicate for a deer. They formed a sort of trough, made by a creature that slogged or shuffled more than pranced. A bear, maybe? A bear that had crawled up under the overhang of the Winklers' deck to get in out of the snow? A bear that maybe, just maybe, smelled whatever was left of the actually fairly delicious beef stew that had been served for dinner, and lurked below at this very moment searching for a way in? It was a sign of Victor's state of mind that under the circumstances, getting mauled to death by a bear didn't seem like the worst thing that could happen—a noble death won out over abject failure any day. On a table near the window sat a pair of binoculars, no doubt left there for watching birds and other woods creatures from this very spot. Victor picked them up and focused in on the tracks. On one side of the trough at regular intervals there were holes in the snow. A bear with a ski pole? Victor was no expert on tracks, but something about these gave him the impression that they led away from the house, not toward it. And the holes were too skinny to have been made by a ski pole. A walking stick, maybe? A cane? "Oh, fuck!" Victor said under his breath. Marco Winkler had walked off into the woods.

[chapter 10]

Victor thought about waking the others, but he didn't know where Lukas and Sasha were sleeping, and besides, a sort of calculus of self-interest had kicked in. Waking the others would mean getting Isabel and Charles involved, and the last thing he wanted was for them to rescue Marco. Rescuing the family patriarch would be a balance tilter. Save Marco and you win Marco's vote.

He found a stairway, which opened into a hallway that led to a boot room, with two small windows on either side of a heavy wooden door. He peered out one of the windows and saw the tracks leading away. He was in the right place. Victor took a deep breath, pushed the door open, and stood mostly out of the snow under the overhang of the deck, where he encountered a cold that was to normal cold what the Grand Canyon was to a drainage ditch. A shearing wind slapped his face like sheet metal. His eyes watered immediately, and what water escaped his eyes as tears froze on his cheeks. He scanned the tree line for a trace of Marco, but aside from the tracks, which had begun to vanish in the blowing snow, he saw nothing. What was Marco doing out here? Was he senile? An insomniac out for his regular evening stroll? Suicidal? A person could die out here.

"Marco!" he yelled out the door, but the wind blew the name off sideways in a swirl of snow. He would have to go look for him. Victor stepped back inside the door and looked for something warmer to put on. He had his overcoat, but it was overmatched by the cold outside. On a bench near the door he found a pair of too-small purple mittens that with some effort he would be able to cram his hands into, along with a matching woolen cap, the kind meant to accommodate bounteous amounts of a woman's hair. He pulled it on. Under the bench sat three pairs of boots, all Winklers, of course. In Goldilocks fashion, Victor tried on one pair that was too small, another that his feet swam in. The third pair was the closest approximation of just right. What people said about the boots was true: they felt amazing. And warm. Next to the bench, on a table full of tools, another stroke of luck: a flashlight. Victor flicked the switch and unlike any flashlight he'd ever found lying about in his own house, it worked. Thus fortified, he headed out.

The wind was erasing Marco's tracks, but enough of the tracks remained visible to give him something to follow. They led off into the woods on what might have been a narrow trail. In the woods, the trees blocked some of the wind and the tracks stood out more.

If Marco had started on a trail, it hadn't been long before he'd abandoned it. The tracks meandered, weaving purposelessly and looping back on themselves, as if he were trying to diagram a large pretzel in the snow. Where was he? Marco was over seventy, and not exactly a picture of health. In these conditions, how far could he go?

After a series of pretzel loops the tracks straightened out and led off into a small clearing, where the blowing wind had made them all but disappear. With the flashlight Victor could make out the barest of indentations left on the surface of the snow. They grew barer with each step into the clearing. The flashlight started to flicker. He shook it and the beam became steady again. He puzzled briefly over why that maneuver worked. He looked around. Behind him the wind was doing an impressive job of covering his own tracks. He scanned the tree line behind him to see if he could make out the spot where he'd entered the clearing. He couldn't. Marco's trail was disappearing in front of him. His own trail was disappearing behind him. "Marco!" he yelled again, but again the wind swept it away.

Victor had no choice but to move on through the clearing and reenter the woods on the other side, hoping that in the protection of the trees he would again pick up some trace of Marco. He found tracks that could have been Marco's tracks, or could have been deer tracks, or some other animal's tracks. He tried not to think about bears. Didn't bears hibernate in the winter? He hoped so. He shuffled around more or less aimlessly, not sure what else to do, and soon couldn't be certain if the tracks he was following were his own or belonged to someone or something else. He stopped and looked around, and a thought that had been abstract until that moment now became concrete: yes, a person could die out here, and that person could be him. As if to underscore that thought, the flashlight started flickering again.

Standing still only made the cold colder, and it wasn't going to help him find either Marco or his way back to the house. Victor started moving again. He hadn't gone far when something beneath the surface caught his ankles and pitched him forward into the snow—soft, powdery stuff, easily two, maybe two and a half feet deep. He managed to drop the flashlight in the process, and it disappeared into the snow, leaving a flashlight-shaped gap on the surface that immediately started to cave in on itself. With some difficulty Victor managed to push himself up onto his knees. He felt around for the flashlight, but his purple-mittened hands instead found what had tripped him. He pulled on what he expected would be a fallen tree branch, and out of the snow came Marco's cane.

Marco's cane! In a panic Victor started thrashing around in the snow. If the cane had surfaced, Marco couldn't be far away. But what if the snow had covered him? How much time did he have? Minutes? Seconds? Was Victor already too late? "Marco!" he yelled. "Marco!"

He saw a faint glow under the snow. He dug for it, and retrieved the flashlight, which somehow had gained new life while being buried. Victor waved it around over the surface of the snow and shined it into the trees, but saw no sign of Marco. He pushed back to his feet and kept shining the light around. "Marco!"

"Polo," a weak voice called from behind him. Victor thought he might be hallucinating. Was that what the cold did right before it killed you? He called again: "Marco!" and stood still to listen. Again came the weak reply: "Polo." Victor moved the light slowly through the trees, and there, maybe twenty yards from where he stood, he saw Marco, sitting in snow up to his waist, his back against a tree.

"Marco!" Victor yelled again, and clumped his way over to him. He knelt beside him in the snow. Marco didn't look like a man in distress, or near death, or almost frozen, but more like a man who simply decided to have a seat and look at the trees and snow. He was staring off at nothing in particular, and had icicles hanging off his eyebrows and eyelashes and beard. "Are you okay?" Victor asked.

"I dropped my cane," Marco said.

"I found it," Victor said, and stuck it in the snow next to him. "Can you walk?" Marco gave him a blank look.

When Victor was seven years old he got his first pet, a stray dog that followed him on his walk home after school one day. He was a mangy dog, collarless and tag-less and of undetermined age and origin, the sort of dog that people would avoid when they encountered him on the sidewalk rather than go out of their way to pet. When Victor got home, the dog was more than willing to follow him inside, where Victor fixed him a peanut butter and jelly sandwich and gave him a bowl of milk. The dog then curled up on the kitchen floor and fell asleep, and he was lying there when Victor's mother came in from whatever errand she had been on. He fully expected her to tell him he would have to get rid of the dog, but she surprised him. She decided to use this dog to teach Victor a lesson about responsibility, and more specifically about how responsibility, having once been taken, couldn't simply be given back. They would keep the dog, and Victor would take care of it.

As pets go, the dog, which Victor gave the uncreative but not inaccurate name Scruffy, was not a good one. He hated other dogs, and if he wasn't tied up he would attack them. Humans he divided into two categories—those he would growl at on sight, teeth bared, tiny bubbles forming at his gums, and those whose legs he would hump. Sometimes he combined these two skills, and would hump with teeth bared, growling and bubbling. He showed no interest in learning any tricks beyond oral self-stimulation, which he practiced with great frequency and enthusiasm. Plus, as the family discovered one morning shortly after they'd adopted Scruffy and Victor came down to breakfast with red welts all over his face, he had fleas. More than once Victor wished he could undo his decision to bring Scruffy home with him, to turn back the clock to simpler, Scruffy-less times, but his mother held firm in her conviction that Scruffy was a responsibility that Victor could not just walk away from.

That same logic applied with Marco. In some parallel universe, Victor may have been lying asthmatically in bed under the relative warmth of a down comforter, listening to sex sounds through the wall and pondering his future, but in this particular universe Victor had gotten out of bed, walked around, spotted tracks in the snow, followed them, and found Marco. That made Marco his responsibility—he couldn't just walk away. Among the more plausible outcomes was that he and Marco would both freeze to death out here.

Marco's head swung to look at Victor. "Annie?" he said, blinking slowly, the icicles hanging heavily off his eyelashes. His lost wife's name. He's delirious, Victor thought.

"No, Marco," he said. "It's Victor. Victor Barstow." Marco's face drooped in disappointment. An icicle fell off. "We're in the woods and we've got to get you back to the house. Are you hurt? Can you stand?" If he couldn't stand, the deep shit they already were in would grow deeper. He sized Marco up. Marco was about Victor's height, but thinner and lighter. He could lift him, probably, but in this snow, Victor doubted he could carry him very far.

"I could use a little nap," Marco said. He had no hat and thin gloves, but a substantial down jacket that Victor hoped had kept him warm enough so that his body could still function. A white down jacket. White. Why would anyone wear a white jacket into a snowstorm? Just to ratchet up the degree of difficulty?

"Marco, look at me," Victor said. "I'm going to get you out of here. Let's try to stand." Victor stood, bent down, looped Marco's left arm across his shoulders, and with some difficulty managed to get them both up to a wobbly vertical. "Try to walk," Victor said.

With Victor's support, Marco managed a couple of shuffling steps. "My cane…" he said. Victor had left it stuck in the snow a few feet from where they now stood.

"I'll get it," Victor said. "Don't move." He let go by degrees, inching away from Marco the way you pull back from an unstable Jenga tower. Victor grabbed the cane, and turned to watch Marco fall.

"Leg's a little sore," Marco said, looking up at Victor from the snow.

"Let's try again," Victor said, and gave Marco his cane. "We'll take it slow. Ready?"

He nodded. Victor looked around for the trail that led back toward the house, but in all his tromping about and flailing he'd managed to disturb the snow in just about every possible direction. They were only a few yards from the clearing, which was more or less circular, and Victor knew that the direction they needed to go was at some point on the other side of the clearing. But that's the thing about circles—they don't have sides—and if the wind had blown snow over his original path, finding the correct route would be guesswork, and they couldn't afford to guess wrong.

They managed to hobble their way back to the clearing. As Victor feared, all traces of the original path had disappeared. He picked a direction that seemed plausible, and they started across.

"No," Marco said, and stood still.

"No what?"

He pointed with his cane to a place about forty degrees around the circle from the direction Victor had them going.

"Seriously?" Victor said. He wasn't at all sure about Marco's directive, and resented the idea of dying on another man's terms.

"That's the way," Marco said, and pointed his cane again at the same spot. Off they went.

Victor tried to think positive thoughts, tried not to dwell on the cold, or the wind, or on what the wind chill might have been, or on exposure, or frostbite, or on how long it took before your organs shut down. He tried not to dwell on how the body would first give up on the extremities in an effort to protect the core, or on how desperately he needed those extremities right now—arms to hold up Marco, legs to walk them both home. Think positive thoughts, he told himself, but thinking positive thoughts when there's so fucking little to think positive thoughts about was hard. Cold hurt. In theory it would make you numb, but if this was numb, then numb cold had a lot in common with pain. And Victor felt numb cold just about everywhere. Except his feet. They weren't exactly warm, but at least he could feel them. Winklers really were amazing boots.

They crossed the clearing and entered the trees at the place Marco had pointed to. They made progress—slow progress, but progress nonetheless, though progress that only really counted as progress if they were headed in the right direction, and Victor still had his doubts. The wind had died down, the on-again, off-again flashlight was on again, and in the trees Victor could make out traces of tracks that he decided were either his from earlier or Marco's. Marco couldn't put a lot of weight on his left leg, so Victor stood on his left side and supported him, with Marco's arm around Victor's shoulder, and they hobbled along that way like kids in a three-legged race at a birthday party. Slow kids. The kind of kids who were funny to watch but stood no chance of winning.

Victor lost all concept of time. How long had he been outside? Minutes? Hours? Eventually he sensed another clearing about to open up ahead of them. If that clearing was the Winklers' backyard, they were in luck. If that clearing was something else, then they'd gone the wrong way and were totally fucked.

"Marco, look! Up ahead. Is that your yard? Marco! Marco?"

Victor felt Marco's weight start to slump against his right side. He shined the flashlight into Marco's face, and in its flickering light he saw that his eyes had closed to slits. Was Marco falling asleep? Or... The flashlight flickered its last flicker and went dark. Victor tucked it into his coat pocket. "Marco!" he tried one more time, but the man's knees buckled, and Victor felt his body surrender to gravity. He held him there for a second, and then they both slumped down into the snow.

This could not be happening. It was simply not conceivable that they would make it all this way only to collapse and die here with the house nearly in sight. If, that is, they had come the right way. I'll carry him, Victor thought. He tried to lift him, but Marco's body was dead weight and steadfast in its refusal to be lifted. Victor considered leaving him there in the snow and running to the house for help, but what if Marco froze to death while he was gone, or what if he couldn't find his way back to him?

He decided it was their only chance. With great effort Victor grabbed Marco under the arms, dragged him to a tree, and propped him up there, sitting in the snow with his back against it. Victor shoved Marco's hands into his jacket pockets for warmth, and in doing so found a wool scarf in one of them, which he wrapped around Marco's face—tight enough for warmth, loose enough so he could breathe. Victor stuck the cane in the snow and put his purple cap on top of it to make Marco easier to locate. Then he trudged off toward what he hoped would turn out to be the house, stomping vigorously to leave as visible a trail as he could.

The wind had picked up again and was now howling through the trees. Victor thought he heard something in the howl that was more than mere wind-howl. He stopped to listen, and heard it again. "Marrr-coooo!" it said, faint and distant. Others were coming to look for them!

"Here!" Victor yelled. "Here! Over here!" He'd only gone fifteen or twenty yards, and could still see Marco back behind him propped up against the tree, the purple cap marking the spot. Flashlight beams darted this way and that, lighting branches in the trees. Victor yelled again.

Lukas Winkler reached him first, followed by Sasha and then Nate and Fiona. Even Charles had joined the search, in his black chauffeur's cap. But no Isabel, Victor was glad to see.

Lukas shined a flashlight in Victor's face. "What have you done with my father?" he said, with no small amount of panic in his voice.

"Over here. He needs help." Victor led him to Marco as the others caught up and gathered around.

"Victor," Nate said, "what the fuck?"

[chapter 11]

Lukas and Charles managed to stand Marco up against the tree, and from there Charles hoisted him fireman's carry over his shoulder, lifting him with no more difficulty than he would lift a sack of laundry. They headed back to the house and entered through the boot room.

Isabel stood inside the door. "Oh, Charles!" she said. "Thank God you saved him!" Victor glared at her. Thank God *Charles* saved him? Really? He knew he shouldn't let her control the narrative, but there wasn't much he could do about it until his frozen mouth started working again.

Marco revived remarkably—he became conscious and aware, wearing the expression of a teenager caught out after curfew. Questions got fired at him and at Victor, though Marco wasn't saying much, and Victor's face muscles hadn't quite thawed. Why did Marco leave? How did Victor know he'd gone? How did he find him? Lukas in particular was aggressive in his questioning, as if he believed Victor to be responsible for, or at least complicit in, Marco's escape. Eventually the consensus emerged that Marco had wandered off, that Victor was stupid for going out after him alone without alerting the others, but also brave to have done so, and in any event it all had worked out well. At some point it was understood that what Victor needed more than an inqui-sition was warmth. Sasha got him a mug of hot chocolate, and Fiona and Nate walked him back to his room while the Winkler siblings took their father off to his.

Victor sat on the bed while Fiona examined him, using the Coleman lamp as a light source. The return of blood flow sent pins and needles shooting through his forearms and hands, which she said was a good sign. "Look at me," Fiona said, and held the light up to his face. A frown crossed hers. "I don't like the look of that nose." Victor reached up to touch it. It felt numb and rubbery, like it was someone else's nose, or a red clown nose. Once again he recalled that guy on Ev-erest who got left behind and his nose froze and fell off. He did not want to be that guy, did not want to contemplate life without a nose. It would be a serious career impediment, even—or maybe especially—for someone who sold women's shoes. Appearance mattered. Plus, there was the whole smell thing. He wiggled it, testing to see if it was secure. "Don't play with it," Fiona said. "That'll only make it worse. There're some spots on your cheeks, too. We'll check everything out again in the morning."

Victor said that what he wanted more than anything was a hot bath, followed by sleep. Fiona went into the bathroom to start the water running in the tub.

"Go to bed," he told them while the tub filled. "Get some sleep. I'm fine. I'll see you in the morning."

Fiona instructed Victor not to submerge his nose in the tub, which she said might be bad for the frostbite, though the advice seemed unnecessary given the importance of the nose for breathing. On their way out, Nate stopped at the door with a funny look on his face that Victor failed to identify as respect. "Victor," he said. "You saved that dude's life."

Victor appreciated the compliment, but didn't want to let his guard down too far. After all, he wouldn't have seen Marco's tracks if he hadn't gone to the study, and he wouldn't have gone to the study if he had been able to sleep. And the reason he couldn't sleep was because of fears that Nate and Fiona were about to turn traitor. He ushered them out, peeled off his damp clothes, hung them to dry on the back of the chair near the woodstove, added a couple of logs, and went to the bathroom to soak. The tub felt incredible, and as Victor relaxed into it he allowed himself to stop worrying about whether his nose would fall off.

At some point he must have fallen asleep in the tub, because he was aware of waking up. Two candles Fiona had anchored tub-side in melted wax still flickered, and the water was still warm, so he couldn't have been asleep for too long. The candles cast the bathroom in an orange-pink glow that in other circumstances might have been romantic, though in the moment it just felt ominous. The house, the snow, the power outage, the bizarre family—Victor felt like he was living in a Stephen King novel, at the moment just before someone threw the hairdryer into the tub. He saw something floating and panicked, certain his nose had fallen off, but he touched where his nose should be with an index finger and it was still there. The floating object was a soap ball. He was trying to decide whether to get out or add more hot water when a voice stopped him.

"You're awake," it said.

Victor shrieked. He flailed. Water left the tub. His head whacked the tile wall. He twisted around to find Marco Winkler sitting behind him on the toilet, with the cover down, thank God.

"Easy, Flipper." Marco said.

"What are you doing here!" What was with people in this part of the world? Was this some local custom to barge in on people when they're in the bathroom?

"Lifeguard," he said. "I was afraid you were going to go under."

"Funny."

"You should keep an eye on that nose, by the way."

"So I've been told. Why are you here?"

"I came to thank you," he said. "And to ask you a favor."

[chapter 12]

"I have…" Marco began, and there was a long pause as he either searched for the right word or wanted Victor to think that's what he was doing, "…episodes."

"Episodes."

"Periods. Spells. Fits. Call them what you want. Sasha's worried they're seizures. Or small strokes. I have times when I don't really know what I'm doing. They come and go. Do you mind if I smoke?"

"It's your house," Victor said. He hadn't expected a cigar, though, whose smell collided with the pleasantly floral scent of soap and shampoo floating about the room, wrestled it down, and held its head under the water until it drowned. Soon the smell was all cigar.

"It's possible I'm losing my mind."

It was an idea Victor had entertained. "You wandered off into the woods in the middle of the night."

"You see," Marco said, pausing to release another smoke cloud, "that's just it. I don't remember going off into the woods. I was in bed. I woke up and Annie wasn't there next to me. So I went to look for her."

"Annie. Your wife. Who left you years ago."

"Yes. That one. To be honest, I didn't even know I'd left the house until you found me."

"You put on a down coat," Victor said, his guard now fully up. He was being maneuvered into something. *I've come to thank you,* Marco had said. *And to ask you a favor.*

"Yes…"

"You called me Annie. In the woods."

"It was dark," Marco said.

"Is it Alzheimer's?" The word drifted up toward the ceiling and hung there with the cigar smoke. The bathroom grew quiet, the only sound the occasional *ploink* of the dripping faucet.

"I've pulled up short of calling it that. Though that's what Sasha suspects. I prefer to think of it as a kind of natural loss of mental sharpness that comes with age. Like forgetting a name, or where you put your keys. No big deal. Nothing to worry about. But the fact is, I was out in the woods sitting under a tree in a snowdrift. So, episodes."

"You said you wanted to ask me a favor." Victor watched another smoke cloud float over the tub. A second smell mingled with the cigar smoke. Marco's arm appeared in front of Victor's face, a silver flask in his hand, the cap off.

"Whiskey?" he said.

"No. Thanks."

"Oh, go ahead. You can't catch Alzheimer's."

"Which you said you don't have."

"Can't catch old age either, though it has a way of catching you. Go on. Go ahead." He wiggled the flask the way you would to entice a small child with a shiny object.

Victor struggled to understand exactly who he was talking to. The Marco in the meeting that afternoon had been a buffoon, a nut-case, a doddering old guy on the brink of irrelevancy. The Marco in the woods had been weak and disoriented, a lost soul both literally and metaphorically. But the Marco perched on his toilet was amazingly lucid, in full control, with all faculties seemingly working as they were supposed to. It set Victor's head spinning. Who was the real Marco? How much was a put-on, and to what purpose? Or were all three the real Marco, the different personalities merely the result of his "episodes"? He decided he could use a drink, after all.

He took the flask and sipped. The whiskey was good. The surge of heat it put in his belly was even better. With the cigar smoke and the whiskey, the bathroom now smelled like a bar. They drank. Marco smoked. The faucet *ploinked*.

"Do you believe in karma?" Marco said.

As someone whose payback for years of hard work and marital fidelity had been to get fired from his job and have good reason to suspect that his wife was cheating on him, Victor didn't put much stock in karma. "Not really," he said. "I take it you do."

"Sasha does. She thinks that's what's happening. You see, Annie came here for boots. That's how we met. Just showed up one day on the road into the property, this wild creature who walked in out of the woods. Dirty, cut, scraped. Completely irresistible. And I didn't resist."

Marco took another swallow of whiskey.

"The problem was, I didn't resist too many others, either. Women would show up here after spending months on a waiting list. Years, sometimes. After all that time, they would do anything to get their boots. And I was inclined to let them. It's such a turn-on, fitting a woman for boots, don't you think? All the leather. The in and out. The leg presented as an offering. It's really quite erotic."

Victor could go days at his job without seeing a customer younger than seventy. The eroticism of footwear had not been an occupational hazard for him. Though he understood the point Marco was making.

"It could be AIDS," Marco said. "I did some reading. There's a kind where you start losing your mind. I'm worried that might be it."

AIDS? Victor had never known anybody with AIDS. He had instant second thoughts about swigging from Marco's whiskey flask. Or was that one of those fears that was out-dated, like the one about toilet seats? Speaking of which… He withdrew his hand from the soapy water and wiped his lips, hoping Marco wouldn't notice.

"You see, as word got out about how boot-fitting went for the girls, some, when they got to the top of the wait list, started paying proxies to come here and get fitted for them. And one of the proxies… Well, I figure that's where I could have caught it."

STD transmission aside, Victor thought the scenario Marco described would be disastrous for proper boot fit.

"Sasha thinks karma is paying me back by having Annie leave without a trace. So I'm left wondering, is she dead, or is she out there somewhere living it up with someone else?"

"Which would you prefer to think?" Victor said. It occurred to him that the logistics of their conversation were not unlike those found in a psychiatrist's office, with the tub substituting for the leather couch. Except inverted, as he, in the role of shrink, was in the tub. And speaking of shrink, his fingers were shriveling from all the time in the water, which was growing tepid.

"Annie's not dead," Marco said. "I'm sure of it. She's too smart to just go off into the woods and let something kill her."

"She would just abandon her kids?" Victor asked, responsibility toward offspring being very much on his mind.

"The kids had moved out. I think that made it easier. She taught them to be independent. She figured her work was done."

The water had grown uncomfortably cool, though Victor worried that turning on the hot water would just signal to Marco that he was ready to settle in for the long haul. He also had to pee, and that would be tricky with Marco sitting on the toilet. He wanted Marco to leave.

"The favor," Victor said, hoping to start wrapping things up.

"Yes," he said, and let out a big sigh. "I want you to find her."

"Find her?" Victor said.

"Yes."

"Do I look like a detective?" The question was beyond rhetorical, seeing as how he was lying pink and naked in a bathtub.

"You look as much like a detective as you do a bootmaker. And yet you came all the way here to ask us to give you control of our company. You'll figure it out. Besides, you found *me*, didn't you? And if you hadn't, I'd be dead. So who better than you?"

"Karma," Victor said.

"Exactly. Though to tell you the truth," he continued, "I don't really care who finds her or how she gets found. I don't care if she walks in out of the woods on her own or gets air-dropped from a helicopter. I'm offering this to you to help you out."

"Help me out how?"

"Help you out with what you came all the way up here to do. Lukas thinks you're a joke. He brought you here to make a fool of yourself. So he'll vote for Nanda Devi. Sasha probably will, too. She's a smart woman. She likes you. She feels sorry for you. She thinks you're a decent guy who's been duped into an unfortunate situation. And she's pissed off that Lukas played her by inviting you. And that girl of yours clearly made an impression. But I doubt that her sympathy towards you will make her want to turn a company that's been in her family for more than a century over to someone who knows as little as you do about running a company, or making boots, or anything you'd need to know to make Winklers successful. But at least she likes you. She might surprise us, but my guess is she'll vote for Nanda Devi too, even if reluctantly."

"That's two out of three. I may as well leave now."

"It's not as simple as that. What Lukas didn't explain is that as long as I'm alive, I have veto power. I can't make them turn the company over to you, but I can block them from giving it to Nanda Devi. Or anyone else they might consider. Lukas and Sasha don't want Winklers to fold, but they don't want to be stuck running it, either. Sasha has her art. Lukas wouldn't mind seeing a competently run Winklers pull him out of the financial sewer he's got himself into, but he's a big-city boy. He's not going to move up here and make that happen. But if they know I'll keep blocking them to clear the way for you, then maybe they'll realize they have no choice but to turn Winklers over to you."

Even Victor could see the flaws in that logic, but he didn't say anything.

"There's one more thing you should know," Marco said. "Technically, because she's a member of the family, Annie has a vote. Nobody thinks about that because everybody thinks she's dead. But if you can find her, and then persuade her to vote for you, it's two to two. And the rules are, if it's a tie, my vote swings it. Patriarchal privilege. So there's added incentive."

"And you're not worried that I'll run the company that's been in your family for more than a century straight into the ground?"

"For fuck's sake, Victor. You're a resourceful guy. Surprise us."

Perfect, Victor thought. All he had to do was find someone who didn't want to be found and may not even be alive, bring her against her will to a place she didn't want to be, and do all of this in a way that persuaded her that he would be the perfect person to turn the family business over to.

"Of course, you could always go back to wherever it is you go back to and sell women's shoes."

Ploink. Ploink. Ploink.

"When you came to look for me, why did you come alone?" Marco said, after they'd listened to the water drip for some time. "Why didn't you bring help? Why, in a strange place, do you come looking for a man you barely know in the middle of a forest in a blizzard in weather that's colder than the freezer where we stock the venison? You could have died."

"The blizzard had stopped," Victor said.

"I think there's a part of you that didn't care what happened to you out there."

"What are you trying to say, Marco?"

"I'm just wondering what motivates you."

"You think I have a death wish?"

"I think you're a middle-aged man selling women's shoes."

"And you think the one leads to the other?" Victor said, though to be fair, there were days. He changed the subject. "Back to Annie," he said. "Any idea where I should start looking?"

"Start close. She may wander, but I'd be willing to bet that wherever she has set up camp is close by. Home matters to her, and for better or worse, this is the only one she's got."

"Assuming she's alive," Victor said, "what makes you think she'd come back to you even if I found her?"

There was another pause, more *ploink*ing, another cloud of cigar smoke. Victor began to wonder if Marco had fallen asleep, or was having another of his episodes. "Marco?"

"You may as well know this now," Marco said. "It's not really Annie that I want back. To tell you the truth, I seriously doubt she'd ever agree to come back here to stay. It's something she has that I want. Finding her is the first step."

Victor turned on the hot water.

★

Marco told Victor a story that Annie had once told him. Annie had been brought up by a single mother in a one-bedroom apartment on top of an Italian restaurant in Canton, New York. Her mother cleaned people's houses for a living, and before Annie was old enough to start school, her mother would take her with her when she worked. One day, when Annie was five, they were at the home of a regular client, a woman named Mrs. Brown, a widow who lived by herself in an old Victorian in the rich part of town. Annie had taken some of her mother's old clothes and a box of her jewelry to Mrs. Brown's house to play dress up while her mother worked. She was in Mrs. Brown's parlor amusing herself with the clothes and baubles when Mrs. Brown came in. She was a kind woman, though lonely, with children and grandchildren who lived far away and seldom came to see her. She stopped for a minute to help Annie create an outfit, and in doing so found a ring in the box of jewelry, a silver band set with a single diamond, simple but elegant. It surprised Mrs. Brown that such a nice ring was in a collection of jewelry that a young child was allowed to play with. She wondered if the ring might have gotten in there by mistake.

"Do you know what this is?" Mrs. Brown asked Annie, holding the ring for Annie to see. Annie replied that it was a ring, of course. "I think it's your mother's engagement ring," Mrs. Brown said.

"What's a 'gage-met ring?" Annie wanted to know.

"It's a ring your father gave her before they were married," Mrs. Brown explained.

Annie was puzzled. "But I don't have a father," she said.

"Oh dear," Mrs. Brown said, and realizing she'd stumbled into terrain where she didn't belong, she backed out of it. "Well, you have to be very careful with it," she said, and left it at that.

"Did my father give this to you?" Annie asked her mother later that evening, when they were home in their apartment above the restaurant. She held out her right hand, and on her index finger she wore the ring.

"Where did you get that?" her mother said. She seemed angry.

"In the jewelry box. Mrs. Brown says my father gave it to you. She says it's the kind of ring fathers give to mothers when they marry them."

Annie watched her mother's face grow sad. Up to that point, Annie had asked very few questions about her father, though her mother knew more would be coming. And now here they came. Her mother sighed, started to say something, stopped, then said that yes, Annie's father had given her the ring.

"Where is he?" Annie wanted to know.

"He left."

"Where did he go?"

Her mother shook her head. "I don't know."

"Why?" she said. "Why did he leave?"

Her mother sighed again, and sought a way to answer that would fall at the intersection of truth and acceptability and could be grasped by a five-year-old. It would be a tricky needle to thread. "He decided he didn't love me anymore," she said.

Annie sat with this a moment. She loved her mother, and her mother loved her, and as she couldn't imagine things being any other way, she found it hard to get her head around the concept of unloving someone. "Did he stop loving me?" she asked.

"No, sweetheart. He didn't stop loving you."

"So he still loves me?" she said. Her mother didn't answer.

Annie searched her memory for a father, but couldn't find one. For all of her short life she'd simply accepted that she didn't have a father. "Why don't I remember him?

"Because you weren't born yet, sweetie. You were in my tummy."

There was much in this scenario that Annie didn't understand, but it was too great a struggle to form the right questions. She waited for her mother to say more, but it soon became clear that nothing more was coming, and eventually Annie went off to her bedroom, where she was left with two thoughts: one, that people could unlove people they loved, and leave them, and two, that doing so was painful. She would leave the mystery of fatherhood and questions about how babies wound up in tummies for another day. When she went to her bedroom, she took the ring with her, and her mother never asked for it back.

From there, Annie's interest in her absent father didn't come in a torrent, but it was consistent. Her mother indulged her less than wholeheartedly. Annie learned he had worked as a fishing guide in Adirondack Park, and met her mother because he was a semi-regular at a restaurant where she worked as a waitress. This conjured for Annie a picture of a free-spirited man of the wilderness, a sort of Adirondack Tarzan. She started wearing the engagement ring on a chain around her neck, and if this bothered her mother, at least she didn't object.

With time, however, Annie's infatuation faded to mild curiosity, and from there to resentment as nothing resembling interest in her or responsibility for her ever became part of the picture she painted. She went through a phase of blaming her mother for driving him away, but that phase didn't last long. Annie found it hard to stay mad for long at the person who raised her. Even as a child she intuited that her mother was a good mother doing the best she could. She focused her resentment on her absent father for leaving her. She stopped wearing the ring around her neck, and put it in a box where she kept special things.

Then when Annie was sixteen, her mother was diagnosed with leukemia. The doctors talked in terms of months, not years. As the cancer and treatments weakened her, Annie took on the house-cleaning work, working afternoons after school and on weekends. Contingency plans were discussed. If the cancer took her mother's life, there was an aunt in Ohio. They both knew that what they really meant was *when*, not *if.*

One day she called Annie to her bedside. "Do you remember that ring you used to play with?" she said.

"Your engagement ring."

"I told you your father had given it to me."

"Yes."

"Well," her mother said, her voice weak, "that may not be entirely true." She took a sip of water from a glass on her nightstand and continued.

There had been another man, a student at SUNY Plattsburgh, a biology major who spent one summer in the Adirondacks. Annie's mother met him one night at a bar. She and the fishing guide had just gotten engaged at this point. She was wearing the ring, though instead of scaring the biology student away, it had the opposite effect. He liked the challenge. They were drunk. He was persuasive. She, a woman of limited sexual experience, had just agreed to spend the rest of her life with one man. What harm could it do to have a little fun with another? No one would know. And it would just be this once.

"Are you saying this other man is my father?"

"That's just it," Annie's mother said, tears filling her eyes. "I can't be sure. When I learned I was pregnant I felt horrible about what I'd done and told my fiancé. So you were right, after all. I drove him away."

"So my father is this college kid or the fishing guide? It could be either one?"

"Yes. The fishing guide," (Annie's mom had been steadfast in her refusal to give the man a name), "he and I had been together for about a year. We wanted children. We weren't exactly trying to get pregnant, but we weren't trying not to get pregnant either. We figured if it happened, it happened, and then we'd get married. But nothing happened. For months. I started to think that I couldn't get pregnant."

"And then you fucked this..." Annie struggled for the right word, "...*student*, one time, and you got pregnant." It was the first time she'd said *fuck* in front of her mother.

"Yes," her mother said.

"Do I look like one or the other?" Annie wanted to know.

"No. You don't look much like either of them." The person Annie most resembled was her mother.

"You're sure those are the only options?"

Her mother looked out her bedroom window. "Oh, Annie," she said, the tears spilling out now.

"Names," Annie said. "I need names."

"No. I can't."

"Why?"

"I don't want you to go looking for them." There was another reason, at least with the biology student. Annie's mother didn't know his name.

"What if they have some horrible disease, and I need to know about it to save my own life."

Her mother fell quiet for a moment. "I need to think about it," she said, but she went and died instead, three days after attending Annie's high school graduation in a wheelchair with an umbrella fastened to it to shield her from the sun.

Annie never went to live with the aunt in Ohio. She organized a simple funeral and then went off into the woods. People figured she'd surface somewhere, especially when winter came, but she never did. For the first year she was technically a ward of the state, and there were some search parties, but they couldn't find her. Once she came of age, people stopped trying altogether. There would sometimes be rumors of sightings, like with Sasquatch. She went from being a real person to a local legend.

"Then one day she shows up at our gate asking about boots," Marco said. "The legend of Annie is that she was this aimless vagabond. But she was more rooted than that. We're less than twenty miles from the apartment she shared with her mother. She drew sustenance from the land, but it was *this* land, the land around *here*, and she stuck close to it. She's a homebody, of a sort. It's just that her idea of home is broader than most people's. I feel her close sometimes. She's like an owl in the woods. A presence. Sometimes you can't quite see it, but you know it's there, and you know it sees you."

Marco took a sip of the whiskey and then passed the flask to Victor, who declined.

"So it's the ring you want, not Annie?" Victor said.

"No," Marco said. "It's something else. My mother came from a family of gypsies, and it's their custom that the groom's family will pay the bride's family a bride price. When I got engaged to Annie, my mother wanted to uphold that tradition.

Isabella gave Annie a necklace—an amber teardrop on a gold chain. It had been in her family for years. It was beautiful and worth a fortune. As a way of saying thank-you Annie gave my mother her mother's engagement ring. My mother tried to refuse, but Annie insisted."

"So you have the ring."

"I have the ring."

"And you want the necklace back."

"I want the necklace back."

Victor moved a hand back and forth in the water, making tiny waves. "You want me to find a woman who may or may not exist, and persuade her to give you back a necklace that has been rightfully hers for more than thirty years."

"It's not rightfully hers."

"How's that?"

"These gifts are meant to compensate a family for losing a daughter to a new family. With Annie, there was no family to compensate. And once she left me, she was no longer part of the new family. So the whole thing is bogus."

"But you're still technically married," Victor said. "If she's alive, I mean. And she's still your children's mother. I don't see how—"

"Just bring her to me," Marco interrupted. "Bring her to me and I'll persuade her to give me the necklace."

"And how will you do that?"

"I have something she wants."

"The engagement ring."

"Yes, but that won't do the trick. I also have information she wants."

"And that would be…?"

"Tell her I know who her father is."

"And do you?" Victor asked.

Ploink. Ploink. Ploink.

"You're bluffing."

Ploink.

"What about Nanda Devi?" Victor said.

"What about them?"

"Do they get a chance to find Annie?"

"Oh, they'll get a chance. Tomorrow when I blow up the meeting by telling Lukas and Sasha to wait on their decision, they'll want to know why. And I'll tell them. I'll tell them I want one last chance to see their mother. They'll think I'm crazy, but they'll go along. They won't have a choice. And it's only fair to give that pretty girl and her big company their shot at finding Annie. But they'll come in all big and brash. Annie will smell them a mile away. They'll never find her. You, however, you found me, so I'm confident you can find her. Besides, I'm giving you an advantage."

"And that would be...?"

"There's an envelope on your bed. There are a few pictures of Annie inside. Granted, they weren't taken yesterday, but they'll help. In one of the pictures she's wearing the necklace. There's also a notebook she kept, from her wanderings. Sketches and notes. Pictures of trees. That sort of thing. There must be more of them, but this was the only one I could find. There's bound to be some good clues in there. I've also put the engagement ring in the envelope. Wherever she is and whoever she is, for years she's done a pretty good job of pretending to be someone else. Show her that and watch her reaction. You'll know you've found Annie, and she'll know you know."

"Remind me again why I should want to do this?" Victor asked.

"Because you want the Winkler contract."

"But I still would only have your vote."

"And Annie's."

"Which I'll get by kidnapping her? I don't think so."

"Somebody else will come around. Probably Sasha. Otherwise I'll hold the thing up forever."

"Or at least until you die. Which, I might remind you, almost happened tonight."

Marco was quiet for several seconds. He smushed out the cigar on the side of the tub, brushed ashes into the water. "Let's look at it another way," he said. "You say *no* to this, and it's game over for you. You say *yes* to this, you have a chance."

Victor sighed. The fact that this needle-in-a-haystack undertaking rose so decisively to the top of the list of options he had in his life right now said a lot about the sorry state of those options. "What the hell," he said.

"Good boy," Marco said. He clapped Victor on his wet and naked back, stood up from the toilet, and left the bathroom.

Victor heard the door click behind him and lay there in the tub, thinking. He tried to sort out what he had just agreed to do. Find Annie? Find the necklace? It had been a long night. He wished he hadn't drunk Marco's whiskey. The bath was getting cold again. Plus he still had to pee. He started to lift himself out.

The bathroom door swung open. "And Victor?" Marco said.

Victor cannonballed back into the tub. "*What!*"

"Remember, I'm counting on you."

For the second time, Marco left the bathroom.

Victor waited a couple of minutes to make sure Marco was really gone, then got out, toweled dry, relieved himself, put on a Winkler-issue bathrobe that had been left for him, and opened the bathroom door. To his surprise and relief, he was alone. A large envelope lay on the bed. Inside was a worn spiral notebook—Annie's journal—and three 8 x 10 black and white photographs of Annie. One was a close-up in profile on a winter day, Annie squinting, ruddy-cheeked, piercing dark eyes with crows' feet at the corners, sort of smiling, but also sort of looking like she was trying to figure something out. The second was at a lake with pre-teen Sasha and Lukas pulling her arms in different directions, everybody in bathing suits, Annie's a bikini, Sasha and Annie laughing, Lukas looking dour, as if whatever his mother and sister were laughing about had been at his expense. The third was a torso shot of a younger Annie leaning against a tree in the woods, wearing the necklace. It was as Victor had described: a simple chain that held a teardrop pendant. Victor was distracted in his analysis of the necklace, however, as it was the only thing that Annie was wearing, and it hung there in the valley formed by her smallish but perfect breasts. He looked at the picture a long time, trying his best to stay focused on the necklace. Everything in the photo was stunningly beautiful.

He turned the envelope upside down. A ring fell onto the comforter. It was as Marco had said—a simple silver band set with a single diamond, a small diamond, a small diamond that may not have even been a real diamond, but Victor figured it probably was, because who would bother making a fake diamond so small? It was an engagement ring purchased by someone who couldn't afford to buy an engagement ring. He picked it up, slid it as far as it would go onto his pinky, and looked at it some more. He had to agree with Marco—whatever value the ring had would be purely sentimental, and the story of its provenance left some doubt as to whether the sentiment in this case would be positive. Victor put the ring and the photos back in the envelope. It was three in the morning. He needed some sleep.

[chapter 13]

The electricity was back in the morning, and following instructions that Kirsten delivered by slipping notes on index cards under each door, everyone assembled in the study at eight-thirty. The day had dawned clear, and a bright sun climbed above trees that to Victor looked less imposing in daylight than they had during the previous evening's rescue mission. Kirsten stood sentry next to a table on which sat an urn of coffee and a plate stacked with muffins, which Fiona, Nate, and Victor helped themselves to—Fiona and Victor taking one muffin each and Nate taking four, then putting one back when Victor gave him a look. They took their seats across from Isabel and Charles, who radiated a practiced confidence as they sat there with mugs of coffee in front of them.

Victor had been awake since six studying the contents of the envelope spread out on his bed. The photos' age limited their usefulness. He'd seen something once where they photographed young people and then computer-aged them into middle age and beyond. He wished he could do that now.

The notebook was full of notes and sketches from her hikes, with commentary about bear scat and eagle sightings and the time of year when the leaves began to change color. Annie had drawn trees and labeled them with Latin names: *Pinus strobus, Tsuga canadensis, Acer saccharum.* Any human presence in the notebook focused entirely on Annie's children—she had written about Sasha being terrified of and enthralled by a box turtle, about Lukas coming upon a large puddle on a day hike and pronouncing it his new swimming hole. There were drawings of butterflies, of a distant mountain range in the snow, of an old cabin in the late stages of collapse. Victor was skimming, but he didn't see Marco's name in there anywhere.

The photos and notebook were supposed to give Victor an advantage, but how? What did any of this tell him about the Annie of today, who might be anywhere, or nowhere at all? Victor stuffed everything back in the envelope, then stuffed the envelope deep in his suitcase.

Nate and Fiona knocked on his door a little before eight. He didn't say anything to them about Marco's nighttime visit. He still wasn't sure how completely he could trust them, and wanted to see how things played out when they were in the room with Isabel. Fiona winced when she looked at Victor's nose, which had gone from pale pink to a deeper rose overnight and had sprouted two modest-sized blisters above the left nostril. She went back to her room for makeup, but returned empty-handed, explaining she'd left whatever it was she'd used before back in Granite in his hotel bathroom. "I could see if I can borrow something from Isabel," she offered. Victor said no thanks.

Down in the meeting room, Lukas asked everyone to sit down. "Thank you all for bearing with us through the unpredictable circumstances we've been forced to deal with. And we owe a special debt of gratitude to Victor and Charles for their heroics in helping to rescue my father last night." Lukas nodded to Victor and then to Charles, who tipped his cap.

Victor *and* Charles? Victor thought. What the fuck? Here he had risked life and limb (and nose) to rescue Lukas's senile father from a mile deep in the woods, and Lukas somehow manages to establish a moral equivalency between his actions and Charles's? He did what? Carry Marco through the backyard? Victor seethed, but tried not to show it.

"Dad," Lukas said. "Would you like to say anything?"

Marco had a glassy-eyed look that worried Victor. He blinked excessively. It was entirely possible that he'd totally forgotten his tub-side visit.

"The northern lights have seen queer sights," he said. He looked like he was about to say something more, but he stopped.

Victor knew the words—the opening line to "The Cremation of Sam Magee," a favorite poem of his father's, who could recite the whole long thing by heart. Was Marco having another "episode"? Marco folded his hands on the table and gave a satisfied nod to no one in particular.

"My father thanks you," Lukas said. "The family thanks you. Now, to get on to the business at hand."

Lukas went on about how grateful the family was that Victor and Isabel had come here to make their presentations. About how each side had its strengths. About how difficult the decision had been. About how the family had wished it could select both teams, but how, well, that just wasn't the way things worked. Blah blah blah blah…

Isabel Forenza sat looking like a queen at her coronation. The green velour dress was gone, replaced by a gray skirt and a white silk blouse. How, Victor wondered, had she managed to change clothes? Had someone mushed in the skirt and blouse by dogsled during the night? Did she always go everywhere assuming she might be spending the night? And where had she spent the night? Troubling images entered Victor's head while Lukas continued.

"I won't drag things out unnecessarily. We believe it's in the best interests of the family and the future of Winkler boots to award the contract to—" He paused for effect, like the guy with the envelope at the Oscars.

Marco leapt in: "He turned to me, and Cap, says he, I'll cash in this trip, I guess; and if I do, I'm asking that you won't refuse my last request."

"Dad, what in the world—?"

"I'm saying just hold on for one goddamn minute," Marco said, and his lunatic glaze sharpened into the determination of an old man fighting against irrelevance.

The room grew silent. Respectful silence wouldn't describe it accurately. Apprehensive silence, certainly. Fearful, even. Or, in Victor's case, hopeful, though he still worried that Marco might be insane.

"You can't go forward without my vote," Marco said. "Those are the rules."

"We just assumed—"

"We."

"Sasha and I."

"Assumed," Marco said.

"Well, based on the information we heard yester—"

"Assumed without giving a shit about what I think."

Lukas glanced at Sasha, who shrugged the slightest of *I told you so* shrugs. Lukas looked back at his father, then folded his hands on the table and said nothing, a man waiting for a storm to pass.

"I want to find Annie," Marco said.

"We all do, Dad," Lukas said. "But Mom's gone." He used the tone parents use to tell their five-year-old that the goldfish has died.

"You don't know that. I don't believe that. And he's going to find her." Marco pointed a bent finger more or less in the direction of Victor.

"Dad, please—"

"Don't 'Dad please' me. He's going to find her, and bring her back. And when he does we're going to turn the company over to him. As an expression of our gratitude."

"Oh, for Christ sakes," Lukas put his head in his hands, then held his hands in front of himself, prayerfully. "First of all, she's gone. If she wanted to come back, she would have come back. Mr. Barstow is not going to find her."

"He found me, didn't he?" Marco interrupted. "Not that any of the rest of you gave a good goddamn about it! It would've fit better with your plans if I'd just gone and frozen to death out there."

"And second of all," Lukas continued. "Finding Mom has nothing to do with running a boot company."

"Shows what he's made of."

Isabel Forenza spoke up: "Can somebody please tell me what's going on? I thought a decision had been made."

Discussion followed. Sasha went over the rules of Winkler family decision-making, explaining the obstructive weight of Marco's vote. Lukas protested, and then Isabel, both of them arguing that Marco's ludicrous desire to see his disappeared and probably dead wife should have nothing to do with the future of Winklers boots. Marco held firm. The fact that he might be insane got danced around. It was business decision-making as if carried out by the Make-a-Wish Foundation. Victor stayed quiet. By supporting Lukas, Isabel was pissing off Marco. The arc of the Winkler boot universe was bending his way. No need to step in and fuck things up.

"How long?" Lukas said, a crack of concession showing in his armor. "How long do we wait to see if he can find Mom? We can't hold things up forever."

Marco blinked and looked off at nothing in particular. "A week?" he said uncertainly.

The Winkler boot-universe arc started to unbend. Seven billion people on the planet, and Victor had a week to find someone who didn't want to be found and might not even exist?

"I don't think that's going to be enough—" Victor began.

"I'm dying, you know," Marco said.

"Here we go," Lukas said. He let out a long sigh.

Sasha spoke up. "You are not dying."

"I have AIDS," he said.

"You have AIDS?" Isabel said. What little color her pale face had held drained out. The woods, his bathroom—Victor wondered where else Marco might have gone overnight.

"You don't have AIDS," Sasha said. "And you're not dying."

"I almost died last night," Marco said. "Would have, too, if he hadn't saved me." He pointed his bent finger at Victor again.

"You have AIDS?" Isabel said again. She looked truly distraught.

All those years of women coming to him for boots, Victor thought. Talk about karma.

"Fine," Lukas said, re-channeling the conversation. "Mr. Barstow, you have a week to find our mother. If you're successful, we will meet back here as a happily reunited family to reach a final decision. More likely, we'll just consummate what we should have consummated today, which is to award the contract to Nanda Devi." He consulted his iPhone and set a date and time to reconvene. "Is everyone agreed, then?"

"What about us?" Isabel said. "Don't we get a chance to find her?"

Lukas looked at his father. "The more the merrier," Marco said. He said nothing about the necklace.

"Fine then," Lukas said. "One week."

"This is just like *Amazing Race*," Nate said.

[chapter 14]

"She's beautiful," Fiona said from the back seat of Nate's car. They had packed up quickly and were headed on freshly plowed roads back to Granite. Victor told them about Marco's visit to his bathroom and filled them in on the details of Annie's story, leaving out for now any mention of the necklace, or of the ring or notebook, which he'd removed from the envelope before handing it to Fiona. She was looking at the pictures of Annie.

"How're you going find her, Victor?" Nate asked, a good question, and Victor didn't have a good answer. Though he figured Isabel Forenza already knew what she was going to do. An image passed through his head of Isabel's black SUV racing in a week's time over snow-covered roads back toward the Winkler property, Annie Winkler drugged, bound, and unconscious in the back seat propped up between two thugs. But still, there was the whole matter of the necklace, which Isabel knew nothing about.

He tried to visualize success, though this wasn't his strength. Once, at the Bootery, in an effort to increase sales, the owner, a short man whose failed hair transplant made it look as though wires were coming out of his skull, hired a woman he introduced as a "productivity consultant" to come and lead sessions on visualization, one a week for three weeks.

The consultant, a short, fit, and perpetually cheery young woman whom Victor recognized as a teacher at the yoga studio Carla went to, ran the sales team through a series of exercises that basically entailed visualizing themselves joyfully serving satisfied customers who beamed with pleasure while trying on shoes and who walked out of the store with so many shoeboxes that they needed help carrying them.

Victor had no problem visualizing the successful sales. His problem was, he was inclined to visualize other members of the sales force making them, while visualizing himself sitting on his little shoe stool surrounded by piles of those tissue-paper things and boxes full of shoes that customers had rejected. Then it got worse. He began to have dreams in which the shoes were wrong for horrible reasons. He would zip up a boot into the skin on a woman's calf and it would get stuck there, or a loose shoe brad would slice a bloody gash in a customer's foot. Victor would wake covered in sweat and gasping for air. The dreams had no basis in reality. In nearly every month he had outperformed the other four members of the sales team—to be fair, higher bars had been crossed—and in no month had he finished worse than second.

On a break in the middle of the third visualization session, he mentioned his dreams to the consultant. She brushed them off as nothing more than the product of healthy anxiety, telling Victor that in his case, visualizing his own failure was a key motivator, and the awfulness of the dreams, by painting worst-case-scenario pictures in his mind, in fact contributed to his success. He nodded as if this made sense, though after he thought about it for a while he decided the woman was nuts.

"Start local," Fiona said from the back seat.

"That's what Marco said," Victor replied. "Why do you say that?"

"For starters, maybe somebody knows her. You can ask around, show them the pictures. But beyond that, for all her wanderings, I'm betting she's a homebody."

"And you say this because…"

"She's a mother. Unless she was a rotten mother, I'd bet she'd want to stay where she could keep an eye on her kids, even if it was from a distance."

"But the kids weren't here. They were off at college."

"Yes, but they didn't go far either. Lukas went to Cornell and Sasha went to RISD. Their framed diplomas are on the wall in the room where we met. It's not like they were at the Sorbonne. They stayed close enough to come home on weekends. They're homebodies too. I'll bet she's still around here someplace. If she's alive, that is."

No one said much for the rest of the ride. Fiona studied the pictures, Victor fretted, and Nate sang badly to songs on the radio. Before long they were pulling to the curb outside the Placid Hotel.

"Well, thanks for all your help," Victor said, unsure if he would get any more of it, and something in his voice suggested he didn't expect any more.

Nate looked at him, puzzled. "Wait—you're dumping us?"

"I wouldn't want to get in the way of your career prospects," Victor said. It came out snarkier than he'd intended.

"Jesus, Victor," Fiona said. "What the fuck? We just drop everything and spend three days helping you out, and now you want to get rid of us?"

"I'm guessing Isabel made you offers that are too good to refuse."

"You're paranoid," Nate said. "And don't lecture us about loyalty."

Victor didn't know what to think. Were they genuinely disappointed? Double agents? Nanda Devi moles? Was he overthinking it?

"I need some time to think," he said, opening the car door and stepping out. "Again," he said before closing it. "Thanks. And I mean that." Victor closed the door and the car spun its tires on a patch of ice and sped away.

★

Victor stopped at the desk and extended his reservation. Staying longer wasn't going to be a problem—it wasn't like the hotel was going to all of a sudden fill up with an ice-fishing convention—though the desk clerk told him they figured to get pretty busy as the week went on. "Something at the college," he explained. He gave Victor the same room from two nights earlier, and told him he would find all of his things right where he left them.

Back in his room, Victor knew he should call Carla and let her know what was going on. Not that she'd been sitting around the house frantic with worry. Victor's phone informed him that he had zero missed calls, the same number of texts, and the only emails he'd received were from his dentist, reminding him he was past-due for an appointment; his insurance company, reminding him he was past-due on a payment he needed to make for Allie's car; and someone guaranteeing that a larger penis would totally change his life.

It was Sunday, and Carla wouldn't be at work, so he tried the house phone first. He was momentarily troubled when a man's voice answered, until he recognized it as his own, on the home voicemail. He didn't leave a message. He tried her mobile, and got a phone-company robot inviting him to leave a message or press one for more options. He left a brief, upbeat, and non-specific message about new developments that could play out in his favor.

Reaching voicemail came as a relief. Relief that he wouldn't have to explain things, wouldn't be second-guessed, wouldn't be lectured to about the folly of his partnership with two students, or the stupidity of barging out into a blizzard to try to find a senile old man, or the ridiculousness of having the whole thing now hinge on his chances of finding a woman who most likely didn't exist and getting her to part with jewelry no one had seen in years.

And voicemail meant he wouldn't have to hear the latest about Karl. Victor had met Karl once, when Carla's car was in the shop and Victor picked her up at school. Karl was younger than Carla—early forties, maybe—and tall. He wore his blond hair in a ponytail and rode a motorcycle to school. Ever since he'd arrived in the fall it had been Karl this and Karl that. How Karl stood up to the principal in an argument over whether teachers could get a Keurig for the faculty lounge. Or how Karl broke up a playground fight between two gang kids (gang kids who were in third grade in a Montessori school, mind you, which Victor thought took some of the heroic edge off of the act). Or how Karl said the funniest thing in the teachers meeting today, ha-ha-ha-ha-ha. Or how Karl told Carla that Victor ought to go back to school in cyber-security, because that was huge right now. And did Victor know that Karl had a tattoo? No, he did not, nor did he want to know where it was or what it looked like. For all Victor knew she was at Karl's now, tracing her finger around it. Or discussing places on her body where she could get one that matched.

He glanced at his phone. Maybe a bigger penis really would change his life.

He tried Allie next, and got, "Hey, this is Allie—leave a message." He heard optimism and hopefulness in her voice, that sense that if she fell, the world would catch her. He felt wistful, but also inspired. "Hi, sweetie. Just checking to see how you're doing," he said into his phone. Allie motivated him. It wasn't the world's responsibility to catch her—it was Victor's.

But not without coffee. Between rescuing Marco and their tub-side chat, he had gotten almost no sleep. He headed down to the lobby to see if he could find some.

Instead he found Nate and Fiona, sitting in two wing-back chairs, next to a fireplace with a dying fire in it. They sat hunched over cell phones, thumbing away. Nate looked up as Victor approached. "You finished thinking yet?" he said.

[chapter 15]

"There's also this," Victor said when they got to his room. He handed Fiona Annie's notebook, distributing evidence in dribs and drabs. He entertained the possibility that she and Nate would relay anything of value they learned to Isabel, but chose to take the risk.

Fiona flipped through the notebook. Nate, next to her on the bed, contented himself with the photo of Annie naked. Victor still hadn't said anything about the necklace, and it was a safe bet that Nate would be too distracted to notice it hanging around Annie's neck. The necklace could wait. They wouldn't find it unless they found Annie, so first things first.

"Huh," Fiona said after a while.

"Huh what?"

"This sketch." She held the notebook so Victor could see a drawing of bushes and trees going from smaller to taller, left to right across a two-page spread. "It's the succession pattern in an Adirondack forest. We studied this in my ecology class."

She kept flipping pages. "Huh," she said again.

She slid closer to Nate on the bed. "Let me see those again," she said, meaning the photos. Nate held them out for her one by one—the nude, the profile, the one with her kids.

"Go back to that first one," she said. The nude. Nate was happy to oblige. She leaned closer for a better look. "Huh," she said again.

"What?" Victor said again.

She shook her head. "I'm not sure." She went back to the notebook and the sketches of the bushes and trees. "Look, I've got to go. Can I take the notebook with me?"

Victor said she could, and hoped she wouldn't just hand it over to Isabel. He gave them a photograph, too, and disappointed Nate by giving them the winter profile, which Fiona tucked into the pages of the notebook. Fiona grabbed the makeup bag she'd brought to work on Victor's nose, and then they left. He stuffed the other two photos back in the envelope and went downstairs to the bar. No need for coffee now—he was wide awake. What he needed now was a drink.

The hotel bar was a sad little bar, with a sad little collection of sad bottles of alcohol and six sad little stools. A TV above the bar had a hockey game on with the sound off. The color was off, too—the ice looked like dead grass. On one of the stools sat a large Black man who looked up when Victor entered and raised a martini glass in salute. Charles.

"Buy you a drink?" he said.

"Sure." Victor sat on the stool next to him and ordered a gin and tonic. When the bartender brought it, Charles lifted his glass to clink a toast. Victor clinked him back, feeling wary and co-opted.

"That was a brave thing you did, going after the old man. Dumb as shit. But brave. It was a real game changer."

"And what game did it change?"

"I'm still here in this icy-ass town. My boss is up in her room getting reamed out by her boss for this not being over. A lot of people are pissed off. This was supposed to be a slam-dunk.

A quick trip up north to close a deal that should have been easy to close. But here we are. So like I said, a game changer."

Charles took the little plastic sword from his martini glass and swallowed the two olives that had been impaled there. Victor twirled ice cubes with a little straw.

"You think you can find her, the old man's ex?" Charles asked.

"What do you think?"

"It doesn't matter what I think. But Ms. Forenza, she's, shall we say, concerned. You know what I'm sayin'?"

Victor sipped his drink.

"It's like we're in the playoffs, you know? Like we were up three-oh in a best of seven series, and were just waiting to close it out in a sweep, and you come out of nowhere and win game four. Then maybe take the lead in game five. It kind of shocked the system. Shook things up."

"So we keep playing," Victor said.

"Yeah, we keep playing. But Victor, you know what? We're still up three games to one. In all of sports, only one team has ever come back to win a championship after losing the first three games, and that was the Boston Red Sox in 2004. That team was loaded with talent. You got that girl, but I don't see you being loaded with talent. The 2004 Boston Red Sox you're not. All you're doing is prolonging the inevitable."

"We'll see."

"You're right about that." He held up his martini glass again, and Victor clinked it.

"What about you?" Victor asked. "Do you think you can find her?"

Charles laughed into his drink. "What makes you think we're even going to try?"

"You're not?"

"Whose name do you think Lukas Winkler was about to say this morning when his old man interrupted him? You think he was going to say he was turning the company over to some guy who sells shoes to old ladies, or to one of the most powerful outdoor companies on the planet? So if you don't deliver this mystery lady in a week's time, everything goes back to the way it was, and we get the contract. So all we do is wait. I get myself a little all-expense-paid vacation. It's not Cancun, but it's not without its charms. Maybe I'll take up a hobby. Dog-sledding, maybe."

"You're not worried that I'll find her?"

"You see, Victor that's the thing. To tell the truth, I'm not sure I buy that this Annie Winkler is even still alive. But you're right. For this to work out well for us, we need to feel confident that if she is alive, you won't find her. So there's steps we can take to boost our confidence level."

Steps they can take. Like send Nate and Fiona to spy on him. The two people he'd just given Annie's notebook and photo to. Were they already on the payroll?

"Steps," Victor said. "Was that supposed to be a threat?"

Charles waved his olive sword in the vicinity of Victor's face. "Let's just say, if you win game five, we're not going to roll over and play dead." Charles finished his drink in one gulp and stood to leave. "Good luck, Victor." He turned to go.

Victor glanced at the TV screen. It was between periods in the hockey game. Commentators commented soundlessly. Behind them a Zamboni circled the dead-grass ice. A hockey statistic flashed on the screen below the commentators. Victor read it, then spoke it. "The Toronto Maple Leafs, 1942," he said.

Charles paused. "Say what?"

"They were down three games to none and won the championship."

Charles glanced at the TV, and a smile spread across his face. "Touché then, Victor," he said. "Touché."

Victor waited until he was sure Charles had gone and took the photo of Annie and her kids out of the envelope. He could show it to people, see if they recognized her. He sat alone at the bar. Behind him, the dining room was empty save for an older couple that sat wordlessly by the far wall, the only other people in a room full of tables set for a dinner rush that wasn't likely to happen. It was late afternoon on a Saturday, hardly the best time to find people to show Annie's picture to—no mid-day drunks nursing beers, no salty old-timers. There was the bartender, but he hovered down at the other end of the bar. He saw Victor looking at him and came over.

"Another?" he said, and pointed to Victor's not-yet-empty glass.

"Do you know this woman?" Victor asked, coming right out with it. He slid the family beach photo around so the bartender could get a good look and pointed his index finger at Annie. In his white shirt and black vest, the bartender looked like a tall, thin, penguin. He was about Victor's age, and had the worn-out look of someone who may have held this job for decades. He studied at the photos, leaned down to get closer, took reading glasses out of his shirt pocket and put them on. Then shook his head. "Sorry," he said. "Pretty, though."

"These were taken over twenty years ago," Victor said, as if that would be helpful information. "She'd be older now."

"Aren't we all?" the man said. He nodded again at Victor's glass. "Another?"

"Sure."

The bartender delivered Victor's fresh drink and went back to watch the hockey game, which had resumed. Victor took the other photo from the envelope—the naked Annie—and began

142

shuffling the two photos, first one on top, then the other, over and over. The bar was so quiet he could hear the ticks of a huge round clock over the doorway to the lobby. One week, and it was disappearing tick by tick. He felt like the hamster in the cage running and running on his exercise wheel and going nowhere. Except Victor wasn't even on the exercise wheel—he was sitting next to it drinking a gin and tonic. He looked back at the photos.

"Mind if I sit here, or would you and your naked woman like some alone time?" a woman's voice said. She settled on to the barstool next to him. Attractive, late thirties, early forties, with a blond bob that Carla would have pointed out was fake blond, and an off-white silk blouse with lacy sleeves. The blouse's top couple of buttons were unbuttoned, exposing freckled skin on which lay a silver necklace, which Victor thought for a second might be *the* necklace, but quickly realized that it wasn't, not even close. He looked away lest it seem that he was looking down her blouse, which in fact he sort of was. The bartender left his stool, assembled a drink, and placed it on the bar in front of the woman. Scotch and soda, Victor guessed from the color and the bubbles.

"Sorry," he said, and shoved the photos back in the envelope.

"Why?" the woman said.

He felt flustered, and blushed. "I'm looking for someone."

"Join the club," she said, her voice deep and a little weary. She sipped her drink.

"What I mean is, I'm trying to find someone, and I have pictures of her, and I'm trying to find someone who might know her. Or know where she is. Do you mind if I…" The chances of her recognizing Annie were remote, but then Victor was on something of a roll when it came to remote chances.

"Let's have a look," she said, and pulled her stool closer to his. A lacy-sleeved arm brushed his hand.

He took out the beach picture and pointed to Annie. "Her," he said.

She leaned in for a close look. Her hair smelled like mangoes. "Let's see that other one," she said.

He hesitated a moment, then took out the nude photo. "It's really the necklace I'm interested in in that one," he said.

"And you like *Playboy* for the articles," she said.

Victor blushed an even deeper shade of red.

"She's beautiful," the woman said.

"She's older now. Those are from a while ago."

"Where'd you get them?"

"From her ex-husband. Erm... husband."

"You an investigator?" she said.

"No, I'm... It's a long story."

"I'm not sure I'd want my ex-husband hiring people to try to find me," she said.

"He hasn't hired me. And it's nothing bad. It's just... He's dying, and wants to see her before..."

"I've heard that song."

"Look, I'm sorry," Victor said, putting the photos back in the envelope. He started to stand up. "I shouldn't have..."

"It's Annie Winkler."

Victor sat back down, nearly missing the stool. He stared at her. "How—?"

"If you know about the Winklers, you know about Annie," she said. "I own a pair of Winklers. Haven't worn them in years. They're overrated, if you ask me. Not worth the effort it takes to get them."

Victor swallowed.

"Isn't she supposed to be dead?"

"Her husband doesn't think so."

"Marco," the woman said, and she said it in a way that Victor couldn't rule out was connected to the effort involved in getting her boots. "Marco's dying?"

"Yes. Well, maybe. It's hard to say. He's not well."

This news elicited a snicker. "I could say I'm sorry to hear that, but I'd be lying." The woman caught the bartender's attention and ordered another drink, a transaction carried out entirely through the movement of her index finger. "What's your name?" she asked when her drink arrived.

"Victor."

"Well, here's to your search, Victor." They clinked glasses. "And you're...?"

"You can call me Molly."

"Molly." They clinked glasses again. Victor felt lightheaded.

The waiter returned with a large plate on which sat what could have been an entire pineapple, peeled and cut into half-circle slices. Victor could only stare.

"I love pineapple. Reminds me of Hawaii," Molly said." You want some?" He shook his head.

"You've been to Hawaii?"

"No," she said. "Someday maybe." She picked up a slice with her fingers and ate it. Victor watched juice roll down her knuckle. "You?"

"No." Though he and Carla had talked about it.

"Here's to someday going to Hawaii," Molly said, and they clinked glasses a third time and drank again.

"You come here a lot," he said, more a statement than a question.

"I like their pineapple."

Victor laughed, and then wasn't sure she'd meant it to be funny. He watched another slice of fruit disappear into her mouth.

Richard Bader

"Are you from around here?"

"Ottawa," the woman said.

"*Ottawa*," Victor repeated, as if it were a foreign land, which, of course, it was. He made a mental note to locate it on a map later. "What brings you to Granite?"

"I have a client here."

"A client," Victor repeated. He said it in a way that invited her to say more about the client, but she declined. He pressed on. "What kind of work do you do?"

It occurred to Victor that if this were a movie of his life, moviegoers would see a middle-aged man having a conversation with an attractive woman he'd met at a bar. He hoped they would read the scene as flirtatious. This is what normal people do, he told himself, and if you discounted the fact that one of those people was eating an entire pineapple, they were reasonably normal people. He congratulated himself for acting like a normal person, and maybe even a flirtatious normal person, in normal-enough circumstances. It felt healthy, good. Then all that changed.

"I'm an escort," she said, and looked straight at him, eyebrows idling, her red lips stretching mirthfully as she watched Victor struggle to figure out how to respond. He swallowed, and felt every centimeter of the rise and fall of his Adam's apple. Of course, *escort* could simply mean she took people from point A to point B. But it probably didn't.

"Hmh," he eventually managed.

She went on. She had come here to meet a regular client of hers in Granite. She didn't say who, and it wasn't like Victor was going to ask. This client was supposed to meet her here at the hotel. They had a system. He would arrange for a driver to pick her up in Ottawa and bring her here to the hotel. He would meet her here, where he'd reserved a room, and then some time later the driver would take her back home. Except this time, and not for the first time, he failed to show. It astonished Victor that she was telling him all of this.

"At least he paid," she said. "I've learned. I make him pay in advance. You sure you don't want some?" she said, meaning, he assumed, pineapple.

"Maybe a bite," Victor said. She speared a slice on her fork and held it out to him. The intimacy of the gesture caught him off guard. He plucked the pineapple off her fork with his fingers, then wondered if that's what she had intended for him to do. Should he have taken the fork from her? Or just leaned over and bit? He fought the urge to ask her how much her client had paid, and ate pineapple instead.

"So it appears I have a couple of hours to kill," she said while he chewed. It was surprisingly good pineapple.

Victor struggled to think of how to respond. "Hmh," he eventually said again. He wiped pineapple juice off his chin with a napkin.

"So why are you here, Victor? Just to see if you can find Annie Winkler, or is there more to it than that?"

"I want to run Marco's company." It was the first time he'd actually said that out loud. It felt good.

"No shit?"

He explained, leaving out the part about the other Victor Barstow, and only vaguely alluding to Nanda Devi, without mentioning it by name. He tried to project confidence.

"How long have you been here?"

Victor thought "Three days?" Was that all it had been? It felt like weeks.

"And you're staying here?"

He nodded.

"So you have a room." She laughed, and then he laughed, and they both were at the bar laughing because asking if he had a room struck him as this sort of inside joke about her profession, a sexy little joke, and Victor said something about how her job seemed to involve very little actual escorting, another little joke, one he regretted saying as soon as he'd said it, though he was relieved when she laughed, which meant maybe the joke worked after all. So he laughed some more.

Banter, that's what they called it, and when they stopped laughing he drank a little more, and she drank a little more, and they ordered another round of drinks, which she put on her client's tab, and they finished the pineapple, and then the laughter died down, and Victor spun his glass in tiny circles with his fingers, which were sticky from all the pineapple juice, very much aware as he did so of his wedding ring on one of those sticky fingers, that plus the feeling that his head had been stuffed with cotton, and soon all he could hear was the tick of the big clock up there on the wall over the doorway, muffled a little bit because of all the cotton, and then she said, "Let's go see your room."

★

Afterward, Victor dreamed. He dreamed he was alone and lost in a snowy woods, and very tired. So he lay down at the base of a tree to sleep. And then after he fell asleep in that dream, he dreamed again, inside the first dream, like a Russian nesting doll of dreams, one inside the other. In the second dream he was back in the Bootery, surrounded by women demanding shoes. And he raced to try to keep up, retreating to the storeroom and coming out with box after box of shoes, but when he opened them each contained only a single left shoe. The women grew angrier and angrier, until finally Victor found a box with a complete pair of red pumps, and when he opened it and the women saw the pair of red shoes there, they charged at him, an ugly mass, like British soccer fans. But the shoes weren't for any of these women—they were for Molly, who sat in languid repose in a wingback chair covered in red velour, waiting for Victor to bring her the red shoes. A man who could have been his boss from the shoe store, but also could have been Marco, stood behind her, dangling slices of pineapple for her to take with her teeth. Fearing for his life, Victor grabbed the red pumps and started swinging them, spinning in circles to keep the women at bay, and they snarled and scratched at him, only now the women were no longer women, but wolves, and he was back inside his first dream, in the snowy woods, and it was dark, and he was cold, and still lost, and Molly was out there somewhere, but he didn't know where, and he wanted to get the red shoes to her, but the red eyes of the wolves glowed in a circle around him so he just stood there brandishing this pair of red women's shoes. He became aware of a dark shape coming toward him, out of the woods, only he couldn't see it clearly, because every time he looked at where it should be it would disappear behind a tree. It lurked, then moved, then lurked, and Victor knew what it was. A bear! A huge, menacing bear, with sharp claws that would slice him like a paper shredder.

In his dream-mind Victor tried think of the things you're supposed to do when confronted by a bear. And another dream opened up and he was sitting on the couch with Allie, an eight-year-old Allie, watching a bear show on the Discovery Channel, and they told you what to do. Then Victor left that dream and was back in the woods but couldn't remember what the man on the show told him to do. But Allie would remember. So as the bear came closer he called Allie on his cell phone. But all he heard was her cheery voice: "Hey, this is Allie. Leave a message."

Climb a tree? That couldn't be right. Bears could climb trees, couldn't they? And besides, there were no trees near him with limbs low enough to reach. Run? He didn't stand a chance outrunning a bear in snow over two feet deep. Should he wait until the bear gets close and then hit him on the nose with something, like a red shoe? Or was that what you did with sharks? Look him in the eye, or was that exactly the wrong thing? What if it was a female? Did that make a difference? Maybe a female who hated males, or one who just hated her male, a male who had run off and left her alone to fend for herself and protect her cub from menaces like Victor with his red shoes. Or maybe a female who had left her male because he was worthless as a bear, couldn't catch a salmon if you dangled it in front of his face on twenty-pound-test monofilament. Victor turned and tried to run because that's what you do in dreams, and besides, what choice did he have? But, dreams being notoriously lousy places in which to run, he went nowhere, just dug himself deeper into the snow. He curled up in the ditch he'd made trying to run, in fetal position, hoping he looked more like a log than a meal, and hoping getting eaten wouldn't hurt too much.

He looked up and what he saw was part bear and part Molly, and he remembered her, remembered going back to his room with her, and now the bear-woman was angry, and Victor wondered why. Had he not met her standards? (Probably not.) Had he remembered to leave her a tip? What did you tip escorts, anyway? Fifteen percent? Twenty? That's what people were doing in restaurants these days, and Victor thought it was nuts. And twenty percent of *what*? He didn't have a clue.

The shape hovered over Victor, and he was looking into a mouth full of impossibly white and sharp teeth. Arms reached toward him. He may or may not have actually screamed, and then all of a sudden it wasn't a bear's face hovering over him after all. It was Fiona's, and she was shaking his shoulders. "Victor!" she was saying. "Victor, wake up! I know where to find Annie!"

[chapter 16]

Victor looked around the room and saw only Fiona. Molly was gone. Had she existed only in his dream? He sniffed the pillow. Pineapple, with an under-note of mango. He lifted the comforter and looked under it. He was naked.

Fiona hopped up onto the bed next to him and propped herself up with pillows.

Outside the window the sun blared, and water streamed off of giant icicles that hung from the roof. Victor's room faced east. If the sun was shining in his window, it was morning, and if it was morning, he'd slept through the night. Was that possible? Had that woman, Molly, drugged him, slipped something into his drink when he wasn't looking? Had she robbed him when she left? They did that in movies. His wallet? Where was his wallet? In his pants pocket. Where were his pants? He looked at the floor on his side of the bed, but they weren't there. He hoped they were on Fiona's side, but being naked, he decided not to get up and look. He fought back through the thicket of his dream, trying to recall what lay on the other side of it. He sensed shame trying to greet him there, shame and guilt, and he didn't want to feel shame or guilt, so he retreated back to the side of the thicket with Fiona and the sunny morning and the dripping icicles.

Fiona wore a white ski cap over hair still damp from her morning shower, and smelled like fresh apples packed in damp wool. Victor hoped this smell overpowered the smells of pineapple and mango and stale sex. If room service had come in at that moment they would have thought Fiona and Victor were lovers enjoying their morning-after in a leisurely if oddly dressed manner. He shook the thought out of his head. Fiona was barely older than Allie.

She had her laptop open. "Look at this," she said, pulling up Granite College website. She clicked on a link for faculty, scrolled down the alpha list, and clicked on a name. Victor looked at the face of an unsmiling middle-aged female professor, her face thin bordering on gaunt, with short, spiky white hair and steely blue eyes. Next to her picture were her name and title: Winona Keller, Associate Professor of Biology.

"So?"

"Victor, look!" Fiona jabbed at Winona Keller's picture with her finger. "Look! *Look!* That's Annie Winkler!"

Victor looked, squinted, tried to reconcile the woman on the website with the beauty in the photos. He didn't see it. Fiona reached into her backpack and pulled out the picture of Annie Victor had given her. She held it next to the computer screen so they could look at the two images side by side. "Those eyes," she said. "The cheekbones, the nose, the whole way her face is structured."

It was hard for Victor to get past the hair—blond and flowing in the picture he'd given Fiona, with wisps floating across her face. Nothing at all like the short, white product-saturated hair of the scowling woman on the computer screen. Fiona used her fingertips to cover Annie's long hair in the photo. Subtract some weight, add a couple of decades. Throw in a new do. Could it be possible? It all seemed too easy. Victor had envisioned a quest! An adventure! Not that he'd gotten very far. Though he had apparently fucked a prostitute. That was new.

"Look at her bio," Fiona said. She scrolled down. "Teaches ecology and environmental studies. An expert on the flora, fauna, and geology of the Adirondack wilderness. Isn't that exactly what Annie would do? Victor, I've taken her class. Even her name—Winona Keller—tell me that's not an anagram for Annie Winkler."

Victor was good at anagrams, a skill honed by doing the newspaper jumbles during slow spells at work, and later during the even slower spells of unemployment. As anagrams go, this wasn't a perfect one—not enough "N's" or "I's," plus that outlier "O"—but it was pretty close, not so close as to rule out a coincidence, but when you factored in all those face bones it added up to a fairly persuasive case. But if Fiona was right about this, that would mean...

"Annie Winkler has been living right under Marco's nose for years," she said, completing his thought. "Put your pants on, Victor. We're going to go pay Winona Keller a visit."

[chapter 17]

In the front of the classroom stood a bespectacled former mid-tier UPS executive who'd been laid off from a solid job that had fantastic benefits and now earned a couple thousand dollars a course to lecture about inflation levels and growth rates to Granite College undergrads, who conveyed no greater enthusiasm for being in his class than he did for teaching it. But Principles of Macroeconomics was a requirement for econ majors, so there they were, all twenty-two of them, one of whom was Nate. Like most of the students in the class, Nate had his laptop open on his armchair desk, and like most of the students in the class, he was doing something other than taking notes—he was playing solitaire. Others were checking email or playing more sophisticated games, games structured on the premises of human slaughter and world domination. Nate liked solitaire, which required minimal concentration.

Inevitably, and mercifully, the class came to the end of its allotted time slot, and the students filed out into the hallway, in which, next to the door, stood a very large Black man. The very large Black man provoked levels of curiosity and interest among Nate's classmates that the former UPS executive could only dream of. Once you got past the basketball team, very large Black men were rarities on the Granite campus (as were

Black men of other sizes), and when this one gestured to Nate there in the hallway, and Nate responded by going over to him, it brought Nate a measure of instant notoriety, like if you were friends with LeBron James or something. Though more than a few of those classmates jumped to the conclusion that Nate's familiarity with the large Black man meant that Nate was involved in some sort of illicit activity, a drug deal, most likely. Such were the knee-jerk thought processes of supposedly liberal-minded white youth isolated up north in white-man country. Still, Nate's classmates were impressed.

"Ms. Forenza would like to see you in her hotel room," Charles's deep baritone voice said into Nate's ear, and Nate followed him outside.

Drug deal was also the number-one thought that crossed the mind of Officer Leonard Fox of the Granite College Campus Security Department, coming in right ahead of kidnapping. Officer Fox had just pulled his overheated patrol car into its usual position across the street from the Habler Hall parking lot, which sat between the Habler Hall dorm and the Academic Building, which was just called the Academic Building because it was ugly and no donor had wanted to affix a name to it. He sipped stale coffee from his thermos cup, watching as the large Black man crossed the lot with that kid he recognized because he'd busted him more than once for trying to buy booze with a fake ID. Nate—that was his name. But aside from the incongruity of the large Black man, Officer Fox's trained eyes could detect nothing in their postures or manner to suggest force or coercion. There were no furtive glances, and neither showed any apparent concern about a patrol car sitting across the street from them in plain sight. Still, Officer Fox had a nose for these things, and his nose told him that somebody was up to no good.

He watched them cross the lot to a black SUV whose engine was running, a modest cloud of exhaust puffing from the tailpipe. Officer Fox chided himself for having previously missed this detail. The large Black man held open the front passenger door and Nate got in—willingly, from all appearances. Then the Black man got in the driver's seat and they drove off. Officer Fox considered following them, but decided against it. He knew perfectly well that his only reason for following them was the Black man, one of just a few of adult age he'd ever seen in Granite and certainly the first one built like a linebacker for the Buffalo Bills, and he didn't want to be accused of profiling, which had been the topic of that fall's professional development seminar. No weapons were brandished, no baggies of weed or wads of cash exchanged hands. There wasn't even a burned-out brake light to justify his pulling them over. Officer Fox could have stopped them for the gray salt-and-slush spray that obscured part of the license plate, but he knew that would be a stretch. Hardly a citizen of Granite could be found not guilty of that infraction, including himself. He did run the plate numbers, just to make sure the car hadn't been reported stolen. A rental, registered to one Charles Conroy. It's all good, Officer Fox told himself, and decided to stay where he was and finish his coffee.

[chapter 18]

At the very moment that Fiona plopped herself down beside Victor on his bed in Room 317 of the Placid Hotel to show him the profile of Professor Winona Keller on the Granite College website, Charles Conroy—who in fact once had been a linebacker, and a good one, though for Yale, not the Buffalo Bills, until a knee injury senior year ended his playing career—opened the door and ushered Nate into Room 202, one floor down in the same building. Unlike Victor's room, which was east-facing and awash in sunlight, Room 202, on the west side of the hallway, with its heavy hotel-supply drapes pulled shut, was about as dark as a room could get on such a sunny morning. Nate blinked while his eyes adjusted. He smelled cigarette smoke.

"Hello Nate," a voice said, low, a little husky, unmistakably Isabel Forenza's voice. "I'm so glad you could come."

"He said you wanted to see me," Nate said. Charles closed the door and stood inside it in an at-ease posture. As Nate's eyes adjusted Isabel came into focus, a shadowy figure across the room in a chair. He saw the glowing tip of the cigarette she held. The Placid was a smoke-free hotel. There were signs to this effect everywhere. Nate took this as an indication that things could happen in this room that maybe weren't supposed to.

"Don't be shy," Isabel said. "Come over here."

He crossed the room and stood a few feet in front of her.

"We need your help," she said.

"Help?"

"For whatever insane reason, Marco Winkler has put us in this race with that shoe salesman to find his runaway bride. We want to make sure it's a fair race, do you understand what I mean?"

Nate considered the question, but the circumstances weren't conducive to quick thinking, which wasn't one of Nate's strengths to begin with. He succeeded, however, in coming up with the operative word from what she'd said. "Fair?"

"We know Marco went to see Victor in his room after his little lost-in-the-woods adventure. We think he gave Victor information that we don't have. Information that has clues to Annie Winkler's whereabouts, if in fact she still exists. We'd like to know what he has." She drew on the cigarette and blew out a stream of smoke. "In the spirit of fairness, of course."

She wanted to know about the notebook and the photos, though Nate doubted that she knew that's what she wanted to know about. He tried to hold his face expressionless while he struggled to decide what to say, with the effect that he looked like someone trying really hard to hold his face expressionless while he struggled to decide what to say. Even in the room's lousy light, Isabel could sense this.

"You know something, don't you?"

Telling Isabel would mean betraying Fiona, who clearly wanted to help Victor. But then there was this physically imposing man standing over by the door who could make him sell out his own mother if he'd wanted to. Nate thought about torture. From what he knew about torture, it sounded dreadful, which he supposed was pretty much the point. Some people, seasoned spies, for example, handled torture better than others. Nate suspected he'd be one of the others. He wasn't eager to find out.

"What does Victor have, Nate?" Isabel said.

Nate looked at her blankly.

"Come closer," she said. He took a couple of shuffle-steps toward her, though it wasn't like he'd been all that far away to begin with. He moved as close as he could without stepping on her feet. He suppressed a shiver. He had no idea what to do with his hands, which flopped around while he tried to decide. He anchored them in his back jeans pockets, but that felt too casual, so he took them out again. With her left hand she grabbed his belt buckle and pulled him even closer. "What does Victor have, Nate?"

Nate gulped. The needle on his will-power tank edged toward empty. "Some pictures, maybe?"

"Pictures. Pictures of Annie, you mean. *We* have pictures. Are you sure there isn't something else?"

"Maybe. I'm not sure."

"*Maybe*," she said. She took her hand away and sat back, drew on her cigarette, and blew smoke up toward his face. "*Maybe* isn't good enough, Nate. *Maybe* isn't the spirit that's driven my employer to be number one in the world. *Maybe* isn't why my employer is letting me offer you a job that will pay about ten times better than anything else you could get with a degree from this third-rate college you attend. I was under the impression that you wanted to be part of our team, Nate. But there are responsibilities associated with that. Obligations. Nanda Devi was built on an attitude. And that attitude is not *maybe*, Nate. She dropped her cigarette into an empty glass on a table beside her chair. A wisp of smoke rose from it.

"Of course if you live up to your responsibilities, there are certain perks associated with being part of our team. Her hand again took hold of his belt buckle. Her fingers slipped inside the waistband of his jeans. "Do you understand what I mean?"

Nate was pretty sure he understood. His dick understood perfectly, and began to salute in solidarity with the cause. Maybe this wasn't going to be about torture after all.

"There might be a notebook," Nate said.

"A notebook," Isabel said.

"One that belonged to Annie. Like a diary or something. Marco gave it to Victor. It's just some notes and pictures of plants and things."

"And you can get it for us?"

"I don't know."

"You don't know."

Nate gulped. "Maybe." Her fingers felt cool against the skin below his belly button.

"*Maybe* again."

"I mean I think so."

"You *think* so." With her right thumb and index finger she took hold of the tab of Nate's zipper. He looked down. The other fingers on that hand flared daintily, as if she were holding a cup of tea in fine china. She tugged gently, and Nate's zipper's teeth started to un-mesh, one by one. He made a noise that could have been mistaken for pain but almost certainly wasn't. He was having a hard time concentrating.

The zipper stopped moving. "Can you do better than *I think so*? We'd really like to have it. To level the playing field."

"Yes!" Nate gasped. "I mean yes! I can get it."

"That's better." More zipper teeth un-meshed. "Where is it, Nate? We think you know."

"Fiona might have it," he said.

"*Might*," she said.

"Fiona has it! Victor gave it to her!" His words came out in a rush.

"And where is Fiona now?"

"I'm not sure."

"Nate," she said, in a tone of parental disappointment. Her right hand paused in its task.

"She may be with him," he said.

"Here? Now? In the hotel?"

"She borrowed my car. I saw it parked outside."

Isabel looked over at Charles. Nate heard him leave the room.

"Do you know why she's here?" she said.

"Maybe she's returning it. The notebook. To Victor." This worked a little bit like torture, in that you told people exactly what you thought they wanted to hear. He fought the urge to tell her to please hurry up. He doubted that's what she wanted to hear. But he really needed her to hurry up.

"Maybe?" Isabel said.

"Yes!" he gasped.

And at that exact moment, Fiona took a firm grip on the stick shift of Nate's car, thrust it into first gear and peeled out of the hotel parking lot with Victor next to her in the passenger seat. Meanwhile, Charles pounded on the door of Victor's empty hotel room.

[chapter 19]

"Professor Keller can be a little…" Fiona said. She drove Nate's car onto the Granite College campus with Victor in the passenger seat.

Victor looked out the window. An underwhelming place, the Granite campus, a seemingly random assortment of buildings in different but equally uninspiring architectural styles arranged around a central quad, in the middle of which sat a huge rock, rendering the quad unsuitable for Frisbee throwing or touch football or any of the other things Victor had seen happy college students doing in quads in the brochures Allie had received by the thousands over the past year or so. To be fair, in all this snow and ice Harvard Yard would have looked dispiriting. Leafless trees suggested death. Weatherworn banners hung here and there with "Granite College – Rock Your World" tag-lined onto them. In the quad, the world was anything but rocking. A couple of solitary figures walked across it, gray and hooded and hunched against the cold. It reminded Victor of pictures he'd seen of Chernobyl.

"Can be a little…?"

"I don't know…"

"Difficult?" he tried. "Eccentric?" She had married a Winkler, after all.

"Odd," she said. "I mean, she really knows her shit, but she's just... I don't know..."

"Odd."

"Prickly," she corrected.

Fiona had taken Winona Keller's Ecology of the North Country a year earlier during spring semester, "spring" being a misnomer as the course had begun in late January. Despite the single-digit temperatures, the class almost always met outside. They had begun by identifying trees on and around the Granite campus, a task made infinitely more challenging—and therefore, Professor Keller said, more valuable—by their leaflessness.

"*Betula alleghaniensis*," Fiona said, pointing to trees as she drove. "*Acer rubrum. Acer saccharum*—that's the one we get maple syrup from." For all Victor knew she could have been speaking in tongues. "When spring thaw started we'd go up into the mountains. She was less prickly out there. Like she was in her element."

"What about her feet? You remember what she wore?" Victor still found it hard to believe that he was about to come face to face with Annie Winkler.

Fiona shrugged. "Boots, I guess. I mean, we all wore boots. There was a ton of mud up there, and still some snow. But you mean were they Winklers. Who knows? Maybe."

They pulled into a parking space in the faculty lot and entered a back door of the hulking concrete cube that was the Academic Building. Fiona led them up two flights of stairs and down an overheated hallway, then down another, stopping mid-hall in front of a closed door that had a class schedule posted on it, plus a pinecone hanging from a green ribbon tied with a bow.

"This is her?" Victor said.

"This is her." Fiona took a deep breath. She knocked and they waited. Nothing. Victor tried a second time, with the same result.

"Try the knob," Fiona said. It was locked. They consulted the schedule. It was ten-fifteen, which placed Professor Keller between a class that ended at nine-fifty and office hours that ran from ten-thirty to noon.

"I guess we wait," Victor said.

So they waited—Fiona sat on the floor, Victor paced. Except for the two of them, the hallway remained deserted. Then at ten-thirty sharp the office door opened and the woman from the website stood there in the doorway, sharp-featured, unsmiling, with boyish white hair that spiked up and flopped over her forehead. She looked back and forth between Fiona and Victor, puzzling over what they were doing there.

"Fiona?" she said.

"Professor Keller," Fiona said. She stood up.

Victor stared. "Annie Winkler," he said.

Without a word she ushered them into her office, closed the door, and locked it, understandable, given the circumstances, though a violation of college office-hour policy.

"Sit," she commanded, nodding toward a worn loveseat. They sat, while Winona or Annie or whoever she was stood, leaning back against her desk with her arms folded across her chest. She glowered down at them, or at Victor, more specifically. They were like two kids in the principal's office. Or one kid and her father.

"Who the hell are you?" she said to Victor. On a shelf behind her desk sat a collection of animal skulls—bleached white, with eye sockets that joined their owner in full glower. None looked human, thank God.

She wore black jeans and a tight white top that hugged a body that persuasively claimed immunity from nearly six decades worth of gravitational pull and the births of two children. An orange scarf hung loosely around her neck. All middle-aged women, Victor supposed, waged war against time and gravity, but for most the battle scars showed. There was an air of effortlessness to Winona/Annie, as though her body was all function and this was the form that necessarily flowed from it.

"My name is Victor. Marco asked me to find you."

"I don't know anyone named Marco," she said.

"I think you do."

"What are you, Victor, some kind of private detective? A 'dick,' they used to call them."

Victor explained himself, tailoring this version of the story so it included the woods rescue and Marco's subsequent confessed desire to see her, but leaving out the part about his not being the right Victor, and, once again, the part about the necklace. He was getting good at framing the story for the audience of the moment. Winona/Annie's expression didn't change.

Fiona took over, transforming what Victor had characterized as a bland business deal. The power outage gained moral weight, thrusting the world into darkness. She spoke of Victor's bravery, venturing out into the wilderness in the teeth of a ferocious blizzard.

"This man risked his life to save your husband's," Fiona said. "The least you could do is stop pretending."

"Whoever this Marco person you're talking about is," she said. "I have no interest in him. You could have left him in the snow, for all I care. Now if you'll excuse me, I have work to do." She circled around to the chair side of her desk and sat, pretending to direct her attention to a stack of student papers on the desk.

Fiona got up from her chair, reached into her backpack, and placed Annie's worn journal on the desk. "Recognize this?"

Professor Keller gave it a stare that aimed for dispassionate but fell somewhat short. "I've never seen it before," she said.

If she'd been hooked up to a lie detector, this would be when the needle went bouncing all over the paper. Victor sensed weakness. He reached into his pocket and held out the ring in his palm, keeping enough distance so she couldn't reach out and grab it.

"What about this?" he said.

Her eyes widened, then shrunk back to normal. Color flushed her cheeks. "Where did you get that?"

"From Marco."

"It's not his," she said, as the last vestiges of Winona Keller dropped away and floated like dust particles to the floor. "What is it that you want, anyway, Victor?"

"To propose a trade," Victor said.

"A trade."

"You have a necklace," Victor said. "One that belonged to Marco's mother. It's my understanding that she gave it to you, and you gave her the ring in exchange. Marco would like to wind back the clock on that one. You give him the necklace, he gives you the ring." He closed his hand around the ring and put it back in his pocket.

"No," she said, shaking her head.

"No? No what? No you don't have it? No you won't trade?"

"Both," she said. "I don't have it, and I wouldn't give it to him if I did."

Victor looked at Fiona.

"He's dying," Fiona said. "Did you know that?"

Annie rolled her eyes. "Oh, God. Seriously? He's still using that one? Did he try to get you to sleep with him when he told you that?"

Fiona looked confused. "What? No. *What?*"

"It's his standard tactic, for when his natural charisma, or the artistic magnificence of his boots aren't enough to get some stupid girl into his bed. He's been dying since he was in his forties. Is it still cancer?"

"He has AIDS," Fiona said.

Annie raised a dubious eyebrow. "AIDS? That's a new one. He told you that?"

"He told Victor. And that's not exactly a line you use to pick up girls."

She let that sink in. "I still don't believe it."

"And he may be suicidal," Victor said. "It could be that he wandered off into the woods in an attempt to kill himself, a sort of preemptive strike against the disease. Or maybe he's losing his mind. Or maybe he associates the woods with where you wandered off. You're the last thing he wants."

"That was always his problem," she said. "He made it clear I was the last thing he wanted."

Victor saw he could have phrased that better. "What I mean is, he needs to see you. It's like a last, dying wish."

"So now I'm confused," she said. "Is it me he wants, or the necklace?"

"Both," Victor said, though he was still a little confused on this point, too.

"And if he had to choose one or the other?"

"Fair enough. If you don't want to see him, then give us the necklace, we'll give you the ring, and we're done here. You don't need to see us, or him, ever again."

"I told you. I don't have it."

"But you can get it."

She just looked at him.

"You cooperate with us, and it's a simple trade. With others, it may not be so simple."

"What do you mean, 'others'?"

"We're not the only ones looking for you. I'm competing for the Winkler job with a big, impersonal corporation. I'm trying to negotiate. They'll come in with muscle. After all, they don't have your mother's engagement ring to offer."

"Are you threatening me?" Annie asked.

"Let's just say I'm warning you. Marco's sorry for what he's done to you. You work with us, he makes things right, and nobody gets hurt." It occurred to Victor that he had started to talk like a mobster.

She laughed. "He's not sorry. He's conniving. He's old and his old games aren't working so well any more. And as you've made clear, Victor, none of this is about mending a broken family. It's about you landing a business deal. That's why you've barged into my life. That's why you've put me at risk. And he's manipulating you. You know why he wandered off? To lure you after him. He wasn't lost. He knows those woods better than anyone except me. He wanted you to come look for him. He wanted to suck you in. And you fell for it."

Victor considered this. The starlit sky. The easy-to-follow tracks. Could he have been set up? He focused on one of the skulls on her shelf, with big round eye sockets and a mouthful of sharp teeth. It looked like it was laughing at him, and who could blame it? What was it? A fox? A squirrel? How much does a creature shrink when you take its skin and muscle and sinew and all that other stuff away? It looked so tiny and fragile. And how did it die? Taken out by a predator, a bear, maybe, or a wolf? Or old age? Had it simply walked off into the woods by itself, alone, apart from its little fox or squirrel friends, to die, and have its carcass picked at by buzzards? Victor imagined Marco's skull up there on Annie's shelf, all shrunken and desiccated, laughing at him with its big, wide skull-grin, laughing at his gullibility, his incompetence, his frostbit nose.

"I'm not going to play his game," Annie said.

"Think about it," Victor said. "The necklace for the ring, a simple transaction, and your little professor charade doesn't get disrupted."

"I have papers to grade."

Victor couldn't stop looking at the skull. It wasn't laughing at him—it was judging him. He was chasing this Winkler thing down a rabbit hole, and it was changing him into someone he wasn't. Someone who made threats. Someone who black-mailed. Someone who encounters a perfectly decent human being and in minutes starts mocking her *little professor charade*. Someone losing perspective about means and ends. *This isn't you*, Victor, was what the skull was saying. And Victor agreed.

He made a possibly rash decision. He stood and put the ring on Annie's desk, on top of the stack of papers. "I'm going to leave this with you," he said. "If I could end things now, I would. But I can't. Those others I mentioned—they're real, and they're going to come looking for you and your necklace." He took a pen from her desk, and wrote 317 on the top paper in the stack. "That's my room number at the Placid. Call me if you want my help. But don't wait too long. Whatever happens is going to happen really soon."

★

"What was all that about the ring and the necklace?" Fiona asked when they were back in the hallway. He filled her in on that part of the story while they walked to the car.

"Is it the one she's wearing, in the photo?" Fiona asked.

"That's the one," Victor said.

Fiona thought about this for a moment. "Then why give her the ring?"

Victor considered saying something about appealing to her sense of fairness, but instead he just said, "I don't know."

He expected some pushback, but Fiona just nodded.

A part of Victor envied Annie, the part that wonders what it would be like to leave the life you have, to pack up and start all over, with a new identity, all the old strings cut. A total, cathartic thrill, as long as you didn't think too hard about the collateral damage it could leave in its wake. For children, for example, though Annie's were grown when she left. For spouses, even if they're cheating on you, like Marco had, and like Victor was pretty sure Carla was, too, though now, post-Molly, Victor had ceded any moral high ground he might have held there. For all those people who didn't see it coming but in some way counted on you and were left to wonder where the hell you disappeared to and why.

Victor remembered reading a story in the paper once about a young woman in Seattle who disappeared. Friends, family—no one knew what had happened to her. It was during a time when a serial killer was on a rampage, and after a while everyone just assumed that she had been one of his victims. Her friends even held a memorial service. Months later, she turned up on a beach in Waikiki. She'd simply gotten tired of the Seattle rain, packed a suitcase, and left. So you didn't need a huge reason for leaving.

Marco's failures gave Annie had a better reason than the Waikiki girl had. And what about Victor's own failures? Failed career. Failed as a provider. No motorcycle like Karl's. He pictured Carla riding off into the sunset straddling the motorcycle behind him, arms around his leather jacket. As long as he didn't think too hard about the straddling part, it surprised him how okay he was of that image. So who was leaving whom?

Ordinarily, dwelling on his shortcomings would get Victor depressed. But he didn't feel depressed. In fact, he felt the opposite. He felt more alive than he'd felt in years. True, getting laid (and with a professional!) may have had something to do with that, but it was also because of the adventure of it all. It really was starting to feel like a quest. Not entirely a quest of his own making, but he'd made enough of it to justifiably claim some ownership. And besides, wasn't that the nature of quests, that they found you, instead of the other way around? He tried to think of the great questers. There was Don Quixote, and that hobbit guy... Those were all he could think of, and he didn't really know much about either of them. By giving Annie the ring, he was questing without losing self-respect. He felt noble, even if it had been a dumb move. It all beat the hell out of selling women's shoes.

Fiona dropped him off at the hotel. As he was getting out, she said, "It sure would be nice to find that necklace."

[chapter 20]

"She says she won't come see you," Victor told Marco on the phone. He'd called him to fill him in on the day's events. If Marco was at surprised by the news that Annie had been discovered so quickly, and basically right under his nose, it didn't come through in his voice.

"Winona Keller," Marco said. "That's clever. If you rearrange the letters…"

"Yeah. I gave her the ring."

Victor listened to a long, slow sigh, like the sound of an air mattress deflating. "Why in the world did you do that?" Marco said.

"Because she deserves it more than you do. It's worth something to her."

"It's worth something to me if it gets me the necklace."

"About the necklace," Victor said. "She doesn't have it."

"Of course she does."

"She says she doesn't, and I believe her. But I don't think it's gone far. It means something to her, which means whoever she gave it to means something to her, too. I think she can get it back. She just needs a little time to come to the conclusion that that's the smart thing to do."

"Which, now that you've given her the ring, she is unlikely to do."

"I'm not so sure," Victor said. "She knows Nanda Devi is looking for her, and that they'll come after her less gently than I did. With fewer bargaining chips, they'll threaten to blow the cover off of the tidy professor-life she's constructed. They may even threaten her with bodily harm, though I doubt they'll go that far. I gave her the ring. Unless she wants to run away now and start all over again somewhere else, she'll have to cooperate with somebody, and it makes much more sense to cooperate with me. She just needs some time to understand that."

"You don't have much time." Marco said.

"We have all the time in the world," Victor said. "It's taken us a day to get this far. Besides, your one-week deadline is arbitrary, and you know it. If you really want the necklace, you're not going crash the whole deal you made just because you don't get it back in seven days. And if you want more than just the necklace, which I suspect you do, that's even more reason to give it more time."

"What is it that you think I want, Victor?"

"I think you're lonely. You have a wife who you drove away, and she's carved out a very satisfying life for herself that doesn't include you. And now you want her back, someone to be your companion, or your nursemaid while you whither away with some disease that you may or may not actually have. She doubts you're sick, by the way. You think if you reestablish contact, you can persuade her. Persuasion's something you're good at. That and manipulation. It may not work this time, but if I'm you, I'm thinking it's worth a shot."

"I'm afraid I'm starting to lose confidence in you, Victor."

"I don't see this taking long. I'll be in touch."

[chapter 21]

Coming back from breakfast Tuesday morning, Fiona had not expected to find Nate standing in her dorm room.

"What are you doing here?"

"I wanted to take a look at Annie's notebook," he said. "To see if it had any, you know, clues."

Fiona set her backpack on her desk. "We don't need it anymore. Oh my God, Nate, we found her! You won't believe it. Annie Winkler is Winona Keller!"

"Annie Winkler is who—?"

"Winona Keller! Professor Keller. She teaches here at Granite. I took a class from her. She never left. She's been right here the whole time. The notebook. It was full of all the stuff she taught us. That's how I figured it out. Victor and I went to see her yesterday afternoon."

Nate thought best in straight lines of cause and effect. Victor found Annie. So Victor gets the Winkler contract. So Isabel loses. So no great job for Nate. Or other perks.

"So that's it. Victor wins." Nate said.

"It's not that simple," she said. "Professor Keller—Annie—she won't go to Marco. She's totally pissed at him, and she doesn't want to see him. Victor gave her this ring that used to belong to her mother, and he thinks that's going to encourage her to cooperate. But I'm not sure that was a good idea. Plus now there's this necklace that Marco wants. I'm still trying to sort it all out. We need a Plan B. It's not like we're going to put her in a trunk and drag her out there against her will."

No, Victor wouldn't do something like that. But Isabel would. Or would have Charles do it. Will do it, in fact, Nate thought, once he gave her the news. And what was all this about a ring and a necklace? He could think about that later. "Where is she now?" he asked.

"Professor Keller? I don't know. In her office? Or teaching?"

Nate was smart enough to know that Fiona was smarter than he was, and it wouldn't take her long to come up with a new strategy for what to do about Winona Keller, so he knew he needed to move quickly. "I've gotta go," he said, and pushed past her, grabbed his car keys from where she'd dropped them on her desk, and started out the door.

"Oh, Nate!" she said. He turned to look back at her. "Isn't this exciting?"

"Yeah," he said. "Exciting!" And he was gone.

★

From his vantage point in a Granite College patrol car across the street from the Habler Hall parking lot, Officer Leonard Fox watched Nate leave the building in a hurry to get someplace. Something no good was up, Officer Fox had little doubt. In fact, to his thinking something no good was usually up with the students at Granite. That was the logical outcome when you took twelve hundred barely post-pubescent kids and set them loose with newfound independence on this depressingly bleak landscape. Maybe their parents had figured it would have the opposite effect. The majority of the entertainments available to them involved something no good.

But this was different. Officer Fox's earlier sightings of the comings and goings of Nate and others had planted a seed of suspicion. First that guy shows up in that big black Lexus SUV with the tinted windows. Like most security professionals, Officer Fox didn't trust cars with tinted windows, which suggested that whoever was inside had something to hide. He enters the Academic Building and exits shortly afterward with Nate. They head toward town. Then an hour later he drops Nate off at the dorm and speeds away. Then the girlfriend shows up driving Nate's car. There could have been a perfectly innocent explanation for all of this, but Officer Fox had his doubts.

Now here's Nate coming out of her dorm, getting in his car, and speeding off back toward town with what struck Officer Fox as an unhealthy sense of urgency. Did these kids never go to class? One advantage of working at such a small college was that you could see all of this from one location if you positioned yourself strategically enough, and Officer Fox's favorite location was on a gravel path in the municipal park across the street from the college, beneath two maple trees. The location was strategic because of the view of campus it afforded—nearly all comings and goings that involved a vehicle came and went from the Habler Hall parking lot, which was the college's busiest lot, serving both the dorms and the main academic building—and because it was only a block and a half from Rosie's Bakery, where Officer Fox could go to fill his thermos and buy a blueberry muffin when he got hungry. Rosie's made muffins the size of softballs. Plus, in the summer the maple trees provided shade.

He swept blueberry-muffin crumbs from his lap onto the floor of the patrol car. His gut told him to follow the boy's car, see what he was up to. But Rosie's muffins could make him a little sleepy—something to do with his blood sugar, probably—and his spot under the maple trees was a good place to take a quick nap.

He was getting too old for this, should have retired by now, *would* have retired by now if he could have afforded to, and any reasonable person at his age should have been able to afford to. And he would have been able to afford to, bolstered by his state-employee pension, if he hadn't made some really dumb mistakes. He might be sitting right now in some ice-fishing shack, reeling in a nice, big northern pike, or better yet, sitting in his cabin in front of the woodstove, feeling superior to those other poor bastards out there freezing their asses off out on the lake in the hopes that a northern pike might bite.

He blamed the Indians, who built that casino out on the river. How was Leonard Fox supposed to know that he would be inclined toward a gambling addiction? He had been a man of few vices. Didn't drink, or at least not enough that it was a problem. Didn't do drugs. Didn't cavort with expensive women, or even with less expensive women, just an occasional date now and then, and not even one of those in, well, a lot longer than he cared to think about. Hadn't really been serious about anyone since that girl all those years ago that he'd fallen for big time. That had ended in a way that soured him on long-term relationships.

The gambling began not long after he had started a job as a cop with the Richland Falls police department, when a former colleague from Fish & Game called and suggested they go check out the new floating casino out on the river. He had protested initially, said no, he didn't think that was his kind of thing. But the guy said how do you know if it's your kind of thing if you don't go and see? Leonard agreed he had a point.

He started with the slot machines, but grew bored with their impersonality and randomness. He moved on to roulette, which wasn't much of an improvement. He knew people had figured out ways to beat it, but he wasn't one of those people, and he still felt at the mercy of a device. He was in his element, however, at the blackjack table, and went home that first night with a hundred and eighty-four more dollars in his pocket than he'd come with. And it was the same thing a week later, when he'd run his total earnings up to something close to five hundred dollars, a tidy sum to supplement his modest cop salary. Winning was heady stuff. He could get used to this.

What Leonard failed to understand was that he was no less at the mercy of a device playing blackjack than he had been with the one-armed bandits. It was just that now the device was the casino system, which was built around the concept of people like Leonard Fox losing money, not winning it. And Leonard obliged them. He lost, and then lost some more, and then lost some more on top of that. Though in the manner of people addicted to this masochistic pastime, Leonard Fox was certain that if he just kept playing, his luck would change and he'd climb back into the black. He even swore to himself that if he ever got back to breaking even, or maybe just a little better than breaking even, he'd stop. Sometimes he'd call in sick and go play cards, not that he was fooling anybody. He got reprimanded, got offered counseling, got told if he didn't straighten up he would lose his job. But by then it was like telling a man to stop breathing. Scratch an itch long enough and all it does is bleed.

One time he took some money out of the safe where they kept petty cash—not a lot, just fifty dollars or so, enough to get him comfortable at a blackjack table—certain he'd be able to repay it in a day or two, and fill up his wallet at the same time.

Of course he got caught, by an office secretary named Sue, though she spelled it Sioux, like the Indians, though she wasn't one, not even close, she was just some New Agey, single-mom white lady, and even as the Richland Falls Police fired him Leonard Fox could appreciate the irony. The Indians got him coming and going, even when they weren't Indians. The whole cluster-fuck of it gave him new appreciation for what Custer had gone through.

And so it was that at age sixty Leonard Fox found himself without a job, and also without a pension, which could be revoked for certain fire-able offenses, theft being one of them. In an act of what they called kindness and compassion his employers agreed to not to press charges against him for theft of public property. Losing the pension hurt—he'd already put in his twenty years, and could already have retired, but he liked his job, so he had put it off. Now with his pension gone, he had no money to retire on, other than the paltry sum Social Security would pay him. He considered giving the casino one more try, but chose instead to give himself over to a higher power. Leonard threw himself into a 12-Step program that met in the basement of the Lutheran church on Elm Street in Granite.

It was there, with his money running out, and surrounded by other people who had gambled their lives into the sewer, that Leonard met Barney, a Campus Security cop at Granite College and a recovering addict who agreed to be his sponsor.

With Barney vouching for him, the college hired Leonard, provisionally at first, and then to a permanent position once they were confident he wasn't going to go back to the casino, which he wasn't. He'd been thrown a lifeline, and he hung onto it. He took responsibility for his weakness, and even stopped blaming the Indians, though he hadn't entirely let go of the grudge he held against that woman Sioux.

That was ten years ago. Ten years of busting up booze-fueled frat parties, confiscating fake IDs, uprooting the occasional dorm-room pot farm, and dealing with random and un-original acts of theft and vandalism.

Poor Barney's life had come to an untimely end (as if there were any other kind). He had climbed on one wagon only to fall off another, and had died of liver failure.

Outside of work, Leonard had pared his life down to a hermit level in order to build a little savings, though now, at seventy-three, with his head and body telling him he ought to call it quits, his gut would ask, then what? He had few friends to speak of, no wife, no kids. He could keep fishing the streams around here, and he doubted he'd ever grow tired of fishing, but fishing didn't add up to a whole life. He'd had to give up fly-tying, as his eyesight wasn't what it used to be and years of working in the cold had left his hands permanently cramped, making it impossible to see and manipulate the tiny knots and wraps the craft required. What was he going to do? Travel the world? Crossword puzzles? Sodoku? Left to his own devices out there in that lonely cabin of his, it occurred to him that he might take his shotgun and blow his head off. So he put retirement off.

In the moment, in his patrol car, with a bite or two of muffin left, Officer Fox succumbed to inertia and just sat, rationalizing sitting by reminding himself that he was the only officer on campus patrol for the afternoon, and if he went off after the SUV he'd be leaving the campus unprotected and vulnerable. There should have been two officers on duty, but young Simpson, that slacker shit, had gone home saying he was coming down with the flu. So Leonard kept eating his muffin, and watched two crows pick at some unidentifiable species of half-frozen road kill out on Main Street.

Then, to Officer Fox's surprise, not fifteen minutes after Nate had driven off, the black SUV was headed back in his direction. It pulled back into the Habler Hall parking lot, and now three people got out: Nate, the Black guy, and a woman he'd never seen before, a woman who even from across the street Officer Fox could tell was gorgeous. He took his binoculars out of the glove compartment for confirmation. He watched them go into the academic building.

Again, Officer Fox decided to sit tight, again telling himself this was totally in line with protocol, and had nothing to do with the potential bodily harm that could result from approaching a trio that included a powerful-looking man who could beat the living crap out of him. Under different circumstances, Officer Fox might have called for backup, but his backup was supposed to have been that slacker-shit Simpson.

It wasn't long before they came back out of the building, only now there were four of them. Nate led the way, followed by the beauty and then the Black man, who had his arm around that hippie professor, Winona Keller. There was something about that Professor Keller. Leonard had had his eye on her since that first faculty reception he'd worked back when he started at Granite. There was something wild about her—not wild as in a drinker and a partier, but wild as in wilderness. She struck him as a wild creature, and as he had spent the early part of his career working out among wild creatures, this made her stand out, especially on a faculty for whom *wilderness* mostly meant the farthest-back stacks in the library. She had long hair then, not that spiky butch cut she'd worn for the last year or so, which caused his colleagues in Campus Security to speculate that she'd gone lesbian. Though maybe not, he thought now. The relative postures of the Black man and the professor could have been explained by romantic attraction. Though it could also have been kidnapping.

The four of them moved swiftly across the parking lot to the black SUV, where the gorgeous woman got behind the wheel and the kid got into the front passenger's seat. The Black man guided Professor Keller into the back and climbed in after her. They disappeared behind the tinted windows.

Officer Fox hoped it wasn't kidnapping, and wondered, as last fall's campus-security retreat had taught him to do, whether he might be profiling. He thought ahead to the report he would have to file, and wished he could come up with a better way to describe the Black man than just to call him "the Black man." African American? The man could have been from Kenya, or Mozambique, or Canada. Man of color, maybe? Officer Fox hated the imprecision of that term, which should have raised a question—*which* color?—but didn't because everyone knew what you really meant was "Black man." The college's modest cohort of "students of color" included just nineteen Black students, eleven of whom were on either the men's or women's basketball team, six who were the product of an overzealous admissions officer's trip to Ghana, and two who for reasons lost to Officer Fox had come from the Bronx, seemingly of their own volition. The nineteen of them had become organized and vocal of late, and had recently delivered to the president a manifesto that outlined their grievances—which chiefly included being steered away from science majors and the dearth of faculty "of color" (there were only two, both adjuncts: a Native American casino manager who taught a course on probability theory and an Inuit lit professor who taught the poetics of snow). Overt displays of racial insensitivity, even the nineteen acknowledged, were few, though the previous spring a giant N been written on a dorm bathroom mirror with what may or may not have been human feces. Students were encouraged not to jump to conclusions—lots of words started with N. In December, the administration installed a Kwanza bush in the quad next to the Christmas tree, but that pathetic gesture had only made things worse.

The SUV pulled out of the lot and headed back in the direction of town. Officer Fox again considered following them, but again decided not to. At the workshop, the security team had been instructed to ask themselves if a person's skin color was fifty percent or more of the reason for choosing to intervene in a situation, and if it was, to think about holding back. Ever since quitting gambling, Officer Fox had distrusted his ability to predict percentages, but he figured that the presence of the Black man was at least half the reason he thought about going after them. So he sat still, sipped his coffee, and watched them drive off, thinking about what a kick his colleagues in Campus Security would get when he told them Winona Keller had a Black boyfriend. Plus, he reasoned, if he did nothing, he wouldn't have to write a report.

★

Marco sat in his chair in his study, first wondering if he had put too many eggs in the Victor basket, and then, asleep. It was a big chair, upholstered in soft dark-brown leather, and Marco was skinny, bordering on frail, just a few thin epidermal layers stretched over a skeleton, and he sank into the chair's folds the way a man sinks into quicksand. He was awakened by the sound of car tires struggling to grab on the gravel of his front drive.

Kirsten appeared in the doorway to the study. She turned on a table lamp. "It appears we have company, sir," she said.

[chapter 22]

"Hello Marco," Annie said. Outside the warm spell continued, melting icicles hanging from the Winkler gutters. Inside things were cooler. "I hear you're dying."

"Annie dear." They were in the study. Marco had extracted himself from the leather chair and now stood behind it, gripping it like a shield. "You look as beautiful as ever."

"You look like shit," she said. "These your thugs?"

Isabel, Nate, and Charles stood on either side of her, cats presenting the mouse to their owner.

"My colleagues," Marco said. "And please accept my apologies if their persuasive tactics got a little rough. I had actually thought you might come with someone else."

"The bald guy and the girl? I met them, too."

"Sit down, please."

"Thanks, but I don't plan on staying long."

"Well, in any event, here you are." Marco sat. He invited the others to sit. "After all these years."

"What is it you want?"

"I'm getting out. We're unloading the business."

"So I've heard. What does that have to do with me?"

"The agreement will be structured in a way so that the family remains in the picture in a behind-the-scenes capacity.

Good for the brand. Keeps the Winklers in Winklers. A healthy percentage of profits will continue to come to the family. Including you, if you decide to come back."

"No thanks," Annie said.

"That's disappointing, but it's what I thought you'd say."

"Can I go now?"

"Profits going forward may be something of a question mark. To put it simply, we haven't made money in years. Things have gotten competitive. It used to be us and a few of the Europeans. Raichle. Vasque. Now everybody's in on the act. Timberland, Merrell, even Nike, for God's sake. There are rumors that Under Armour is about to start a line. You can buy boots on Amazon—never mind whether they actually fit. And people are hiking these days with all manner of ridiculous things on their feet. Sandals. Shoes with toes in them. They look like apes. We're hoping our new partners will be able to turn things around, but who knows? And as you said, you met the bald guy."

"He's going to run your company?"

"Your arrival here with these charming people makes that less likely. His name is Victor, by the way. Victor Barstow. Does that name mean anything to you? Barstow Bootery?"

"Don't tell me he's *that* Victor Barstow."

Marco laughed a laugh that devolved into a hacking cough. "Sadly, no. A case of mistaken identity. Or, more accurately, a case of intentionally manipulated false identity. Manipulated by your son, by the way, to insure that your companions here gain control of Winklers. They are Nanda Devi, in case they haven't properly introduced themselves. Surely you've heard of them. Big. Corporate. Everything our little enterprise has stood so steadfastly against all these years. But it looks like that's about to change."

"And kidnapping? That's a service they offer?"

"I said I was sorry. That wasn't supposed to happen. But that brings us back to why you're here. As you noted, I'm dying, Annie."

"AIDS, I hear? That's new. Talk about chickens coming home to roost."

"It's progressing slowly, you'll be glad to know. Thanks to some very good drugs. And I can keep things going slowly as long as I can afford them. Which I can barely do now, and which I will not be able to do if the company continues to do as poorly as it's been doing."

Annie doubted everything he said. Marco had two skills: making boots and spinning webs of manipulation. "What has this got to do with me?" she asked.

"You have something I want."

"The necklace. The bald guy told me."

"It's worth a lot of money," Marco said.

"You'd never sell it."

"I might if it meant the difference between living and dying."

Return the necklace, and save Marco's life. Keep it, and it's a death sentence. Marco the manipulator, playing to his strength. "So this isn't really about me, is it?" she said.

"You have always grasped things so quickly. I'd love to have you and the necklace," Marco said. "But if it's got to be either/or, then yes—I want the necklace."

★

Annie and Marco got married in the meadow behind the Winkler mansion on a perfect day in May of 1982, after winter had retreated and the mud it left in its wake had mostly dried up.

The day before, Isabella had given the workers the day off from their regular jobs and dispatched them to attend to wedding details—setting up the reception tent, planting flowers, and so on. To show her appreciation, when the work was done she threw them a pre-wedding party—out in front of the mansion on the driveway, so as not to wreck the wedding ground—with good wine and food from an Italian caterer in Syracuse.

As the workers enjoyed a rollicking good time, Annie sat by herself on a stone wall, watching. Any bride could be excused for having a reflective moment on the day before her wedding, but Isabella knew that what Annie really felt was a mixture of sad and angry. And she knew why.

Isabella sat beside her. "Annie, dear," she said.

"Unbelievable," Annie said. "Just unbelievable."

"He's working. He has a pair of boots to finish. He'll be here soon."

"We both know perfectly well what he's doing," Annie said. The boots Marco was finishing were for the feet of a leggy model from Boston. She and Marco were in his "work room" where he could "fine tune the fit."

Isabella released a sigh. "It's his last day as a single man. Tomorrow he marries the woman of his dreams, the most beautiful woman on the planet. He'll change. You'll see."

Annie made a noise. She picked up a pebble from the driveway and threw it at nothing in particular.

"I want you to have something," Isabella said. She reached into her vest pocket and withdrew a white silk bag tied shut by a purple ribbon. She handed it to Annie. Annie untied the ribbon and took from the bag a necklace whose simple beauty made her gasp—a thin gold chain holding an amber teardrop the color of cognac and set in a ring of gold.

"It's beautiful," Annie said.

"Look." Isabella held the necklace up so it could catch the sun's rays. Imbedded in the amber was a twig with its tiny leaves still intact. "It is of the woods. It reminds me of you."

"Isabella, I can't—"

"You can, and you will. Here, turn." Annie presented her back to Isabella, who fastened the necklace around her neck, causing her to shiver with delight. "Let me see," Isabella said. Annie turned back to face her. Isabella nodded. "Perfect," she said. She kissed Annie on the cheek.

Annie felt her eyes fill with tears. "I don't know how to thank you," she said.

"It was my mother's," Isabella said. "She gave it to me on my wedding day."

This was both part of family lore and a lie. The necklace was less a gift than a payment, an exceedingly grateful payment, years before, and it came not from Isabella's mother, but from a young soldier from Verona, a boy of eighteen, who had joined Italian forces helping the fascists to gain control of Spain in the Spanish Civil War. He was riding an incredible wave of good luck, which began with the discovery of the necklace, in perfect condition, wrapped in a double layer of cloth in what had likely been the jacket pocket of a soldier who had had the misfortune of being on the receiving end of artillery fire. It was a miracle that the necklace survived undamaged, as little else about the soldier did, making his allegiance impossible to determine. The Italian boy, whose name was Paolo, thought it would have been insane to carry around something of such obvious value as a keepsake or good-luck charm, and so concluded that the dead soldier must have plundered it, most likely from the Italians, given its beauty, and therefore the act of taking it from his body wasn't theft so much as a matter of restoring the necklace to its rightful owners.

Paolo's string of good luck included sustaining an injury—a bullet wound to the thigh—serious enough to get him sent home to recover but minor enough to leave him neither crippled nor permanently deformed. On his third evening home he made his way into the city and wandered the streets, his limp barely noticeable. He came upon Isabella, plying her trade. She felt sorry for the soldier, so clearly just a boy, and liked the way his light-brown hair fell across his forehead. In the hours that followed she didn't just take his virginity, but treated him to a night of pleasure that left him limp, drained, and immensely grateful. Keen even at his young age to the transactional nature of his initiation into manhood, and believing his night of ecstasy to be worth more than the few paltry coins he had in his pocket, young Paolo expressed his gratitude by giving Isabella the necklace.

With time, Paolo might have grown to regret his decision, but within the week he was deemed healthy enough to return to the fighting, where the winds of fortune shifted. Just nine days after his night with Isabella, he got in the way of another bullet, and this one pierced not his thigh, but his heart.

But as far as Annie knew, the necklace was a family heirloom, passed from mother to daughter on the occasion of marriage. So it surprised her the following day, when she wore it to her wedding, that as she and Marco stood on the small wooden platform that had been constructed for the occasion, his eyes seized upon the necklace where it lay against the pale skin of her chest, and filled with what could only be interpreted as rage.

"How did you get that?" he hissed into her ear later, having pulled her outside the reception tent.

"Your mother gave it to me."

"You need to give it back." Marco's neck bulged angrily against the starched white collar of his tuxedo shirt. "It belongs to the family."

"And now I am family," she said. She had never seen him so mad.

"Give it back."

"Why?"

"Give it back."

"Let go of my arm."

Marco released Annie's arm, and they both watched as the white finger marks he'd left on her skin started to fade. The violence of his grasp surprised even him. His tone changed, softened, went from fury to pleading. "Give it back and I'll…"

"You'll *what?*" Annie said, and glared at him, waiting for him to complete the thought. "You'll what, Marco? Stop fucking the clients?" Annie walked away from him and returned to the reception, rubbing her arm where he'd grabbed it.

★

"It's not yours," Annie said. "Your mother gave it to me."

"It's a family heirloom. A Winkler family heirloom. The key words here being *Winkler* and *family*. A family you decided to abandon. And by doing so, gave up your right to the necklace. And I'd like it back."

"A *former* Winkler family heirloom," Annie said. "I gave it away."

"You gave it away? Seriously? You just gave away a necklace worth… Do you even have any idea—?"

"I gave it to someone who could appreciate it more than I could."

Marco tilted his head sideways, like a German Shepherd trying to decipher a confusing command. "You gave it to a lover, didn't you? Christ, Annie. Don't tell me that now you're a dyke. I should have known from the hair."

"You're the last person who should go all judgmental about who people sleep with," Annie said. "Aren't you the one who's supposed to have AIDS?"

"It's all very cute to watch you lovebirds quarrel," Isabel said. "But Marco, we had an agreement, and we've fulfilled our end of it."

"The agreement was to persuade my wife to return. Not to muscle her into the back of a paddy wagon. And I need the necklace."

On the drive to the Winklers, Nate had told Isabel that Fiona had said something about a necklace. Its significance was only now becoming clear. "You never said anything to me about a necklace," Isabel said. "It was never part of our deal,"

"Well it is now."

"If it's about money, the profit-sharing in our arrangement will be more than enough to cover your medical—"

Marco interrupted her. "We won't see profits out of this for years, if ever. I'll be dead by then."

"I can assure you we'll find ways to advance you whatever you need—"

"What I need, Ms. Forenza, is my mother's necklace."

Charles touched Isabel on the arm. She tilted her head toward him while he whispered something into her ear. A brief conversation followed, and ended with affirmative head nods.

"Very well then," Isabel said to Marco. "We'll find your necklace."

[chapter 23]

Officer Fox eased his patrol car into the Habler Hall parking lot and parked near the curb next to the faculty building. He'd been wise, he assured himself, not to follow Professor Keller and those others, despite his lingering questions about whether the professor had gone willingly or been coerced. Besides, Winona Keller was one tough broad. She could take care of herself. He belonged on the campus. His allegiance was to the students and faculty here. To be lured away was wrong. And now that the good professor had left the campus, it would be a good time to search her office to see if it held any clues about just what the hell was going on.

A class had just ended, which kicked into motion a flurry of campus activity. Students scurried to their next class, or back to their dorms, or simply scurried. There was noise, hubbub, energy. Give it five minutes to subside, and things would revert to their usual state of desolation. The admissions office timed tours to coincide with class changes, to give the impression that the campus was more than just a lifeless, frozen wasteland.

Officer Fox waited five minutes, climbed the stairs (better for his heart than the elevator), and walked the now-empty hallway to Winona Keller's office. He knocked twice to reassure himself that the room was empty, then tried the doorknob.

It was unlocked, which wasn't unusual, though it went against recommendations issued by the Campus Security office. He glanced down the hall in both directions to make sure no one was watching, let himself in, and closed the door behind him.

The room held no signs of struggle, nothing to suggest that Professor Keller had left against her will—no overturned chairs, no spilled cups of coffee, no papers scattered on the floor. Skulls on her shelves sat in neat rows, leering witnesses to his sneaking about.

It would have overstated things to call Leonard Fox's thinking about Professor Keller a fixation, but he certainly kept an eye on her, even though he felt sure that he meant no more to her than that giant rock that sat in the quad. At least students sometimes painted the rock. He felt her presence in the bright colors of the paintings on her walls, in the abundance of plants, in the shelves full of skulls. He sat in her desk chair, and even through his campus security overcoat he thought he could feel how its contours and indentations had shaped to her body.

He flipped idly through the student papers on her desk, eyed the red-ink feedback she'd scribbled in the margins. "EVIDENCE!!" it said in all caps and underlined near the bottom of the first page of the top paper, but alas, he could find none. Also, in different handwriting, "317," whatever that meant. Nothing in her office suggested anything out of the ordinary.

He kept flipping through papers, taking care not to disturb them too much, though the stack lay haphazardly to begin with. Something was buried in the pile, the pea in the princess's mattresses. He lifted more papers, and several layers down he found a ring, and it left him stunned. It was an engagement ring, and a ring he recognized, because he had bought it.

[chapter 24]

Back at the Placid, Victor sat on his bed propped up on pillows, thinking. The warm spell continued, with temperatures in the high forties. Sun and warmth felt all wrong for this place, whose natural state was cold and gray. The clear skies, however, brought with them a return of reliable cell phone service. He decided to try to call his daughter again, and to his surprise, she answered.

"Hiya pops," Allie said. "How's the Arctic Circle?"

"Melting. I suspect global warming. How're things there, sweetheart?"

"Good! Sea-level rise has not yet breached the living room. I've ordered sandbags."

Victor's daughter. Bright, positive, funny, preternaturally upbeat. A kid destined to change the world, if Victor could just afford to send her to a good college. "You hear from any schools?"

A sigh. "I got into Maryland," she said.

A school where the average SAT score topped 1200, but for Allie, a safe school, with in-state tuition that was supposed to make it an affordable alternative, but that was still beyond financial reach for the daughter of a school teacher and a shoe salesman. "That's great!" he said.

"Thanks. I won't hear from the others for a while."

The others. Vassar. Swarthmore. Amherst. Brown. Great schools orbiting in a price-range galaxy far, far away.

"So, do we own a shoe company yet?" she asked.

"Boot company. No. Not yet. But there are some new developments. Positive ones. I'll be up here a little while longer. Tell your mom."

"Okay. Have you talked to her?"

"I haven't been able to reach her. The phone service up here isn't great." He waited for his daughter to say something, but when she didn't, he asked, "How is she?"

"She's good. Busy at school. I haven't seen a whole lot of her. I've been late at rehearsals." Her school play. *The Crucible*. She played one of the girls the townspeople thought was a witch. Victor could relate to the concept of people thinking you're something you're not.

"Do you know Mr. Swenson?" she asked, a tentativeness in her voice.

"Mr. Swenson—?"

"He's a teacher? At Mom's school? He was here for dinner the other night. Rehearsal ended early because Mr. Dressler wasn't feeling well. I came home and Mom was eating dinner with him."

"Was there a motorcycle outside?"

"Yeah. Big and shiny."

"That would be Karl." Fucking Karl.

"It looked good. The dinner, I mean. Some kind of pasta. I think he cooked it."

"You didn't eat with them?" Victor asked.

"No. I went upstairs to do homework. It felt weird."

"Weird," he repeated. He could imagine.

"Are you and Mom okay?" Allie asked.

"Of course we're okay. What makes you ask that?" Karl. Karl's what made her ask that.

"I don't know. It's just that… You know my friend Melissa? Her parents are splitting up. And she says with her sister's boyfriend Ryan it's the same thing. It's like they wait until their kid is about to head off to college and say, 'Well, there, done with the whole kid-raising thing. No point in staying married to *this* person anymore.'"

"Are you asking this because of Mr. Swenson?" Victor said.

"No. Well, maybe. Sort of. Things have been strange between you and Mom."

"Sweetheart, we're fine," he lied. Though *strange* was the perfect word for it. Even he had been trying to figure out what was going on. Though with Karl, the picture was becoming clearer.

"Dad, I don't care where I go to college. It really doesn't matter all that much to me."

It was her turn to lie. Victor knew it mattered enormously to her where she went to college, though she would never say it. She was breaking Victor's heart. It was painful, but also motivating. Tend to what's breaking your heart and maybe you yourself won't break. Was that a saying? Victor would not be a broken man.

"Allie, stop worrying about it. Everything's going to be fine."

"What was that man doing here?" It sounded like she was starting to cry.

"He was just a friend who came over for dinner. Nothing more than that." Allie's bedroom faced the street. If she went up to do her homework, even with the window closed she would have heard when the motorcycle left. Victor didn't ask her when that might have been—if it was after dinner or in the middle of the night or sometime the next morning. He hoped she'd been up in her room with the drapes drawn and her little white earbuds stuck in her ears with the music blaring. "Look," he said, "I've got to take care of a couple more things here before I can come home, but I'll be back for opening night of your play. I promise."

"Okay. Love you."

"Love you, too."

He hung up with Allie and called Sasha Winkler.

"I hear you found my mother," she said. Victor listened for some surprise and enthusiasm in her voice, but heard neither.

"I did," Victor said. The thought entered his head that she'd known where her mother was all along.

"I need your vote," he said.

"You want to run our company?"

"You know I do."

"Then find the necklace," she said. "I'm next in line for it."

[chapter 25]

"You're acting weird," Fiona said to Nate. They were sitting in her dorm room, Fiona in a chair, checking Instagram on her mobile, and Nate on her bed, flipping through pages in Annie's notebook. "Something's up."

Nate kept flipping pages.

"Tell me," she said, firmly, not pleading, almost maternally, a mother coaxing a confession from a small child. He ignored her.

"Why are you still on Victor's side?" he said.

"You're not?" She put her phone down on her desk.

"There's not much in it for us. With Nanda Devi, there's jobs, careers, lots of money, other stuff."

"Other stuff."

"So why are you?"

"I like Victor," Fiona said. "I trust him, and I like helping him. He needs our help a lot more than Nanda Devi does. With him, what we do matters. He wouldn't still be in the running if it weren't for us. I don't want to bail on him now."

Nate leaned back, supporting himself on his elbows. "You know how we said it's like David and Goliath? Well, guess what. This time Goliath's going to win."

"You don't know that."

"We took Annie to see Marco," Nate said.

"What are you talking about? We who?"

"Me. Isabel. The big guy, Charles. We took her to see him."

"So I tell you that Professor Keller is Annie Winkler, and you go behind my back to take her to Marco?"

"All's fair in love and war, as they say."

"What the fuck, Nate? Which is this? Love or war?" He examined his fingernails, and said nothing. "So now Nanda Devi wins, and you get to be on the winning team? High fives all around?"

"Not quite," Nate said. He sat up. "It got more complicated. You mentioned a necklace. It turns out Marco wants it because it's some family heirloom. He gave it to her, and now he wants it back. I guess it's worth a fortune. Only Annie says she doesn't have it. She says she gave it away, to her lesbian lover, it sounds like. Even if that's true, she knows where it is and she can get it back. It's just going to be a matter of time." He held up his right hand, thumb and fingers about an inch apart. "We're this close, Fiona."

"*We*," she said. "You and Isabel."

"It could be you, too."

This was a new Nate, different from the one she'd been dating for four months. That Nate was fun, easygoing, not the most motivated guy on the planet, but she had enough motivation for both of them. The new Nate was greedy, calculating. And still a follower. Just that now he followed Isabel Forenza. And still not too bright. Here he was looking in the notebook for clues to the necklace, when he had stared at the nude photo of Annie for who knows how long without realizing she was wearing it. But then, he may not have noticed her face in that picture, either.

"Find anything in there?" She nodded at the notebook.

"Nah, it's all bugs and leaves and shit. But we'll find it."

"What comes next?" Fiona asked. "Thumbscrews?"

"You see, Fi," he said, grinning at her, "you come up with the best ideas. That's why you should join us."

[chapter 26]

Winter Carnival was about the biggest deal of the year at Granite College, a week-long event celebrated with massive ice sculptures, performances by the college's many and various music and theater groups, a polar-bear plunge in a section of the college pond cut out of the ice with chainsaws, a hockey game against the vastly more talented cross-town SUNY school that typically found Granite on the short end of a score more common to football games, and an unsanctioned but highly popular clothing-optional cross-country ski race promoted by the campus Outdoor Club as a mid-winter antidote to vitamin D deficiency. A highlight of the festivities was the by-invitation-only Snowflake Gala, held mid-week in conjunction with the Winter Show, a juried art exhibition of work by students, faculty in the art department, and selected professional artists who lived or at least semi-regularly vacationed in this part of New York. Despite its being held in such a tiny and out-of-the-way place, the show featured quality art and attracted savvy buyers. For students, it was a high honor to be included, and a chance to be seen by people who understood what they were looking at.

Guests at the Snowflake Gala who weren't artists or weren't affiliated with the college tended to be rich. The Gala was a major event for the development office, an opportunity to mine the surprising vein of wealth in the region—a vein full of city people, mostly, high-net-worth folk who traveled upstate in the summer months to lakeside second (or third, or fourth) homes. They made this midwinter trek to support a good cause and enjoy a good party. In exchange for the privilege of having their work displayed, student artists agreed to a seventy-thirty split of the proceeds from any art they sold, with the seventy going to the college endowment. Some students found the financial split exploitative, but the Gala was good exposure—enterprising students could make good connections, and they could take comfort from knowing that their work might hang on the wall of a semi-famous rich person, where other semi-famous rich people might see it and inquire about the artist. Plus, the food was good, drink was plentiful, and at a classy event like this, no one bothered to card them.

They held the Gala in the upstairs ballroom of the Carrbridge Student Center, a bland space under ordinary circumstances, but transformed handsomely by an event-staging outfit paid an obscene sum of money to drive up from Brooklyn in the dead of winter. There were ice sculptures and a fountain and a disco ball and a jazz quartet and lots of waiters and waitresses scurrying about with trays full of expensive champagne and exotic-looking appetizers. A theater major posed as a living statue, made up like a Norse goddess and wearing a Viking helmet, a toga-like thing, and lots of green body paint.

Fiona was all kinds of glad to be there. She needed a break from Victor and Nate and the Winklers and all the nonsense that came with them. She needed the external justification that her decision to major in studio art wasn't entirely a waste of her and her parents' money. She welcomed an excuse to wear her one fancy dress, black and sleeveless (to show off her tattoo) with a lacy hem that helped steer the attention of staring eyes to the cowboy boots she wore with it. They were light brown with paisley swirls carved into the leather, and she had found them ridiculously underpriced at a Goodwill store in Schenectady. She had two paintings in the show: large canvasses, abstract, otherworldly, and ferocious with color, something of a cross between the incandescent sunsets the North Country occasionally managed to achieve and those origins-of-the-universe images sent back to Earth from the Hubble.

Fiona saw several people she knew. A group of student artists congregated near the fountain, trying to look sophisticated with their champagne flutes. Her painting professor was there, a flashy man in his mid-forties with a shaved head, a purple sports coat and shirt, and a yellow bowtie, explaining his own paintings to two men in dark suits. She saw Eliza Willis, the president's wife, deep in conversation with an older couple whose wealth couldn't have been more obvious if a neon dollar sign had blinked on and off over their heads. The McKenzies, Fiona guessed—the science building was named for them. Just past the president's wife, it surprised Fiona to see Winona Keller. Annie.

The good professor looked lost and uncomfortable, out of her element, but also stunning, in an emerald dress with her spiky hair styled so it looked to be disobeying at least a couple of the laws of thermodynamics. She held in a life-preserver-ish way a tumbler of something on the rocks that looked to be stronger than champagne. Fiona felt bad about the encounter she and Victor had had with her. The woman had justifiable grievances. Who could blame her for creating a new life for herself? Who could blame her for resenting intrusions into that life by people demanding things of her? Fiona thought about going over to talk to her, to apologize, but then a voice spoke in her ear.

"I like your boots," the voice said, a woman's.

Fiona turned to find herself looking up at a tall and attractive woman about her own age or a little older, with long reddish-brown hair and the kind of ruddy complexion you associate with people who spend a lot of time outdoors or have had too much to drink. She held a jumbo shrimp in one hand like a question mark. "Oh!" Fiona said. "Thank you!"

The woman ate the shrimp in one bite and deposited its tail on the tray of a passing waiter. "Let me guess," she said, licking her fingers. "Those two over there are yours." She pointed across the room to where Fiona's oversized canvasses commanded a disproportionate share of wall space.

"Guilty as charged," Fiona said. "How'd you know?"

"The color. The energy. I see the same things in your tattoo. I like them. They're different from most of what's here. They feel western."

Fiona hadn't thought of them being western, or being like her tattoo, but didn't disagree.

"Melody," the woman said and extended her hand. Fiona shook it. "And if that card next to your paintings is accurate, you're Fiona."

"Yes," Fiona said. The woman wasn't a student, or at least not one she'd seen, and wasn't faculty, and Fiona was fairly sure she wasn't a townie. She looked too young to be a big donor, but you never knew.

"What am I doing here?" Melody said. "Is that the question you want to ask?"

Fiona laughed. Melody laughed with her.

"You see that man over there?" Melody pointed across the room to where a short, stocky man in a charcoal suit and a white cowboy hat was lecturing Eliza Willis about something. "He invited me. You see his feet?" Out the ends of his trouser legs poked a pair of wine-colored cowboy boots. "I made those. I make boots."

"You've got to be kidding," Fiona said.

Melody laughed again. "Why do you say that?" she said.

"It's just that everywhere I turn these days someone is making boots."

"Well, that's what I do. I have some on display over behind your paintings. I sell them in Colorado. That man wearing my boots is Clinton Packard. He invited me. He has a house here. He has a house in Colorado. He has houses all over. He's insanely rich. He came to our shop in Telluride on a ski vacation and bought four pairs. He said if I came to this show with him, he'd see to it that I'd get orders for forty more. So, here I am. I would guess Mr. Packard is expecting more from me than simply the satisfaction of helping me expand my business, but if so he will be sadly disappointed. Would you like to see my boots?"

Fiona followed Melody past Mrs. Willis and Clinton Packard, who was blustery and red-faced as he talked, gesturing with his short, thick arms. They passed close enough to Winona Keller for Fiona to attempt a nodded greeting. She got something between a blank stare and a scowl in return.

In an alcove past where Fiona's paintings hung were three left-foot boots perched on white pedestals, one with a green tint, one bluish, and one rust-colored. They were exquisitely beautiful, with all the craftsmanship of a Winkler boot, but with more attention to art along with the craft, with intricate designs and motifs carved into the leather and accented by thin lines of color—red and purple and turquoise. They were unlike anything Fiona had seen before. "They're gorgeous," Fiona said. She wanted to hide her own boots under a carpet. They seemed to belong to a different species.

"Thank you."

"Can I touch them?"

"Of course." Melody took the green-tinted boot from its pedestal and handed it to Fiona. It was soft and supple, with none of the stiffness you associate with a new boot (a cardboard support inside helped it stay vertical). She turned the boot upside down, and in the hollow where the heel met the sole saw a signature burned in a simple script like a cowboy's brand: M. Barstow.

"You're Melody Barstow," Fiona said.

"Yes."

"Of Barstow Bootery."

"You know us!"

"Daughter of Victor Barstow?"

"Granddaughter," Melody said, her face brightening. "I'm amazed you've heard of us. You're like one of four people east of the Mississippi who has. It's a really small operation."

Fiona put the boot back on its pedestal and tried to think, but the only thought that came to her was *fuck fuck fuck fuck*. Melody Barstow. Granddaughter of Victor Barstow. The *real* Victor Barstow. As if things weren't complicated enough.

"Come with me," Melody Barstow said. "I want you to meet somebody." She took hold of Fiona's arm and steered her back across the room to where Clinton Packard and Eliza Willis stood talking. Annie/Winona had moved in close enough so that now she was plausibly part of the conversation.

"Clint, I want you to meet somebody," Melody said. "This is Fiona…"

"O'Brian," Fiona said.

"Fiona O'Brian. She's one of the student artists."

Fiona offered her hand to the man, and he took it, kissed it, and held on to it for several seconds before returning it to its owner. He then introduced Fiona to Eliza Willis.

"Delightful to meet you, Fiona," the president's wife said. "And perhaps you know Professor Keller?"

"Fiona was in one of my classes," Annie said. Her tone was cordial, though Fiona detected subtle shards of ice laced through it.

"Fiona's paintings are the best ones here," Melody said. "Those big paintings over there are hers." She pointed and everyone in the small group turned to look. She put her hand on Clinton Packard's arm. "Clint, don't you just love them?"

"Spectacular!" the man said, flinging an arm and nearly overturning a passing tray of empanadas. He was clearly drunk.

"They are beautiful," Mrs. Willis agreed.

"They look western, don't you think?" Melody said. "The way she uses color? I think you should buy them, Clint."

"Sold!" he said after a moment's hesitation.

"Oh Clinton, that's wonderful," gushed Mrs. Willis, opening the faucets on her fundraiser charm. Fiona smiled along with the others, but the irony of having just raised nearly a thousand dollars for a college that was already sucking away every penny she had for tuition wasn't lost on her. On the other hand, she had just sold her first two paintings.

"And you should commission two more," Melody said. "Now, before she gets too famous."

"Young lady, I would be honored," Packard said to Fiona. He held his cowboy hat over his heart and gave her a little bow.

Fiona glanced back and forth between Packard and Melody to be sure this was really happening. "Of course!" she said. Amazing, she thought. Just like that, she was a professional artist.

"Deal, then," Packard said, and he and Fiona shook on it, no kiss this time.

The dean of students announced that dinner was about to be served and asked everyone to please take their seats, which were marked by nametags. Mrs. Willis asked Fiona to join them—President Willis had had to cancel due to another engagement, she explained, so she had an extra seat at her table. Fiona gratefully accepted the invitation, but doubted the rationale. The president and his wife seldom appeared together at events, and the train wreck of their marriage—widely blamed on the president's extracurricular proclivities—had become an open campus secret. Mrs. Willis engineered the seating at her table so that she sat with Clinton Packard on her left and Annie/Winona on her right. Melody sat to Clinton's left, and Fiona sat next to her. President Willis wasn't the only no-show—there was an empty sixth chair between Fiona and Annie. Fiona was glad for the extra space, as she did not much want to have to talk to Annie Winkler. Still, she puzzled over what was up with Annie and the president's wife.

Fiona directed her attention toward Melody, which worked out well, as it quickly became clear that Eliza Willis would monopolize Clinton Packard. Melody, thrilled to meet someone who had actually heard of her family's business, gave Fiona an abbreviated history of the rise and fall of Barstow Bootery—the company started by her great-grandfather, who made boots for miners; the boom years of the mining era; the struggle to survive after mining collapsed; the boom as Telluride became a ski town; more struggle as bigger companies moved in—in all a shorter but more deeply personal version of what she had heard before from Victor.

Melody had learned the craft from her grandfather. She explained boot anatomy to Fiona, going over welts and spur ridges and upper and lower vamps, tongues and throats and collars, front and back shafts, piping, lasts. An eavesdropper would be excused for thinking Fiona was talking to a well-resourced dominatrix. No wonder people formed fetishes over footwear. It struck Fiona that for all the talk of boots lately, she actually knew very little about them. Did Victor—the other Victor, *her* Victor—know all this stuff? Did Isabel Forenza? Did any of them have a clue about the actual work of making boots?

"I'm building a website, working on social media," Melody said. She sipped her wine. "And we may try some new styles, hiking boots, that kind of thing. Have you heard of Winklers?"

Fiona coughed up half of a Brussels sprout.

"You okay?" Melody said.

"Fine." Fiona took a gulp of wine and waved for Melody to continue.

"They're super-nice hiking boots. Made by a small, family-run operation somewhere around here that's not too different from ours, I would guess. The first pair I saw was on a hiker I ran into on a trail outside of Durango. I asked him to take them off so I could examine them. Really beautiful boots. Exquisitely made. Since then I've seen people come into our store wearing them. Even Granddad concedes they're great boots, and he's stingy with praise. He said once that if the Bootery and Winklers merged, they'd rule the boot world."

"Hrmh," was all Fiona could think to say. She drank some more wine.

"I brought him with me on this trip," Melody said.

"You brought... who?" Fiona felt panic rising inside her.

"My grandfather. I thought maybe we'd figure out a way to go visit Winklers. But that's not going to happen unless he gets it in his mind to leave the hotel."

"The Placid?" Of course the Placid. She envisioned her Victor and Melody's Victor in adjacent rooms. Bumping into each other in the hallway. Striking up a conversation.

Melody nodded. "He was supposed to be here, but he didn't want to come. This kind of thing isn't his thing." She swept her hand to indicate the Gala, the fancy food, the incoherent din of conversation. The empty chair next to her was for Melody's grandfather, Fiona realized. "He's probably in the hotel sitting at the bar."

Fiona tried to think. The words *collision course* came to mind. *Burst bubble. Fraud.* But hadn't Lukas Winkler intentionally invited Baltimore Victor? And hadn't Baltimore Victor had saved Marco's life? Wasn't the whole family indebted? And wasn't the whole business of who gets to run Winklers now focused more on Marco's mother's stupid necklace than on anything to do with actual boots?

While all of this churned through Fiona's mind, she felt a hand squeeze her right knee, gently, more a caress than a squeeze, but only for a second or two before it withdrew. She looked at Melody, whose hands at that moment were both involved in cutting the beef tenderloin on her plate. Fiona looked at Clint. Clint looked at her. Clint winked at her. Son of a bitch, she thought. And with those short, stubby arms.

She swung her legs away from him and felt something fall from her knee to the floor. He'd placed something there. Fiona dropped her napkin to give herself an excuse to look under the table, and there on the floor next to what she now knew to be the spur ridge of her right boot, she saw a wad of bills held by a brass money clip. Startled, Fiona sat up. She looked over at Clint, who despite being deep in conversation with Eliza Willis managed to send a grin her way, along with a slight nod. She looked away quickly. Was it money for her paintings, to compensate her for the Gala's unfair business model? Did he have some other kind of transaction in mind?

Well, she could just get the money and sort out the nuances later. She folded herself back under the table, grabbed the money clip and slipped it into her boot. While down there she glanced over to check on what Clint's hands were up to. Only one was visible, and it rested innocently enough in his own lap. But a couple of chairs over, another hand had strayed, and if Fiona was counting hands correctly it belonged to Eliza Willis, and it rested not so much on a knee, but on the fleshy interior of a thigh made accessible by the pushing up of a dress, and that dress belonged to Annie Winkler.

Fiona bumped her head on the underside of the table as she sat back up, sending plates and silverware rattling and drawing expressions of concern from around the table.

"Oh dear," Eliza Willis said, in her best president's-wife voice. "Are you okay?"

"Yes, sorry, fine." Fiona locked eyes with Mrs. Willis. Did the president's wife know that Fiona had seen her with her hand practically in Winona/Annie's crotch? Did she care?

The first lady looked away. Her right hand went back under the table as she turned her attention to Clinton Packard, who was telling her a story that had something to do with a horse. Fiona looked back and forth between Eliza and Winona/Annie, trying to wrap her head around the fact that they were lovers. Well, why not—both of them had total shits for husbands. This got her thinking about Nate, and his defection to Nanda Devi. Was he too a total shit? A shit in training? Maybe she should consider the two women sitting across from her role models. Here they were building lives on their own terms. And Eliza Willis was pulling it off while living in a president's-wife fishbowl. Yet there she sat, the very image of poise and grace, managing to make guests (especially the rich ones) feel like they were the most important people in the world while her hand roamed inside her girlfriend's panties. What an elegant woman, Fiona thought, with her gift for multitasking, her professionally colored auburn hair, her light-blue dress with its scoop neck and tastefully appropriate décolletage, set off by the amber necklace on the gold chain that lay against her pale skin.

Holy crap! Fiona thought. Her eyes went wide. The necklace! Eliza Willis was wearing Marco's grandmother's necklace! There it was, hiding in plain sight, just like Annie Winkler had done for all these years. Fiona had found it—now how in the world was she going to get it? She tried by an act of will to drain the excitement from her face. She glanced at Annie. Did Annie know that Fiona now knew? But Annie's eyes were vacant, unfocused, staring off into the middle distance in the manner of someone daydreaming, or someone with someone else's hand in their pants.

A waiter swept by to ask Fiona if she was through with her dinner. A half-moon of perfectly cooked beef tenderloin lay on her plate, but she let him whisk it away. She was too agitated to eat, her focus now on the necklace not more than six feet away from her. It took effort not to stare at it.

Conversations resumed, though Fiona was too distracted to give them much attention. Before long dessert appeared where Fiona's steak had been. Under different circumstances, the artist in her would have been impressed. The presentation was an aesthetic triumph—a gleaming poached pear standing skinless in a pool of red that, after she dipped in her pinky and licked it, she discovered to be a puree of raspberries.

As food, however, the dessert turned out to be less of a triumph. Unlike the steak, the pears had not been cooked perfectly. In fact, some of them seemed as though they had hardly been cooked at all, or even left out to ripen, and from around the dining room there came the clanking of plates and silverware, startled shrieks, and bursts of laughter as attempts to dig into the pear with the modest dessert fork that had been provided for that purpose sent several of the glistening fruit skittering off of tables and onto the floor, flinging raspberry puree in their wake and making whole sectors of the event look like the triage unit of an emergency room.

At Fiona's table, everyone waited politely for the president's wife to begin. Eliza Willis, keen to what was unfolding around her, held the pear in place by its stem, and with only slight difficulty managed to carve out a bite-sized portion, which she dipped into the red sauce, placed in her mouth, and pronounced delicious. "Please, everybody eat," she said.

Clinton Packard had less success. A lefty, he hacked at his pear as if he were splitting kindling, and sent it flying off his plate toward Eliza Willis, who saw it coming and pushed her chair back forcefully—too forcefully, it turned out, and as a spray of raspberry sauce Jackson-Pollocked her pale blue dress, Eliza Willis and the chair tumbled over backwards.

Around the room, the shrieks and giggles turned to gasps of concern. At Fiona's table there was a flurry of activity as everyone rose from their chairs and gathered around the president's wife, who lay startled on her back, her dress having climbed up her legs to an undignified height. Clinton Packard moved in to help her up, but Winona/Annie cut him off and got there first. A cut on Mrs. Willis's elbow was bleeding, though with all the raspberry sauce it was hard to tell how badly. With Winona/Annie's help, Mrs. Willis worked her way up to a sitting position and paused there on the floor to further assess physical damage. Packard, inexplicably, was telling people he knew CPR.

The clasp on the necklace Eliza Willis had worn around her neck was a simple hook-and-eye number, and her fall managed to dislodge the hook from the eye and send the necklace skittering across the floor through some raspberry spray to come to a stop a near an adjacent table, whose occupants, mostly mid-level development staff, plus the few second-tier major-gift prospects they were entertaining, had sprung from their chairs and rushed to Mrs. Willis's aid.

You hear athletes talk about being in the zone, about how everything slows down and the baseball pitched to them or tennis ball whacked at them looks to be the size of a cantaloupe. Such was the necklace for Fiona, and she followed its path from Mrs. Willis's neck to the floor to its resting spot by the nearby table with Zen-like focus. She got up, backed away from the hubbub, stepped discreetly over to the necklace, and stood with one booted foot on either side of it, pinning it between her insteps. She bent gracefully, picked up a stray fork for cover, and deftly palmed the necklace and slipped it into her boot, where it disappeared somewhere next to Clinton Packard's money clip. She looked up to see if anyone had noticed, but all the attention remained on Eliza Willis. She placed the fork on the table. Now she was both a professional artist and a jewelry thief. The evening was full of surprises.

Now what? It wouldn't take long for Mrs. Willis to realize her necklace was gone. What then? Would they block the exits? Strip-search the guests? She looked around for something, a potted plant, anything, a place where she could hide the necklace and come back later to retrieve it. But it seemed that every decoration and receptacle was made of clear glass—the Winter Carnival theme was ice—leaving her with no good options.

A Campus Security guard materialized at Mrs. Willis's side. Here it comes, Fiona thought. She drifted farther away, considered making a run for it. But it was Mrs. Willis's well-being that concerned the guard, not her jewelry, whose disappearance remained unnoticed. Blood from Mrs. Willis's cut soaked a napkin someone had placed over it, and it was the Security guard's opinion that the wound required professional attention. He insisted that she come with him to the infirmary. She may need stitches. She protested—with all these wealthy people, it would mean leaving money on the table. But the guard persisted, and off they went, with Winona/Annie following them.

This is too good to be true, Fiona thought.

Trying to restore a festive mood, the band started in on a swing tune. The raspberry splotches got mopped up, and couples migrated to the dance floor. Melody materialized at Fiona's side. "You wanna dance?" she asked, and Fiona, trying her hardest to make it look like nothing was out of the ordinary, said sure.

Dancing with Melody confused her. Who was this stranger who had just inserted herself into her life? She wished she could just enjoy it, but the circumstances—including, but not limited to, the discomfort of having both the necklace and Clinton Packard's money clip inside her boot—left her distracted. After one song, Fiona begged off, worried that her window of opportunity for a clean escape would close fast. "I have to go," she said into Melody's ear. "Eight o'clock class." Melody made a hurt face and gave Fiona a kiss on the cheek, which maybe lingered a little longer than a standard cheek kiss and made Fiona's eyes half shut until she managed to pull away.

Fiona walked away across the ballroom, doing her best not to race out and make it look like a getaway, but also doing her best not to limp. The money clip dug into her ankle, and the necklace had slipped painfully down under the arch of her foot.

★

The campus had been thick with security cameras for years, ever since a convicted murderer had escaped from Riverview, so Fiona waited until she was safely back in her dorm room with the door locked before she emptied the contents of her boot onto her bed. She needed to think.

She would have thought that the first thing she would think about would be the necklace, but in fact it was Melody. What was going on with this bootmaker's granddaughter who had materialized out of the west? A stranger comes to town. Wasn't that one of the two plot lines they'd discussed in her Russian lit class? Once in town, the stranger stirred things up. Fiona definitely felt stirred. Shaken, even. And by a girl. That was new. It was an evening of firsts.

Then there was the money clip with all the money in it, confirming that for the first time in her life she had sold paintings. Not only that, but she had been commissioned to sell more. Ben Franklin's face looked out at her from the wadded bills. Had she seen Ben Franklin on currency before? Maybe in movies, but not in real life.

And then there was the necklace, a thing of covet-worthy beauty. And power. It was like an amber-colored black hole that could suck her future into it.

She could simply turn the necklace in to Campus Security, claim she'd just found it on the floor near where Mrs. Willis had fallen, and wash her hands of the whole Winkler thing. Become an artist. Let Melody wax into her life where Nate waned. But was that fair to Victor, after all they'd been through? She had the necklace. The necklace meant Victor could win the Winkler deal. Wasn't that the whole point? But then, whose point? And wasn't that point pretty pointless if it meant she could go to jail? For Winter Carnival the college had increased the number of shuttles it ran into town. Fiona needed to catch one and go see Victor, and hoped that on the way there she would figure out what she wanted to say to him.

[chapter 27]

At six o'clock on Wednesday evening, the dining room at the Placid was full. Victor wondered if this was a Granite tradition—a hump-day dinner at the Placid providing a little spirit boost before the townsfolk finished out their workweek at whatever jobs they would return to on Thursday morning. At least they had jobs.

The only empty seat at the bar put Victor next to an older guy with long reddish hair, a matching beard, a handlebar mustache, and a bolo tie cinched tight at his neck. He looked like a cross between Salvador Dali and Yosemite Sam.

"Anybody sitting here?" Victor asked. The man stared at the empty barstool as if its emptiness were a matter of existential importance. Bushy eyebrows cantilevered off his forehead. He sat hunched over a bowl of chili, a half-drunk beer on the bar in front of him. He shrugged. Victor sat.

"You from around here?" Victor asked, being polite, making conversation. It's what you did at bars. And his luck meeting strangers in this bar had been pretty good of late.

There was a pause between spoonfuls of chili. "Nope," the man said, more to the chili than to Victor.

"How's the chili?" Victor asked, and got a shrug in reply.

The bartender came over and Victor ordered a beer and a hamburger. He persisted with the guy. "What brings you to Granite?"

The chili spoon hung in the air long enough for a word to escape. "Boredom."

Victor laughed. "Well, you picked the right place for that."

The guy clearly wasn't a talker. Victor decided to leave him alone. The bartender delivered his beer, and a few minutes later, his hamburger. The old man ordered another beer. Victor reached over for the ketchup and squirted a small pool of it on his plate next to his French fries.

"I lost my work," the man said, suddenly loquacious.

"Yeah, me too," Victor said.

"What'd you do?" One eyebrow bush lifted slightly.

"HR."

"The hell's that?" the man said.

"Human resources. I hired and fired people," Victor said. "Or did. Until they fired me."

The man took one of Victor's French fries, dipped it in the ketchup, and ate it, an act of sudden intimacy that took Victor totally by surprise.

"It ain't right, taking a man's work away," the man said.

It ain't right taking a man's French fries without asking, either, Victor thought but didn't say. "What kind of work do you do?" he asked.

The man turned sideways on his barstool and swung a leg out. He pulled up his jeans a few inches to reveal a shiny black cowboy boot inlaid with thin silver accent stripes. "That's my work," he said.

Victor looked from the boot to the man and back to the boot as he let the pieces fall into place. An older eccentric guy who looks like a cowboy and makes boots. Here in Granite, home of the Winklers, headed by their patriarch, another older eccentric guy who makes boots. It made no sense and perfect sense all at once, or as much sense as anything had made since he'd left Baltimore—and possibly his marriage—to come up here. Uh-oh, he thought. This can't be good.

"You make boots," Victor said. The tingling sensation in his spine was hope draining away.

"I do."

"You're Victor Barstow," Victor said.

The man's eyebrows rose in tandem surprise, like tectonic plates shifting to form a new continent. "I am," he said.

"Me too," Victor said.

★

They drank and talked long enough for them to lose track of how long they drank and talked. Victor the Elder told Victor the Younger the story of Barstow Bootery—the boom, the bust, the boom, et cetera. The Silicon Valley billionaire who bought his storefront and in its place opened a boutique that sold Hermès scarves and had Diego Rivera canvases on the walls. Victor relocated to a side street tourists seldom walked down, next to a stack of shelves where people unloaded free stuff for poor people to take. Business slowed, then all but stopped. "I can't sell shit anymore," he said. "My granddaughter—she has some luck, but not me. It used to be a good town. But it's turning into fucking Aspen."

"You may have a hard time believing this. but…" Victor began, and came clean. He explained how he came to be in Granite, the coincidence of their names, the offer from the Winklers, the competition from Nanda Devi.

"So you're impersonating me?" the Elder asked at one point, one eyebrow raised at an accusatory angle.

The Younger sighed. "No," he said. "I was impersonating someone who thought he deserved to run a boot company, but it wasn't you. I never pretended to be you." He explained how inviting him with his woeful qualifications to bid on the family business was all part of Lukas Winkler's strategy, a way to ensure that the Barstow bid would lose and Nanda Devi would win. "In fact," he said, "Lukas Winkler thinks you're dead."

The Elder looked away, stared at his beer. "Might as well be," he said.

"I really didn't stand a chance," the Younger said. "But then there was this girl."

He told him about Fiona and Nate, about how Fiona rescued his bid from the dung pile it had been headed for. He skimmed through the blizzard rescue and the complications—Annie, the necklace, Isabel Forenza, her muscle man, the shifting alliances. He couldn't tell how much of the story was sinking in, but at least he had a sympathetic audience.

"I know Nanda Devi," the Elder said, twirling the tip of his mustache in gesture of disapproval. "They're next door to the *boo-teek*."

"We should join forces," Younger Victor said. He said it un-seriously, an offhand comment delivered with no more of a goal than to affirm bar-side solidarity. But the idea hung there between them and gained traction. "You know," he said, "Maybe we really should. I've managed to get pretty far with one major skill missing from my résumé. I don't have a clue how to make boots. You make boots—really good boots. So what if we teamed up? Winklers by Barstow. Or the other way around."

The Elder gave him a dubious look, but it fell short of outright rejection. Don't press it now, Victor told himself. The Elder was at least a couple of beers ahead of him, and his eyelids were starting to droop.

"How long are you in Granite?" the Younger asked.

"Couple a days. Came with the granddaughter. She's off at a thing."

"Think about it," Younger Victor said.

He paid the bill for both of them and walked Elder Victor out of the bar, through the lobby, and down the hall to his first-floor room. "Sleep on it," he said when they reached the door. "We'll talk again."

Passing back through the lobby, Victor saw a familiar face. "Molly!" he said. She was sitting on the lobby couch.

"Victor." He thought he heard brightness in her voice. "You're back."

"You're still here. How goes the quest?"

"Never a dull moment," he said. His beer-sodden brain made space for the possibility that she'd come to see him. But as she sat there unmoving, he realized that was unlikely. "You're here to meet someone."

She nodded. "I have a date."

"Well... Can I buy you a drink while you're waiting?" Hope, springing eternal.

"That's sweet, but my date has actually showed up this time." She nodded toward the door. Victor turned and saw a man headed their way. Medium height. Thick dark hair combed back and held in place by gel. Burberry overcoat. Black leather gloves that he was peeling off. His cologne reached them first. Victor hated cologne, and judged those who wore it badly. Molly stood.

"George, this is Victor. Victor, George. Victor's in town on business, George. We met the other night. When you had something come up."

"Victor," George said, and extended his now un-gloved hand. Victor took it, and there ensued a little hand-squeeze battle, two elks bashing antlers for mating privileges. The introduction surprised Victor. This must have been light years beyond protocol for someone in Molly's line of work, yet it she seemed to delight her. It did not seem to delight George.

"George is a very busy man," Molly said. "Sometimes things come up."

George looked back and forth between Molly and Victor. "Well then," he said. "Martha?" He extended a bent arm to Molly, and she hooked hers through it. *Martha?* Victor thought. What happened to *Molly?* "Pleasure to meet you, Victor," he said. They walked away toward the elevator.

George and Martha. Victor could only imagine, though he tried not to.

★

Victor needed to pee, so when he got back at his room he headed straight for the bathroom. When he came out, Fiona was standing by his bed.

"What?" he said. The cause and effect linking bathrooms to materializing people no longer surprised him. Beneath her down coat, Fiona was more dressed-up than usual.

"You'll never guess what just happened," she said, talking fast and giving him no time to guess. "There was this art thing at school? With a fancy dinner? You know how the Winklers said there was this other Victor Barstow, who makes boots? I just met his granddaughter."

"Well, how about that," Victor said. "I just met Victor himself."

"She's an artist, and... Wait—you *what?*"

"I met Victor Barstow. The one who actually knows how to make boots. I'm working on getting him to join us. Then even Lukas won't have an excuse not to choose us."

She let this sink in for a second, then went on. "That's great, but listen. Her name's Melody, the granddaughter. She makes boots, too. Really gorgeous boots. She introduced me to this guy. He bought two of my paintings. He paid good money."

"Fiona, we can win this thing."

"Okay, but..."

"But what?"

"Victor, somebody saw my work and liked it a lot and paid a lot of money for it," she said. "My *art* work, Victor. I want to be an artist. Not a cobbler."

"Bootmaker."

"You know what I mean."

"What do you mean? That you want out?" Fiona made his ideas sing. Actually, she made her own ideas sing, but she sang them in a way that left room for him on backup vocals. He needed her. Yet here she was entertaining yet another reason to leave him.

"I don't know," she said. "I need some time to think things through."

"Why not do both? Help me with the Winklers and do your art at the same time?"

"I can't dabble," she said. "I owe it to myself to fully commit. I'll hate myself if I don't."

Was he really about to lose her? And replace her with what? A codger with birds-nest eyebrows?

Fiona inhaled deeply and blew it out. "I have something for you," she said.

She took the necklace from her coat pocket and laid it on Victor's pillow. He froze.

"Is that...?"

"It is."

"How did you…?"

"Don't ask," she said.

"You stole it."

"Let's just say an opportunity presented itself, and I took advantage of it. But look, Victor, if you want to give this to Marco, you need to move fast. What happened with the necklace is complicated, and those complications may buy you some time. But people are going to realize it's gone, and they're going to be looking for it, and they just might figure out that I took it, and they're going to be mad."

"Isabel. Does she know?"

"No. I don't think so. At least not yet. Just hurry."

[chapter 28]

In the chaos of the dining room, the attention focused on liq-
uids—the splatter of raspberry puree on Eliza Willis's dress, the
blood dripping from her elbow. Melody held a linen napkin on
the cut to slow the bleeding. Clinton dabbed at the raspberry
stains with a cloth soaked in San Pellegrino, until Winona
stopped him. Deploying too much water and too little pre-
cision, he threatened to turn the evening into a wet T-shirt
contest.

It wasn't until they were in one of the infirmary's four
exam rooms and the on-duty nurse had begun cleaning the cut
on Eliza's elbow that Winona, seated on a yellow plastic chair
under the glare of fluorescent lights, realized that the necklace
was gone.

"Eliza—the necklace!"

Eliza put her hand to her throat, and finding nothing
there but skin, gasped. "Where…?" she said, her voice frantic.

"I know where," Winona said. That girl, Fiona, who was
mixed up with that guy, whose name she couldn't remember,
who was mixed up with Marco. "I know exactly where."

"We need to call security!" Eliza said.

"No. Let me handle it."

"Handle it how?"

Eliza Willis had met Winona Keller at a faculty party. They became friends, and then became more than friends. Eliza knew the quiet scowl that scrunched Winona's face when she was mad for reasons that would go unsaid. She knew the constellation of tiny moles along her rib cage on the right side, which reminded Eliza of the Pleiades, and which she once connected with a blue Sharpie to demonstrate. She knew the scar on Winona's left butt cheek, where she'd once fallen crossing a stream and cut it on a jagged rock. She knew all kinds of things about Winona Keller, but she didn't know a thing about Annie Winkler. She didn't know that that stream crossing had occurred when Annie, not Winona, was a teenager, or that what triggered the fall was her grief over her dying mother, which caused an uncharacteristic lapse in focus. Annie kept that part of her life hidden, and she wasn't about to start pulling back the covers on it now.

"Don't worry," Winona said.

"Don't worry?"

"Trust me."

★

Fiona was coming out of a Thursday morning art class, talking in the hallway with friends, when Professor Keller intercepted her, quickly and surgically—an elbow grab, a few words about a "project" she needed to talk to Fiona about, and in a split second Fiona had been separated from the pack and steered down one corridor, then another corridor, and then into the professor's office. "I want it back," Annie said.

"Want what back?"

"Don't play games."

"I don't know what you're talking about," Fiona said, though even she could tell she didn't say it very convincingly.

"You know exactly what I'm talking about—the necklace you stole Saturday night."

"Necklace," Fiona said. "Were you even wearing a necklace?"

"Like I said, don't play games."

"But what if I like games?" Fiona said.

"I'll have you arrested."

Fiona may not have had total confidence in the cards she held in her hand, but she played them expertly. "I don't think so," she said. "Let's do a hypothetical. Let's assume for the sake of argument that the necklace in question is a Winkler family heirloom, and let's assume it's the very same one your husband, or ex-husband, or whatever he is, is demanding to have returned to him. And let's further assume that the necklace is also the same one that hung around the neck of the Granite president's wife at the Gala on Saturday evening." She paused a moment to let Annie connect the dots, then proceeded to connect them for her, in case there were any doubt.

"So, wouldn't drawing attention to me as a possible person in possession of this necklace—and notice I said 'possible,' I'm not confessing anything here—also run the risk of drawing attention to the provenance of the necklace itself? And wouldn't that kind of blow the cover off the fraudulent identity you've managed to leverage into a tenured professorship? And that's to say nothing of the whole series of steps that led to the necklace hanging around the president's wife's neck in the first place. Wouldn't the news that Mrs. Willis is having it off with one of the ladies of the faculty be disconcerting for some people—like, maybe, and again we're being totally hypothetical, Mr. Willis? Or donors?"

It was true what they said—college really was a time to explore the measure of your powers. Annie was about to say something when Fiona cut her off.

"Besides," she said. "It doesn't matter. Whatever necklace it might be that you're talking about, I don't have it."

★

When Leonard Fox got a call from Eliza Willis telling him that she needed to see him, and soon, and that it involved a matter that needed to be kept quiet, he went to see her hoping to get some questions answered. For more than a year, figuring it could be in his professional interest to look into persistent rumors about George Willis's extramarital affairs, he had deployed the investigative powers that his office afforded and discovered to his surprise that the president wasn't the only one with varied and voracious appetites. Others on campus may have been blind to the spark between Mrs. Willis and Winona Keller—the eyes tend to see only what the mind expects them to see—but not Leonard Fox, with his professionally honed observational skills and wide, empty expanses of time with nothing better to do than deploy them.

And Professor Keller was just the latest in a string of flings for the college's first lady. Earlier it had been that short, abrasive assistant professor of English, with her pink-streaked hair, an authority on Cuban cigars and Virginia Woolf, dismissed just as she was coming up for tenure, for unspecified "actions detrimental to the profession." There was the theater professor, male, pressured to resign as part of a deal to prevent a junior theater major, female, from going public with accusations that he traded lead roles for sexual favors, a deal that may also have involved the strategic deployment of a not-insubstantial amount of college funds. At least the president had the good sense to take his liaisons off campus, where they got expensed to "fundraising."

And now there was the troubling matter of the ring he'd discovered in Professor Keller's office, a ring he had once given to the only woman he'd ever really loved, who had accepted the ring and agreed to marry him, but then had gone and fucked someone else. What was Winona Keller doing with it? Had she bought it at some pawnshop? Had Eliza Willis given it to her? Was she planning to give it to Eliza Willis? Where had it been for the last fifty years?

So now, as he found himself standing with Eliza Willis in the foyer of the President's House, Leonard Fox hoped the fog of confusion swirling around some of these questions was about to lift.

"I've been robbed, Leonard," the president's wife said. She said it without emotion, a simple observation of the state of things, in the way one might say to a spouse, "We're out of milk." She looked disheveled with her haphazard hair, gray sweatpants, and gray GRANITE hoodie, which had one sleeve rolled up above a bandage on her elbow.

She led him to her living room. They sat, and he took notes in his flip-pad as she explained—the Gala, the unripe pears, her fall at the table, the elbow, the infirmary, the necklace, its disappearance. The development office would have a list of everyone who attended the Gala. Leonard made a mental note to ask them for it.

"Do you know what it's worth, this necklace?" he asked.

"I don't. A lot, I would think."

"You didn't buy it, then."

"No."

"So you got it… how?" he asked.

Eliza fidgeted in the manner, Leonard knew from experience, of people worried they're about to give away potentially incriminating information. "It was a gift," she said.

"From Mr. Willis?"

"George? Oh, good God no."

"From who, then?"

"Leonard, is this really relevant?"

It was, and was becoming more so by the second. "Knowing who gave it to you could help us establish the motive someone might have had for taking it," he said.

She puffed her cheeks and blew out a stream of air. "Winona Keller gave it to me," she said. "She's a professor of biology."

"Hmmm…"

"Hmmm *what*, Leonard? Just what the fuck do you mean by *Hmmm*?"

"Nothing. And was she at the Gala?"

"Yes. She was at my table."

Leonard pursed his lips. He tapped his pen on his flip-pad. "Who else was at your table?" he said.

"Professor Keller, a gentleman named Clinton Packard, who was there as my guest. He has the potential to become a major donor, and he's richer than God, so there wouldn't be much point to him taking it. He brought a young woman with him. An artist he met out west. Melanie…Melody… something like that. I don't know anything about her. And there was a student. Another artist. A girl this Melody person seemed to know."

"A Granite student?" Officer Fox asked.

"I believe so. Yes. She had two paintings in the show. They were talking about them. Mr. Packard bought them."

"Do you remember her name?"

"No, I don't. I suppose I was told, but I can't remember. It would be easy enough to find out. Her paintings are hanging in the ballroom. Big paintings with lots of color."

"What'd she look like? Any distinguishing features?"

"Pretty, she said. "Average height. Dark hair. Dressed in black like all the art majors do. She had this huge tattoo running down her arm."

Leonard Fox nodded. He was pretty sure he knew who the student was at Mrs. Willis's table, and he could check the paintings to confirm his hunch. And all of this, he suspected, had something to do with the comings and goings of the girl and her boyfriend and the beautiful woman and large "person of color" he'd been keeping an eye on. The universe of possibilities had narrowed to a manageable level. He asked a few more questions and then he stood to leave.

"And Leonard," she said, walking him to the door. "I would appreciate your discretion on this. I'd like it to be kept out of the campus crime log, do you understand? If it shows up there, it'll wind up on page one of the student newspaper. Are we agreed on that?"

He nodded in what he intended to be a noncommittal manner, muttered something about "getting to the bottom of this," and drove across campus to the Student Center to take a look at the paintings. "Fiona O'Brian – Studio Art," it said on a small card affixed to the wall next to them, confirming his hunch. Marijuana possession, underage drinking—he knew the name well enough. And now, jewelry theft.

He called in to his office to find out her dorm room, then went there and knocked on her door. No one answered. Students milled about, male and female, in pajamas, oversized T-shirts, boxers, most of them coming from or going to the bathroom at the end of the hall, getting ready for classes. A few were dressed in actual clothes. Leonard felt a bead of sweat trickle down between his shoulder blades, partly a result of being overdressed in an overheated space, but also because coed dorms were a concept that made him uneasy. Coed bathrooms even more so.

"You looking for Fiona?" a young woman said. She had emerged from the room next to Fiona's in sky-blue pajama bottoms with yellow ducks on them and an orange T-shirt with the name of a band Leonard had never heard of. And she was braless, he couldn't help but notice. She held a toothbrush in one hand, toothpaste in the other.

"Do you know where she is?" he asked.

"I think she's got a morning class. Is she in trouble?"

"No, no, nothing like that," he said, trying his best not to look at her T-shirt. Clapper, the other senior officer on the Security staff, always wore sunglasses, even when he was indoors. Was this why? "I just need to ask her about something."

"If I see her, do you want me to tell her you were looking for her?"

He tried to think if that was a good idea. The band on her T-shirt was called the Post-Its, which wasn't at all helpful. "Yes," he said finally. "Please do."

"Okay," she said. "Well, I gotta go pee."

He considered using his master key to enter Fiona's dorm room and see if he could find the necklace, but that was against protocol and there were a lot of students in the hallway, so he left. Besides, if she had this necklace, it's not like she would have just left it lying out on her bed. He decided to pay her boyfriend a visit instead.

★

Nate was lying in his bed dreaming that he was at an Arcade Fire concert with Isabel, and he was stoned and the music was loud and he was behind her and pressed up close against her with his hands on her hips and she had her arms up in the air and they were both swaying to some song that would have been really awesome if the drummer had been playing the right beat instead of the out-of-synch *rap-rap-rap-rap-pause*, *rap-rap-rap-rap-pause* that he was playing instead. Parts of this dream had a toehold in reality. Nate, for example, really was stoned. And Arcade Fire really was playing, on a stereo in the room next to Nate's, but plenty loud enough to fill Nate's room too. And the disturbing percussion, Nate realized as he began to emerge from his dream, really was happening, only it wasn't coming from the Arcade Fire drummer, but from someone knocking on his dorm-room door. He dragged himself from bed, plodded across the room in his boxers, and opened his door to find the large, uniformed frame of a Campus Security cop standing there silhouetted in the too-bright hallway lights. And not just any Campus Security cop, but one he'd met before, often enough that he should know the guy's name, though he didn't, but it was right there on the nametag on his coat: Leonard Fox. Discovering a cop in his doorway deflated the last vestiges of the boner that dream-Isabel had given him.

"Where is it?" Officer Fox asked.

Nate scratched his scalp through his bed-head mess of hair. "Where's what?" He yawned.

"You know perfectly well what. The necklace. I want it back."

The word *necklace* got his attention. "I don't know what you're talking about," Nate said.

"I think you do. Why don't you let me in so I can have a look?"

Nate glanced with unconvincing nonchalance back over his shoulder into his room. There was no necklace to find, but he did have a baggie of very good weed in the bottom drawer of his desk that he did not want discovered. "No, I don't think so," he said.

"Well I think so."

"Don't you need a learner's permit or something?"

Officer Fox looked confused. "A *what?*"

"You know…" His right hand flapped in the air.

"You mean a search warrant?"

"Yeah, one of those."

Not for the first time, Officer Fox understood the desperation of the Granite College admissions office. This kid was Exhibit A for those who argued that the "accept" bar had dropped too far. "Let me explain something about the pros and cons of search warrants," he said. "If you force me to go get one—and I will get one—then I'll come back and I'll tear the hell out of your sorry room. And if I find anything that shouldn't be in here, there's a very good chance you'll get kicked out of college. Maybe worse. And make no mistake—I guarantee I will find something. Or we can do this nice and neat now. Your call."

Nate sensed a bluff. They both knew that even if he had the necklace, it wouldn't be in the room when Officer Fox returned with a search warrant. Nor, Nate at least knew, would the pot. "Whatever," he said.

"Whatever what?"

"I guess go get your search warrant."

Officer Fox's face pruned in on itself, like he was fighting a sneeze.

"Look, Leonard," Nate said. "Do you mind if I call you Leonard? Maybe I can help. Just whose necklace is it that you think I stole?"

"Who said anything about stealing? Have you stolen a necklace, Nate?"

"Sorry, *have*. Whose necklace do you think I have?"

Officer Fox started to say something, then stopped, then thought, then settled on, "It was last seen in the possession of its owner at the Snowflake Gala."

"You do realize, don't you, that I wasn't at the Snowflake Gala?" Nate said.

"Your girlfriend was there." Officer Fox said.

Yes, she was, Nate thought. Fiona was at the Snowflake Gala, and so, apparently, was the Winkler necklace. And now it was missing. Too often, Nate learned in his econ stats class, people made the mistake of looking at a simple correlation between events and assuming cause and effect where there was none. But Fiona, the Gala, the necklace... Nate felt certain that in this situation cause-and-effect was a factor. "Maybe you should talk to her," he said.

"I tried to. Do you know where she is?"

Nate had a good idea of where she was, or at least what she was up to. And he realized that if he was going to do anything about it, he had to act fast. "No idea," he said.

★

After leaving the dorm, Leonard Fox returned to his usual spot in his patrol car across the street from the Habler Hall parking lot, the best possible vantage from which to keep his eye on Habler, where Fiona lived, and Kendall, Nate's dorm, and the Academic Building. With the unseasonably warm weather, he rolled his driver's side window down about halfway, allowing the vehicle to fill with the promise of spring and a fresh-cinnamon-roll aroma that wafted downwind from Rosie's. He needed to think.

That stoner kid was hiding something, and if he just bided his time, that something would reveal itself. It wasn't all that different from fly fishing—you stand still in the creek in your hip waders trying to cast just the right fly at just the right moment so a trout will find it too appetizing to resist and bite on it. Leonard was pretty sure he'd used the right fly—he'd seen the way the kid's eyes lit up when he'd mentioned the necklace—and now he just had to wait, a not altogether unpleasant task on such a fine day.

He didn't have to wait long.

It wasn't Nate, but that girl who appeared first, Fiona, on foot, heading to her dorm. He sat debating whether to go ask her a few questions when a silver minivan with Pennsylvania plates coming from town sped past his patrol car, squealed its wheels turning into the Habler lot, and pulled to a stop next to where Fiona was standing. After a few seconds, she got in. The minivan pulled away from the curb, squealed its wheels again, and sped off back toward town. A woman he didn't recognize was driving, and an older fellow sat next to her in the front seat.

Officer Fox was considering whether to follow the minivan when he saw the black SUV with the tinted windows headed his way, also coming from town. The SUV pulled into the cutaway in front of Kendall, and the stoner kid came out and climbed in. The SUV also headed back toward town, also moving fast.

Then a third car appeared, this one coming from somewhere on the other side of the Academic Building, and easy to identify. It was Winona Keller's beat-up Subaru, and it too was headed toward town. Well, Officer Fox thought, things are getting interesting. He let the Subaru get a block ahead of him, then pulled out to follow the parade.

[chapter 29]

Victor sat on his bed, thinking. So much had gone so well. He had found Annie, and it had only taken a couple of days. He had met the other Victor and cobbled together an admittedly shaky alliance, but one that figured to solidify if Elder Victor remembered it when he sobered up. And now he had the necklace. The Winkler deal was within his grasp. The last remaining thing to do was to return the necklace to Marco. But that's what he sat there thinking about. Was that the right thing to do? Not just right from the perspective of securing a business deal, but right ethically, right morally? Right like returning Annie's ring to her had felt right? Whose necklace was it, anyway? Marco's? Annie's? The college president's wife's?

Victor personalized his dilemma. If his own mother had given Carla some gift to welcome her into the Barstow family, and Carla had subsequently left him for Karl, and then she had given the thing to Karl, Victor would want it back, especially if it was something valuable, like jewelry, as opposed to, say, a lamp. More than just *want* it back—he would do whatever was within his power to get it back. Following this logic, he agreed with Marco. By choosing to remove herself from the Winkler family, however justified that decision might have been, Annie forfeited her ownership rights. And Marco was justified in wanting his mother's necklace back. This was straightforward, rational thinking, a conclusion that rested on solid ethical ground, independent of its connection to business prospects, or to Victor's loathing of Karl.

While he sat there congratulating himself for his clear thinking, his hotel-room telephone rang. "Meet me in the lobby, and bring the necklace," Fiona said when he answered. "We're going to go see Marco."

Fiona led Victor to a minivan out front. She and Victor climbed into the back seat. A young woman he'd never seen before sat behind the wheel, and next to her was Elder Victor.

"Name's Victor," Elder Victor said, turning in his seat and offering his hand to the new passenger, with not faintest glimmer of recollection in his face. The minivan lurched off.

"Right," Victor said, shaking his hand. "Me too. Remember? We met last night, at the bar? We have the same name? We talked about boots?" Elder Victor blinked, then turned to face forward. Younger Victor worried about the partnership he'd worked out, but decided to sort that out later. "Fiona..." he said, "what...?"

"It was her idea," Fiona said. "Victor, Melody. Melody, Victor. She's his granddaughter. I told her what was going on. They hate Nanda Devi."

Melody drove like a madwoman. The recent warm spell had melted most of the snow off the roads, but large patches of mud had flowed in off the hillsides to take its place. The minivan fishtailed occasionally, but Melody kept them on the road.

"We're being followed," Melody said. The black SUV was behind them.

"Isabel," Victor said.

"Who's Isabel?" Elder Victor wanted to know.

"Nanda Devi," Younger Victor said.

Elder Victor's eyebrow ledges rose, and a thin smile spread on his lips. "Pick it up a bit, darlin'," he said. Melody hit the gas. The gap between the minivan and the SUV widened.

"When we get there, you go in and find Marco," Fiona said to Victor. "We'll stall and try to hold them off."

"That won't be easy," Victor said. "She's got Charles with her."

"I can help with that," Melody said. She pulled back her coat and there gleaming on her right hip was the pearl handle of a revolver nestled in a gorgeous leather holster.

"Damn!" Younger Victor said. In the front seat, Elder Victor cackled with glee and slapped his hands on his thighs.

They slipped and slid their way to the Winklers, Melody's driving skills keeping them out of roadside ditches while putting even more distance between them and the SUV. Victor wrapped his fingers around the necklace in his coat pocket. They pulled onto the drive that led to the Winkler compound.

"There's a metal gate," Fiona said to Melody. "I'll get out and open it."

That would cost them a few valuable seconds. In movies cars just plow through gates like they're not even there, but Victor doubted that would work with in real life with an iron gate and a rental minivan.

When they reached the gate, Melody skidded the minivan to a stop inches in front it. Fiona leapt out and pulled on it, but it didn't budge. She looked back at Melody, palms raised. "It wasn't locked last time we were here," she called out. On the other side of the fence, a Winkler gatekeeper stepped halfway out of a tiny gatehouse. Melody pointed her pistol at him out her window. "Open it," she ordered. He raised his hands and froze. "Open the gate!" she said again. He reached back into the gatehouse and did something that resulted in the metallic clang of a lock disengaging. Fiona got back in the minivan.

The gate slid back slowly, showing an excruciating lack of respect for the importance of haste in this situation. The black SUV was maybe a hundred yards behind them and closing as fast as the muck would let it. When the opening was just a few feet wide Melody hit the gas and they plowed through, sacrificing a left front headlight in the process. A second casualty was the gate mechanism itself—the collision left the gate stuck open, with plenty of room for the SUV.

When they reached the house, Melody spun the minivan in the gravel into a one-hundred-and-eighty degree stop, leaving the vehicle facing back toward the road they'd just come in on. She opened her door and stood behind it with her gun pointed through the open window in the direction of the approaching black Lexus. "Go! Go! Go!" Fiona shouted, and Victor went, with Fiona close behind.

"Marco!" Victor yelled once they were inside, and they listened to his name echo off the walls. The house felt empty. Victor patted his jacket pocket, to reassure himself that the necklace was still there.

"Upstairs," Fiona said. As they raced up the stairs Lukas Winkler came racing down.

"Where's Marco?" Victor said.

"No idea. He's gone off again."

They followed Lukas through the house to the back door that opened onto the field with the woods behind. Sasha sat tying the laces on a boot—not a Winkler boot, Victor couldn't help but notice, one of those clunky things with the rubber soles and the fur bulging from the top.

Sasha led them along the same path Victor had traveled the night he'd gone searching for Marco. With the warm spell, patches of grass showed in places where Victor had struggled through thigh-deep snow, and the trail had turned into a mixture of ice, slush, and mud.

From behind them, the sound of a gunshot ripped through the sky. They all froze.

"Was that a *gun?*" Lukas said.

Victor and Fiona looked at each other in disbelief. Had Melody actually shot somebody? Was Charles lying in the driveway, bleeding out? Was Isabel?

"Just go!" Fiona said, and they went.

In the slush and mud Marco's tracks weren't hard to follow. Deer paths branched off in all directions, but only one path had boot prints on it, and the forest was a lot easier to navigate in broad daylight with the sun out. Sasha stopped when they came to a fork in the path, with boot prints coming and going in both directions. "He got confused here," she said.

"To the right's where I found him last time, I think." Victor said. He was covered in mud from slipping and falling, and breathing heavily from trying to keep up with Sasha.

"To the right's the meadow," Sasha said. "To the left is the pond."

"Go right," Lukas said, and started off up that path.

"Wait!" Fiona said. Lukas stopped. "You smell that?"

They all raised their noses and sniffed. To Victor it smelled like wet dog—between the sweat pouring off of him and falling in the snow, his wool coat was soaked. Fiona turned in a slow circle, facing one direction and then the next, tracking a scent the rest of them couldn't yet detect. "It's cigar smoke," she said, and once she said it they all could smell it. "That way." Fiona said, pointing left, and they all headed off in that direction.

The trail rose and then started a gradual descent. From high up they got glimpses of the pond below—a big shimmering disk of white snow layered on ice—but as they descended a thickening forest of fir trees mostly blocked their view. The descent grew less gradual, and with all the mud there was a lot of slipping and falling as they made their way down toward the pond. It was a big pond, and the path led them to a cove, where out on the ice, maybe thirty yards from shore, sat Marco, in the kind of low chair you'd take to the beach, with a cigar in one hand, a glass in the other, and his silver flask sitting on the ice beside him. He faced their direction, and raised his glass to toast their arrival.

"Just what the hell do you think you're doing!" Sasha yelled to him.

He blew smoke into the air. "Smoking a cigar," he said. "Having a drink. Enjoying the sunshine. The simple pleasures of a dying man."

"You're not dying!" Sasha called. "Get back here!" Marco made no move to get up. He blew more smoke. He seemed not the least bit ruffled by their arrival. It was more like he had been waiting for them.

"I'm going to get him," Lukas said, but Sasha grabbed his arm.

"Wait! "Look," she said. She pointed to Marco's left where a crescent of black water arced from the shore out toward where Marco sat. "The ice could be thin."

"It supported him," Lukas said, pointing at his father.

"He's a hundred and thirty pounds," Sasha said.

Lukas persisted. "We ice fish here," he said, and started out onto the ice. He hadn't gone ten feet when they heard a crackling noise that reminded Victor of the sound his nose had made when he'd gotten off the plane at the Granite airport.

"Lukas!" Sasha yelled. He froze. A spider-web crack spread under his feet, thin white lines etching the blue ice.

"It's a little thin in places," Marco called from his chair.

Lukas took another tentative step toward his father, unleashing another round of cracking noises and starting a new spider web.

"Lukas, don't!"

He cast a troubled look in Marco's direction, then turned slowly and walk-slid his feet back to the shore, arms out to his sides like a tight-rope walker. "We'll need a rope," he said once he was back on the bank.

"A rope won't do us any good if he won't grab hold of it," Sasha said. Besides, they hadn't brought one.

"Well, what do we do, then?"

Victor watched helplessly. Even Fiona had no good ideas.

It was late morning, and the already warm day would get warmer before it got colder again, which meant the ice would get thinner. At any minute Marco could plunge into the freezing water like the principal in the dunk tank at a school fair.

"We convince him to come in, and hope the ice holds," Sasha said.

"How?" Lukas asked.

From behind them came the sound of something crashing through the underbrush. A small posse of people slipped and slid their way down the hillside—first Charles, then Isabel, followed by Nate, then Melody Barstow (who had holstered her gun), and then Elder Victor. Just behind them came Annie Winkler, navigating the hillside with fawn-like ease, followed by Kirsten, and behind her stood Leonard Fox, holding onto a tree while he caught his breath.

"Mom!" Sasha said.

"Mom?" Lukas said.

"I brought some more help," Kirsten said.

A dozen of them were now gathered there in the mud of the shoreline, looking like a large and dysfunctional family on vacation, staring out at Marco in his beach chair. He lifted a hand to shield his eyes from the sun. "Annie?" he called out. "That you?"

He stood when he saw her, and took a step toward her. The ice responded with another crackle, which elicited a collective gasp from those on the shore. But the ice held. Marco stopped. He looked wobbly, like someone taken by surprise by one of those moving walkways they have in airports.

"Marco, what in God's name do you think you're doing?" Annie yelled back.

"I'm old, Annie," he called. "Old and stupid."

"You'll get no argument from me," she said. "Now come back here."

"Can't," he said. "Seems I'm on thin ice." He cackled at his own little joke, then drew on his cigar and blew out a cloud of smoke. "What are all those people doing here?"

"Everyone's worried about you," Sasha said.

"Ha!" he said. "They want my business, is what they want. They don't give a good goddamn about me."

"Of course we do," Sasha said.

"Who's the old guy?" Marco called out.

Fiona answered: "That's Victor Barstow, Mr. Winkler."

"Victor Barstow? I thought *he* was Victor Barstow?" He waved his cigar in what he intended to be Younger Victor's general direction.

Younger Victor was about to say something when Fiona spoke up. "He's the *other* Victor Barstow. The one who makes boots in Colorado," she said. "Barstow Bootery."

"I thought he was dead," Marco said.

"Not yet," Elder Victor replied.

"It is a day for surprises," Marco said. He sat back down, picked up his glass, and drank. Birds sang. Ice melted. Tendrils of tree-branch shadows receded as the sun rose higher in the sky. "Why's there a cop?"

Nobody had a good answer for that.

"Come back in, Marco," Annie said.

"You always said it was a disgusting habit, smoking cigars," Marco said. "Called me a narcissist for smoking them, fouling everyone's air for the sake of my own pleasure."

Annie didn't respond. Nobody said a word. From somewhere behind them came the *tat-a-tat-a-tat-a-tat* of a woodpecker working a dead tree.

"And yet you still bought them for me," Marco said. "Good Cubans. Gave them to me at Christmas. You used to care about me. Guess I fucked that up."

"People still care about you," Annie said.

"But not you," he said.

"Including me."

"I'm going to die, Annie."

"Not if you get off that ice."

"When I'm gone, you all can do whatever you want with the company. Even shut it down if you want to. It makes everything a lot simpler."

"You know that's not what we want," Lukas said.

Victor decided it was time to play the only card he held. He took the necklace out of his pocket and held it up so Marco could see it. "Marco," he said. "See this? It's your mother's necklace." Marco leaned forward in his chair and squinted. Annie tensed, but Fiona, standing beside her, raised a palm to hold her in place.

"Well, what do you know," Marco said. "How'd you get that?"

"I'll tell you later." Victor glanced at Annie, who glared at him. "Come here and I'll give it to you."

"I don't think so," Marco said. "Could be a fake. How 'bout instead you throw it out here to me so I can take a closer look?"

"I can't do that," Victor said. "Too risky."

"Throw it to me. If it's the real deal, I'll come back in." He stood again, unsteadily, either because of the ice or the alcohol or just because he was old.

"Throw it to him," Annie said.

"No," Victor said. "He'll come for it. Just wait."

With his concentration focused on Marco, Victor failed to hear Isabel coming up behind him. She snatched the necklace from his hand and kept going, stopping when she was in water up to her ankles. She cocked her arm back like you do to skip a stone and threw.

The necklace skittered across the surface of the ice and come to a rest to Marco's left, maybe five feet from the edge where the ice stopped and open water started. There was nothing to do but stand and stare and see what Marco would do. It occurred to Victor that now Isabel could claim that she had returned the necklace, so the Winkler contract would go to Nanda Devi. *Well played*, he thought.

But then, Isabel hadn't actually returned the necklace to Marco. All she'd done was throw it out on the ice. Marco took a few shuffling steps toward it.

"This isn't good," Charles said.

"Pop, don't move!" Sasha said. "The ice won't hold. Just leave it there. You can see it. You know it's real."

"We can't just let it sit there," Isabel said. "What if it falls in?"

Sasha glared at her. "What if *he* falls in?" she said. Isabel didn't respond, but looked troubled.

Out on the ice, cigar in hand, Marco ignored the shouts of protest from the shore and shuffled along toward the necklace, and despite a couple of disturbing crackling sounds from the ice, soon he had moved to within ten feet of it. Suddenly the shouting stopped—as if the twelve people watching had become a single organism holding its breath. The air grew still.

The woodpecker pecked. Marco shuffled. The ice held. He was six feet away, then four, then almost within arm's reach.

He got down on all fours. Good, Victor thought. It would distribute the weight more broadly. Marco began to crawl, but then stopped suddenly, responding to some movement those on land couldn't detect. There came another cracking sound—louder than the others. Marco spread himself wider. He put down his cigar. He looked like a skinny stranded polar bear.

"*Marco!*" Annie yelled.

He looked up at her, a confused old man who had made some good decisions in his life and some bad decisions, and was right now coming to grips with the reality of what was turning out to be a very bad decision. "Polo?" he called back, and then the ice gave way and Marco Winkler disappeared into the freezing water.

[chapter 30]

Six months later.

The tiny plane banked into its final turn and lined up for the approach to the runway. Below, the verdant green of the Adirondack landscape took Victor's breath away. It looked so different in late August than when he'd first seen it back in February, when it came wrapped in drab gray cotton that had been sprayed with water and set out to freeze. The plane was full, which meant five people, plus the pilot, who, like seemingly every pilot on this route, couldn't have been too many years out of high school, if in fact he'd ever graduated. Victor sat in the back row next to an older woman on her way back to Granite after a visit with her son in Atlanta. After takeoff in Albany she went on and on about Atlanta's oppressive heat, and how glad she was to be returning to a more reasonable climate. Victor wasn't disappointed when she fell asleep.

The plane's other occupants were three students flying in for freshman orientation at Granite College. In the row in front of Victor were a Middle Eastern guy and a Black girl, who sat there as living testament to the college admissions office's tireless work to boost diversity percentages. They sounded giddy with excitement, which made Victor smile, though he wondered how they'd feel in mid-January. They discovered they had gone to rival high schools in Northern Virginia, and sat comparing the overlaps in their Instagram networks. The third student, up front, occupying the co-pilot's seat, had less in common Instagram-wise, but sat turned sideways toward the other two so she could be part of the conversation. This student was Victor's daughter, Allie.

Allie's turned-sideways posture put her in even closer proximity to the pilot, whom Victor had kept a wary parental eye on throughout the flight, lest his right hand wander past the controls and onto Allie's knees. Several inches below those knees were two gorgeous cowboy boots, black with crimson and teal inlays, a pair that had been custom made for her by Melody Barstow. Victor thought the boots might be overkill for late August, but Allie had barely taken them off since they arrived from Colorado by FedEx a couple of weeks earlier.

Allie's college dilemma had resolved itself nicely. She had been dubious when Victor first flew her up to take a look at Granite. Her concerns were the common ones—it was too small, too remote, too cold—but after meeting Fiona and Melody and Sasha and Annie, attending Granite was all she could talk about. Plus, thanks to her father's surplus of new connections, Granite had made her a financial aid offer that was too good to refuse. Allie had decided to design her own major, in something Victor didn't understand called sustainable art, a concept she had worked out in consultation with those four women. It didn't seem to involve theater, which Victor thought was a wise decision after having seen her performance in *The Crucible*.

"So what's your major?" the pilot had asked just after takeoff. Over the roar of the plane's engine he tried to follow the explanation his daughter gave the pilot. It befuddled the poor kid even more than it had Victor, but it made sense to

Allie, so that's all that mattered. Victor hoped the pilot was better at aviation than he was at pickup lines.

The plane bounced a couple of times after coming in contact with the tarmac, but otherwise landed smoothly, and as they taxied around, Victor caught a glimpse of the black Lexus parked over by the Quonset hut that was Granite International Airport, with the river beyond and Canada beyond that. Charles stood beside the vehicle, resplendent in black slacks, a peach and lime green Hawaiian shirt, and aviator sunglasses. "He looks like Idris Elba!" Allie had gushed after her father had first introduced her to Charles, and Victor had nodded his agreement, though he hadn't been sure if Idris Elba was a person or an obscure African nation.

Marco's plunge through the ice had taken on a significance similar to that of the birth of Christ, in that everything got divided into those events that occurred pre-plunge and those that occurred post-. One thing that did not occur post- was that Victor did not become the CEO of Winkler Boots. Nor did the company get folded into Nanda Devi. Post-plunge, wiser heads had prevailed (Sasha Winkler's and Melody Barstow's, mostly), and it was agreed that the whole unfortunate necklace thing was something of a red herring that drew attention away from more important issues. Winkler Boots and Barstow Bootery would merge. It was too soon to tell how this would play out in the marketplace, but the merger increased exponentially the number of prospective feet that could find their way into the company's boots, and initial signs were encouraging. As for the necklace, it was never found. For all anyone knew it wound up inside the stomach of an actual red herring.

Victor may not have become CEO of Winkler Boots, but he was the new chief operating officer of the newly merged

W&B Boots, LLC, and Charles, as the new director of marketing, reported to him. There had been consideration of calling it W&B Footwear, to leave open the possibility of branching out at some point into other kinds of shoes, or even, God forbid, sandals, but ultimately it was felt that that would be diluting the brand too much, sort of like Starbucks selling beer. Besides, neither Melody nor Sasha wanted anything to do with a company that made flip-flops.

Charles, with his imposing stature but basically gentle demeanor, had had great success so far in broadening the number of locations that agreed carry one or the other or both lines of W&B boots (hiking boots with the Winkler brand, or Barstow cowboy boots). He was a great bear of a man in the fullest sense of that expression, leaving those who met him to wonder if he leaned more in the teddy direction or the grizzly. This made him hard to say no to.

Victor reported to none other than the Evil Princess herself, Isabel Forenza. The Winklers decided that from a practical standpoint this just seemed to make the most sense, and the Barstows agreed. Once he got used to the idea, even Victor had to agree. Isabel had more business savvy than all of the rest of them put together, plus the single-minded ruthlessness characteristic of leaders of successful brands, like Steve Jobs, or Attila the Hun. And once you were teammates with her, she turned out not to be such a horrible person after all. As Victor had long suspected, she turned out not to be Isabel Forenza, either. That phony name had been a shameless tug on the Winkler family's heartstrings. The nameplate on her desk on the third floor of the Winkler mansion read Ellen Pine, Chief Executive Officer. This explained the "EP" Victor had seen monogrammed on her purse back months ago on that night when they'd first landed at the Granite airport.

Kirsten, her unpaid-intern years behind her, became Ellen Pine's well-paid executive assistant.

Ellen Pine quit Nanda Devi for the new W&B gig. She brought a newfound confidence to the newly restructured business, a confidence underscored by her decision to request, in lieu of salary, a generous percentage share of net company profits. This signaled either that she was crazy—neither Winkler nor Barstow had generated much in the way of profits in years—or that she saw potential where others did not. Her first goal was to bring the business forward into the twenty-first century; step one was establishing a presence online. She retained the services of a Boston-area tech firm to develop boot-fitting software that allowed buyers to upload precise images of their feet, from which bootmakers would fashion boots. In this way she managed to throw out the pilgrimage-to-Granite bathwater (and, for women, the skeezy conditions that went with it) while retaining the custom-fit-mystique baby that had long been at the heart of the Winkler brand. It worked for Barstow boots as well, though for those with time and money, traveling to a pretty town like Telluride was viewed as less of a hardship. In June a reporter for *Outside Magazine* had spent two days in Granite and three in Telluride working on a story about W&B's revival. It would run in the October issue, and the publicity it would generate figured to make Ellen Pine's compensation arrangement look like genius.

Melody moved back to Telluride, and once spring semester ended Fiona joined her. The spark each had felt at the Winter Gala ignited—they were now a couple. Melody ran Barstow Bootery out of a new storefront on Colorado Ave., in a building she was able to buy thanks to generous terms from Clinton Packard. The ground floor was the store—cowboy boots in the front, hiking boots in the back—and Melody and Fiona turned the second floor into a cozy two-bedroom apartment, the second bedroom serving as a studio for both of them if no one was visiting. Fiona's only remaining graduation requirement involved completing her senior portfolio, a task she happily undertook with the backdrop of southwestern Colorado's San Juan Mountains providing inspiration.

The ruggedness of the Western landscape brought out new layers of creative expression in Fiona's work, helping get her nascent professional career off to a strong start. Her work sold well and for good money, mostly from a gallery a block and a half from Winkler & Barstow that Clinton Packard was a part owner of. He visited Telluride at least a couple of times every year, always with some new girl on his arm who looked to be roughly a third his age. The gallery showed a variety of mostly Western artists—some of Melody's boots were on display there—but Fiona's work was always featured prominently, as was work by Sasha Winkler, who was delighted to have a new outlet and an excuse to spend time in a town as cute as Telluride.

Fiona helped out in the Bootery from time to time, and W&B also had her on retainer as a creative consultant, in which capacity she worked to build awareness on social media, where some catching up was called for. W&B now not only had a website, but a Facebook page, an Instagram account, and nearly fifteen hundred people following on Twitter.

Nate stayed in Granite for the summer. His academic career had suffered in the chaos of spring semester, so he remained there to catch up on his degree requirements, one of which he fulfilled with an internship at W&B. He started out as an apprentice bootmaker at Winklers, but after finding he had neither aptitude for nor any real interest in bootmaking, he restructured the internship so he could work remotely with the tech firm Ellen Pine had hired to run W&B's digital operations. Working with digital fitting software turned out to be a much better fit for Nate, and the firm told him they had a full-time job waiting for him when (if) he graduated. Nate turned twenty-one in May, and could now buy his own beer.

In June the trustees made Eliza Willis interim president of Granite College. The board expressed public astonishment at the revelation of George Willis's indiscretions, though it was unlikely that their reaction was genuine. Many had long known what was going on, but were willing to keep quiet about it as long as he continued to be a tremendously effective fundraiser. Everything had blown up when a prostitute President Willis solicited turned out to be an undercover cop. The trap that caught him had been laid after one of his trustee detractors called in a favor with a police-detective friend. Ultimately the charges were dropped, but the scandal brought an end to George's tenure as president, which had been the point all along. The college severed its connection to him, and his wife put in motion divorce proceedings to do likewise. Eliza Willis came out, and she and Annie became an official couple. Annie became Annie Winkler again, dropping the Winona Keller façade.

The news about George Willis had triggered a wave of panic in Victor, as the faux prostitute behind the sting was of course Molly, whose real name wasn't Molly, or Martha, but Maureen, and she wasn't from Ottawa, but Albany. He feared that the same sting that stung George Willis had stung him, too. But as news about George Willis spread, Molly/Martha/Maureen paid Victor a visit and assured him he was in no legal trouble. What had transpired between them at the Placid Hotel had been between consenting adults, and since George Willis had stood her up, when she had walked into the bar and sat next to him she had been officially off duty. And, importantly, no money had changed hands. Victor was hugely relieved that he hadn't left her a tip.

The revelation about Molly/Martha/Maureen, however, left Victor with two questions. One, if her meetings with George Willis were part of a sting, why did she see him multiple times? She explained that it took several liaisons for George, a former professor of American history, to get around to some sort of bedroom activity that qualified as illegal. His initial desires ran toward Colonial-era role-play involving tri-corner hats, breeches, ruffles, and petticoats, plus one non-abusively wielded riding crop, and those things, however kinky, were not illegal. Victor's second question was what, on that evening when George stood her up, made her decide it would be a good idea to have first a drink, and ultimately sex with him?

"I like you, Victor," was her reply, and it left him speechless. "You were irresistible, you and your quest." Things continued to develop between them. One evening she even allowed herself to be persuaded to bring out the petticoats.

Carla and Karl broke up, which gave Victor less satisfaction than he'd expected. Allie told him what happened. At Carla's suggestion, Karl had begun coming with her to her Saturday morning ashtanga yoga classes. One rainy Tuesday during spring break, after he had cancelled a lunch date by saying he wasn't feeling well, she decided to skip lunch and see if she could fit in a yoga class instead. A CLOSED sign hung on the front door of the studio, which was unusual, and even more unusual was finding a motorcycle that looked an awful lot like Karl's in the parking lot. Whoever hung the CLOSED sign had neglected to lock the door, and inside Carla discovered Karl and the new young yoga instructor engaged in an ambitious tandem variation of downward dog. They were lucky they were in a yoga studio, where Carla could find only soft and round-edged things to throw at them. It could have turned out very differently if this had happened in the tool aisle at Home Depot.

The end of Carla's relationship with Karl did not mean the rekindling of the one she had with Victor. They separated, more or less amicably, and divorce proceedings were underway. Allie, though hardly thrilled by this turn of events, wasn't surprised either, and was handling the break-up pretty well. She loved them both, flaws and all.

On a drizzly day in early March, not long after Marco's icy plunge, Annie summoned Officer Fox to her office to report a theft. She explained to him how she had hidden a ring under a stack of student papers the day Isabel and Charles had dragged her off to the Winklers, only to find later that it was missing. She said she didn't hold out much hope that it could be found, and she doubted it was worth much, but she felt it wise to report it anyway, if for no other reason than to add some substance to the college's pathetic weekly crime log. She had barely begun describing the what/when/where of things when Officer Fox placed the ring in front of her on her desk.

"You...? How...?"

"I found it in your office the day you went off with that woman and her sidekick. I didn't steal it. I took it for safe-keeping. I was afraid someone else would take it."

"Why didn't you tell me?"

"It's a little complicated."

"Tell me, Leonard."

His shoulders rose and fell, the epaulets on his uniform jacket going up and down with them and making him look helpless in the manner of a large, flightless bird. "When I came into your office, I recognized the ring," he said. "I know it. I gave it to someone once. Not one like it. *That* ring."

Annie processed this. Her mouth fell open. "My mother."

"It was a long time ago. I was in love with her, and I thought she was in love with me, but... well, let's just say things didn't work out."

"You're the fisherman."

He started to say something, but stopped.

"She told me stories about you." Those stories struggled to reassemble themselves inside her head. "But that means..."

Leonard Fox inhaled deeply and blew it out slowly. "Yeah. I don't quite know how to say this, but I think I might be your father." A DNA test confirmed it.

Leonard subsequently became the college's first emeritus security officer, which meant he could keep an office and hang out on campus, but they didn't have to pay him much. Being on campus meant he could be closer to Annie on a daily basis. He had a daughter—a daughter closer to sixty than sixteen, but a daughter nonetheless. He started teaching Annie to fly fish.

Lukas—who moved back to Boston to take an investment job but stayed involved as a W&B financial consultant—arranged his vacation days so he could join his mother and grandfather out in the trout streams.

Victor the Elder split time between Colorado and Granite, and the bootmakers on both sides of the Mississippi were thrilled whenever he decided it was time to go where they weren't. He pestered workers in both locations about what he perceived to be their sloppy craftsmanship. In Telluride, after he left it would be Melody's job to soothe their fragile, creative egos. In Granite it was less of a problem, because when he was there he spent the bulk of his time drinking and smoking cigars and bullshitting with Marco.

Yes, Marco. He hadn't drowned or frozen to death after falling through the ice. Within seconds after he had gone under Charles had taken off from the bank with the same long, purposeful strides he once used to track down Harvard tailbacks. About ten yards into the pond the ice gave way beneath him, but he just kept going, as it turned out that the pond where he fell through was only maybe three or four feet deep. Who knew? More and more of Charles disappeared underwater the farther he went, but the water never went past his shoulders. When he got to the spot where Marco had fallen through, he dove beneath the surface, remained there for what felt like minutes but probably was no more than a few seconds, and emerged with his arms around Marco, who spat and flailed like a drowning cat. The place where Marco had fallen through had been about five feet deep.

After all the things that hadn't managed to kill him, Marco lived with a buoyant sense of his own indestructibility. Elder Victor was good for him because he offered companionship, but also because their combined physical maladies limited the amount of trouble they could get themselves into. So they smoked and drank and cursed at one another, and others were content to let them.

After she de-planed Allie raced over and jumped at Charles, who caught her and spun her around with a big grin on his face before setting her down gently. Then everyone stood around and waited for their bags to be unloaded. Allie was now BFFs with the Middle Eastern guy and the Black girl, whose names were Khalid and Rachel.

"Can we give them a ride?" Allie asked her father. Victor looked at her. How long had it been since he stood just about where she stood, only in the freezing cold, and in the dark, with hardly a clue as to what he was doing, and even less of a clue of how to go about doing it? Could that really have just been six months ago? He thought about how different his life would be right now if he hadn't gotten into Nate's piece-of-shit car that night. He thought about how Allie's life would unfold from this point forward, hinging on decisions just like this one, about how the interplay of intention and serendipity would define that unfolding, about how she would need him less and less, and about how opportunities like this one, to play a role in her life, however minor, would be fewer and farther between.

"They were going to take an Uber," Allie said, "but that's expensive. If they even have Uber up here."

Victor started to laugh.

"What?" Allie said.

"Long story."

Acknowledgements

Thanks to:

– My wife, Catherine, who wins the contest for most profound influence on my life by such a wide margin that I can't even imagine what second place would look like.

– Our three children—Matthew, Lauren, and Julia—who are a greater source of inspiration than they may realize. Extra thanks to Lauren, whose early read and advice has helped make this a better book.

– Colleges (and college towns) everywhere, especially those I've had the good fortune to attend or work for or with. These communities within communities are intriguing, valuable, and frequently zany, often for overlapping reasons.

– Lisa Catalone Castro, a gifted graphic designer and a good friend, for her contributions to the cover design of this book.

– Adelaide Books, for bringing this story into the world of readers.

About the Author

Richard Bader grew up north of Baltimore, moved away for college, and then circled the U.S. for a couple of decades during which he worked as, among other things, a restaurant cook and a whitewater rafting guide. He made his way back east and eventually launched a business helping nonprofit organizations tell their stories. At other times he makes up stories of his own. His fiction has been published by a variety of literary magazines and by National Public Radio. This is his first novel. He lives with his wife not far from where he started out, in Towson, Maryland.

CPSIA information can be obtained
at www.ICGtesting.com
Printed in the USA
LVHW032107080321
680887LV00009B/2035

9 781954 351110